Love letters
to the
Virgin Mary

Love letters to the Virgin Mary

The Resurrection of King David

DAVID RICHARDS

Published by Mjolnir Productions LLC

ISBN (paperback): 978-0-578-27593-2
ISBN (ebook): 979-8-88862-195-0

Cover design by Gareth Richards
Interior design by Christy Day, Constellation Book Services

Printed in the United States of America

For the woman in the black dress.
Merci. Vous m'avez aidé à définir l'amour
inconditionnel; tu as mon éternelle
reconnaissance

Contents

Preface

Albert Einstein once remarked, "Imagination is more important than knowledge. For knowledge is limited, whereas imagination embraces the entire world, stimulating progress, giving birth to evolution."

Each one of us is equipped with an imagination. At some point, usually in our teen years, we begin to divorce ourselves from our imagination. Part of this arises from peer pressure and the desire to "fit in," while an education system that is guided by standardized testing also bears some responsibility. In the West, and most particularly in the United States, the nation that produced the assembly line, conformity has long been a hallmark of corporate culture, driving many of us to embrace the tenets of left-brained pragmatism for the sake of efficiency at the expense of individual creativity. Thankfully, that is changing.

Today, imagination is in abundance. When I was a kid, and we had televisions with antennas, we were limited to four channels. Now, there are countless channels and streaming services, and hundreds if not thousands of shows and movies available daily—as of 2018, YouTube has more than 23 million channels.

Thanks to technology, billions of people have smart devices that provide virtually unlimited access to the world's information. We are producing, exchanging, and consuming information at a rate previously unknown in human history, and social media apps like Instagram and SnapChat are allowing people to craft individual expression and identity to a greater extent than ever before. Thanks to the abundance of information and incredibly fast access to it, we are learning faster than ever before. Forty years ago, it might take me days or even weeks to find out answers I now have available at my fingertips instantly. What is paramount is putting that learning to use via Imagination. The only cost to imagination is time and focus; otherwise, it's free.

While this story will be labeled a religious story, at its heart, it is a love story.

It operates on the grand stage that Judaism, Christianity, and Islam are all chapters of one great love story, and that the first god was a slave. With that as the platform on which the story rests, I'll use the remainder of the preface to orient the reader as to the framework around which the story is built.

First and most notably, the three Abrahamic faiths share the common lineage of such historical figures as Abraham, Moses, Isaiah, and King David. Like Christianity, Islam believes Jesus returns at the end of days. Islam does something fascinating in its veneration of the Virgin Mary; she is the only woman mentioned by name in the Quran, and is recognized as the greatest woman to have ever lived.

Secondly, these three great faiths are delicately intertwined with one another. What would Christianity be without Judaism? Jesus was Jewish. What would Islam be, if it could not differentiate itself from the foundations laid before it by Judaism and Christianity? Islamic beliefs are specific: Jesus did *not* die but was saved by God. That story would not exist if it were not preceded by the story of Jesus' death and resurrection.

Every good story finds the protagonist seeking a single key by which their journey might continue. There is seemingly only one solution, and the hero/heroine must grow into the person needed to realize that remedy. In the original *Star Wars: A New Hope,* Luke must get his photon torpedoes into the narrow opening that will destroy the reactor at the heart of the original Death Star. Though a novice X-Wing pilot, Luke uses the force, the torpedoes find their mark. The galaxy is saved. In 2017's *Wonder Woman,* the Amazonian princess must deflect Ares' light torrents back at him to defeat him. In *Avengers: Endgame,* out of fourteen million possible outcomes in fighting Thanos, only one leads to victory. Tony Stark, long the supreme narcissist of the Marvel Cinematic Universe, makes the ultimate sacrifice, and Thanos vanishes.

This story is like that.

While the story does not spend any significant time in the biblical period of Jesus' life or his teaching, it is built around several verses, many that focus on his relationship with King David. In the verses where Jesus is speaking, I have italicized the text:

"Not so with you. Instead, whoever wants to become great among you must be your servant, and whoever wants to be first must bbe slave of all" (Mark 10:43-44).

"But about that day or hour no one knows, not even the angels in heaven, nor the Son, but only the Father" (Mark 24:36).

"He must become greater. I must become less" (John 3:30).

Jesus answered them, *"Is it not written in your Law, 'I have said you are gods?'" (Mark 24:36).*

(It should be noted here that Jesus is referencing the Old Testament, quoting Pslams 82:6.)

"Jesus saith unto him, *I am the way, the truth, and the life: no man cometh unto the Father, but by me"* (John 14:6).

Jesus said to them, *"How then does David in the Spirit call Him 'Lord'? For he says: 'The Lord said to my Lord, "Sit at My right hand until I put Your enemies under Your feet. So if David calls Him 'Lord,' how can He be David's son?"* (Matthew 22:43-45).

"And about the ninth hour Jesus cried out with a loud voice, saying, *'Eli, Eli, lema sabachtahani?"* which means, *My God, My God, why have you forsaken me?"* (Matthew 27:46).

(Here, Jesus is quoting a Psalm of David: Psalm 22.)

"He will be great and will be called the Son of the Most High. The Lord God will give him the throne of his Father David" (Luke 1:32).

"I am the both the source of David and the heir to his throne" (Revelation 22:16, NLT).

Revelation 12 in its entirety also factors heavily into the story. The great dragon. Satan. The woman clothed in the sun.

Finally, because it factors so significantly into the story, a word on quantum physics.

The classic model of the world is based on Newtonian physics and the idea that everything is separate from everything else. This is the model of the world that most of us were raised on; it's the world we can see and the world that dominates our senses. Newtonian physics focuses on the external environment. In this model of reality, people wait for their external circumstances to change to feel a certain way internally. People become dependent on external factors to manage how they feel inside.

Quantum physics turns traditional physics on its head. It observes that 99.9% of an atom is nothing but empty space. Even the nucleus of an atom isn't as solid as we previously understood under the traditional model. When we take this concept of an atom being mostly space and expand it up to people, the same rules apply. Despite the very solid feel of your skin, your skeletal system, and your hair...it's mostly space. Quantum physics drives focus on the internal environment. In my view, quantum physics is the science of imagination. In the quantum model of reality, we feel a certain way to create the outside world we wish to see. People "feel" from the place they want to be, drawing that place to them. That is the power of imagination. The starkest distinction between these two models of the world is one thing—belief.

Without pulling too much detail from the story, quantum physicists know that the universe responds to observation. If someone believes they are not part of the universe but rather separate from it, as in the traditional Newtonian model, the universe will support this belief.

A person who believes in the classic model of physics will see everyone as separate from them. Because of this, they will normally be attracted to people who share similar values and beliefs, and oppose those who think or believe differently from them. In this model of the world, like attracts like. Prejudiced people remain prejudice if they are unwilling to open their minds.

On the other hand, someone who accepts the underlying principles of quantum physics realizes that there is no separation between observer and observed. This is a fundamental tenet of yoga, and flirts with the precepts of Buddhism. When I am speaking to another person under the auspices of quantum physics, the more "tuned in" I am to them, the greater connection we will establish between us. The greater the sense of oneness.

In the classic model, differences are enough to divide and segregate. In the quantum model, the universality of the human condition enables us to see beyond physical differences or even differences of belief. We all have our own models of how the world operates; connecting with another person is simply a matter of accepting their view of the world will be different from ours. To quote the Persian poet Rumi, *You are not a drop in the ocean, you are the entire ocean in a drop.*

It is not too far a stretch to suggest that, as more and more people learn to appreciate the underlying fundamental nature of reality as being quantum, the world will experience a grand enlightenment. If our bodies are vibrating energy and mostly space, what is consciousness, and who is asking the question? Said differently, the sooner we can make the quantum world easy to understand, people will start to appreciate, there really is a soul inside us, this seed of consciousness that directs our attention and focus. Quantum physics leads us to the law of attraction. The law of attraction leads us to our divinity.

The premise behind this story is simple enough. As a slave to humanity, the first God would be one of the last beings to awaken to its own identity. The David here is a mortal man who has spent his entire life searching for a single woman. Upon seeing her, he is overcome with joy. As he awakens to his identity however, he realizes how far his journey to find her has taken him from the Cross. That journey, with all its challenges and tribulations, is the heart of this story.

Finally, this story was inspired by a picture posted on Instagram early in the pandemic. I heard it recently said that every heart has a key that unlocks it. If I never again saw the woman who posted it, I'd know that she had the key to unlocking mine. That, to me, is real freedom.

To believe in the story of Jesus is a personal decision; it can't be forced on anyone, despite the multitude of attempts throughout history to do so. Attempting to force our beliefs onto anyone misses the point of Jesus' story entirely. To believe in his story outright is to come to a grand realization; following Jesus to the cross means believing that you too will be resurrected. That thought leads me to one last Bible verse worth mentioning as essential to the story:

"Then Jesus said, "*Father, forgive them, for they know not what they do*" (Luke 23:34).

Finally, two revelations that occurred during the pandemic helped this story finally come into form. The first was the discovery that I have a slight trace of Jewish ancestry in my DNA; I learned that in 2020 from the genetic testing website 23andme.com

The second revelation was rather magical, as a team in Sweden determined that the egg chooses the sperm in the moments leading up to conception, upending biology and sex-education classes around the world which, for generations, had taught that one sperm manages to beat out all the other sperm, overcoming the egg's seemingly impenetrable defenses.

*Think of yourself as dead. You have lived your
life. Now, take what's left and live it properly.
What doesn't transmit light creates its own darkness.*
–Marcus Aurelius

Beauty awakens the soul to act.
–Dante

BOOK ONE

Darkness: The Creation of Silence

M~

This is the last letter I'm writing. I'm putting it at the front as a way of expressing my eternal gratitude.

Thank you for putting up with me. For your patience. Your strength. For the majestic, resplendent way you celebrate life. As I suspect you'll see in the letters that follow…seeing you hiking with your friends, or lifting weights in the gym, or wearing girly clothes, as you like to say… that my eyes get to see something so immaculate daily is heaven.

I am not at all ashamed to say, it took me a few months to believe you were real. After a lifetime spent searching for you, I have come to relish how delicious the end of this journey has been.

These letters are far from perfect, but I'm certain they're better than the previous versions I've shared with you along the way. I still haven't thrown myself into learning French. I could benefit from some tutoring.

I am excited for what comes next.

Happy birthday, M.

The First Love Letter

Every man struggles with what it means to surrender. While many men will attest to being followers of Christ, precious few have demonstrated the courage needed to surrender to him.

I was one such man. While I readily surrendered to others, acquiescence becomes an artform when you lack courage, Jesus was, for much of my life, hidden in the background.

At the same time, I knew something like courage. Early in my life, I possessed an overpowering sense of God's love. God's existence was a certainty, that was without question. That same existence set my life on the strangest trajectory; I would realize this love in the eyes of a woman. Of this, I was equally certain, though I lacked any kind of context, or identity of just who this mysterious woman might be. At no time in my life did I reason that, on a planet of nearly four billion women, such a thing was inconceivable.

In my childhood, my relationship with Jesus was unparalleled.

In time, that relationship changed. Like Santa, God started to become a myth. Most certainly, as I will explain in the letters that follow, I felt myself drifting from the safety of his presence by the time I made it to college. The world in which I lived was very physical and material. A hard world. A world of division. A world of haves and have nots. I learned to be selfish with my affection, even as I searched for a woman I knew was out there.

As a man, I saw the disparity in the world. I competed, delighting in my victories over others, and beating myself up when I lost.

Through my upbringing, I had developed a mindset of scarcity; take what you can, as there isn't enough to go around. As I began my military career and traveled the world, meeting people from different backgrounds, cultures, and faiths stirred my imagination; how could one God account for us all? It was a distressing cocktail of curiosity and doubt, hammering at the increasingly weak foundations of my poorly tended Christian faith.

I still believed the reservoirs of love inside me would find their release, even as I sacrificed my integrity at the expense of fitting in.

I had no idea how to find you, nor did I know that it was for you I looked. I hadn't thought to look in the Bible for romance. Why would any man?

The idea that the mere picture of someone could make me question my belief in God was something that had never crossed my mind. Yes, I people watched. With unconscious assessment, I looked at everyone I encountered. I scoured the internet, blindly driven by some unseen force, without understanding what I expected to find, or when I would know it had been found.

The moment I saw you in that black dress, I knew my life would be forever altered.

Surrender.

As the pandemic settled over the world in the Spring of 2020, I had the first real sense of who I was. I also had the oddest sense of orchestration, particularly as I reviewed the tumultuous events that saw the end of another relationship as 2019 came to an end. It felt like my life was unfolding for me on a scale I could scarcely comprehend. From this wellspring, I drew such rich waters. I felt in command of my destiny.

You were more than I could imagine. Some days, I would look at a post you had shared, or revisit one of your stories, awestruck by what I saw. My heart sang with a vibrancy I did not know it possessed. The spectrum of emotions I began to feel exceeded my greatest expectations.

Seeing you elicited in me a happiness, a joy, that was rapturous. How could I know such abundant bliss? Yes, bliss was the word. As the pandemic exhaled its terrible pollen over the earth, I was adrift with possibility. How could I fathom what I was witnessing?

Jesus.

Over the course of my mortal life, though I was unconscious to the fact, I had sought my own destruction.

What else can account for all the broken relationships, failed marriages, and infidelities?

Looking for you, I lost myself.

I initiated my divorces, and hardly contested their proceedings. I sabotaged my moments of happiness, forfeiting material possessions and financial stability. I lost friends and pushed family away. I twisted my life in knots, losing myself in desperate bouts of drinking, uncertain why lasting happiness was so elusive, even as each broken relationship strengthened my belief that such happiness was out there, waiting to be found. Destruction.

I lost my faith.

That reality would express itself in the starkest terms in the summer of 2020.

That would be the summer I began to face the truth; I had started the war in heaven. I had declared war on love.

Lost.

A sheep, in wolf's clothing.

I didn't consider "God" as family. It was just "God." This...entity, something very much outside me. The creator of heaven and earth. Ostensibly, Jesus' Father. The only catch was, Jesus' Father didn't have a name. Jesus was just...Son of "God." God...some mysterious figure that was all-knowing, and everywhere and nowhere at once, or sitting on a throne, passive and unmoved by the struggles of his creation. I did not find myself alone in this thinking, and found refuge with likeminded people, who questioned the existence of God from a great distance.

I cloaked myself with the shame of my missteps. No one ever enters a relationship, hoping it will end. Invariably, after a few dates, a few months, a few years, I would come to the same conclusion; this relationship wasn't it. Something was missing.

Or someone.

It has been hard for me to acknowledge a relationship with our Son. The reason for that is quite simple. I was looking for his Mother, without knowing it…not until I saw you. And yet, unable to find you, how could I ever accept him?

The truth was, I never could fully understand how Jesus fit into romantic love. Honestly, his isn't the first name that comes to mind. It wasn't just that. It was praying to a God that seemed impersonal. That was how I addressed many of my prayers…"Dear God." I was like an ape, praying to "Human." It didn't make sense. I didn't appreciate that developing a personal relationship with Jesus was the only way to get to Heaven, and it certainly took me a long time to gather that Jesus' Father *must* have an identity, and that his path to believing in his Son would need to be unique, and quite purposeful. What would be required for the Father who sent his Son to die on a cross to accept responsibility? How would Jesus' Father become a Christian?

How would that Father explain his existence?

When my mortal life was spiraling out of control, and there were at least three good occasions where it went sideways quite severely, I would just think of or cry out to God. But what good is there in praying to an abstract entity?

Jesus is a name. An identity. The Son of God. No man comes to the Father except through Him.

For much of my life, it never dawned on me to look at the story told from the Bible and how that story might have continued to evolve throughout modern history. Yes, Christianity advanced. Islam was born. Countless wars have been waged in the name of these religions. Could the story of Jesus' Father be explained through history?

The answer seems obvious now, but in truth, the journey that led to this understanding had its share of trials, consequences, and blunders. All because of love.

I knew, in some vague sense, that Mary was the Mother of God. Easy enough to digest. Mother of Jesus. Jesus, Son of God. Mary, Mother of God. God, the Father.

But looking in the Bible for romance? The King David of the Old Testament existed a thousand years before the time of Mary and Jesus. Even when the archangel Gabriel appears before Mary to tell her she's going to give birth to the Son of David, most people…most Christians…don't take Gabriel's statement at face value.

The funny thing is, why would an angel tell a woman she's pregnant through the power of the Holy Spirit, name someone as the father, and *not* name *the* Father?

It's the idea of one. It's difficult enough to comprehend that Jesus died for all the world's sins. It's as equally as hard to believe that *someone* sent him to die on the cross.

So then, who is King David? And how is it possible, that he could have a story to tell in the twenty-first century? Going back three thousand years, he was the shepherd boy who felled Goliath. He wrote poems. He was a brilliant strategist. He was a king. He also had an affair, and sent the woman's husband off to battle, where he was killed.

I have had the strangest fascination with love, ruled as I have been by my heart. When I was a boy, it was cute. When I was a teenager, it became something both odd and somehow, I believed, admired. By the time I became a man well, you would have thought left-brained practicality and pragmatism would have won the day. No. Not entirely.

I have spent my entire mortal life, walking on a beach, looking for a single, specific grain of sand.

I was a romantic…I just didn't know I was *literally*, the biggest one ever created.

I was convinced there was *one* person I was *destined* to be with.

My friends humored me in my youth. When I was an adult, people appealed to my sense of reason, especially after my first divorce.

You know there's not really one person meant for another, they'd say. I wanted to agree with them; I *knew* what they said made sense. There are billions of people on the planet. The odds that two people share something so grand a story as ours is beyond astronomical. It borders the farthest reaches of existence and imagination.

I *understood* what my friends said, but I couldn't believe it. Logically, I agreed with them. In the U.S. the divorce rate is on the high side of 50 percent. Still, there was something inside me I could not vocalize that resisted such an idea with absolute certainty.

As a result, I kept looking. In some odd way, it was as if each broken relationship was preparing me for something. As I grew older, I took relationships more seriously. In my late thirties, I felt like it was time to settle down. When my second marriage didn't turn out to be the "one." I went looking again. This time, I was in my mid-forties. The Persian poet Rumi once said, you have to keep breaking your heart until it opens.

Breaking my heart open took fifty long, very mortal feeling years.

April 4, 2020. A week before my birthday.

I will remember that day for all eternity.

I was exhausted. My life had gone ridiculously off track because I refused to settle on mortal love. It seems ridiculous to say. I so enjoyed watching couples who genuinely liked being around one another. I wanted what they had, yet contented myself with their company. I wanted the nice car, the fancy house, the vacations to nice places, and the warm sense of family. I wanted to live without worrying about life.

What *did* I have? Most would say I had commitment issues.

I'd say, I had the grandest expectations of love one creature could ever possess. I'd seen so many things on my travels around the world, much of them while in the military.

But I'd never seen anything like the picture of the woman I saw on April 4, 2020. The woman that made me question what I believed.

It was the first time in my life I saw *absolute certainty*.

At my age, with my track record in love, I'd had my doubts. So many doubts. Tearing relationships apart was painful. I drank. I agonized. I tried my best to forget what I had done by focusing on what was in front of me. It sometimes felt heartless, but I knew to some degree, each failed relationship was burning a layer off that wasn't serving me. It wasn't serving anyone.

I was consumed with the material world. Own stuff. Make as much money as you can. Plan for retirement. Physical pleasure and comfort. Stay healthy in the hopes of putting off death as long as possible. But something, *someone*, always vectored me back towards love. Love was my prime directive.

That seems so obvious now, but I couldn't piece it together. I was looking for someone without ever bothering to look to the Cross. For romance? The Cross seems to be the absolute *last* place one would think to look for a romantic love story. If Google is to be believed, there have been more than one hundred billion people throughout human history. The odds are nothing, if not extravagant. Faith can be extravagant.

I felt like it took me a long time to come to Jesus. I was fifty years old when I first saw you. Fifty. And I felt it.

Reconciling visual proof of absolute certainty is no easy task. Quite literally, for the first three or four months of the pandemic, I couldn't believe what I'd seen. I looked at you with sheer awe. It took commitment, perseverance, and dedication just to reconcile myself to the fact that you were *real*. It demanded an introspection that was uncompromising, and sometimes, downright scary. I would learn that absolute certainty, once realized, is non-negotiable, inviolable.

That is the price of an eternal soul. That is the cost for everlasting life. Yes, these things demand the removal of all our limiting beliefs, our prejudices. Someone must bear witness to the journey needed to remove these deficiencies.

Yet, you are real. You have a life. Friends. Family. You own a cat.

I see you every day. Separated by an ocean, you are as close to me as heaven will allow. For so long, that felt so very far away.

It has been more than two years since you posted that picture. Given what preceded the viewing of that post the week prior, I hope you can forgive me for struggling the way I have in writing to you.

I started work on this story instantly. *Gladiator*. Maximus.

I have his armor next to me, on display, as I write.

When I saw your picture, I thought of his wife. There was no hesitation, no bothering to address the implications of the journey I would have to take, and whether it was worth taking. You *were* the wife of Maximus, wearing a black necklace with a black dress, drenched in a field of golden wheat. Black and gold. Two of my favorite colors, together. The writer in me danced at the idea of finding a story there.

But there was something so odd about the picture as well.

It afforded me the strangest sensation, as though I'd seen the picture before.

I did not know what I had done. How could I?

Gladiator was one of the first movies to come out that really seemed to take advantage of computer-generated special effects in a realistic setting; it didn't involve spaceships, outrageous creatures, or wizards and magic.

I remember watching an HBO special on the making of the film. This must have been in the early 2000's. They showed the rendering of the Colosseum, and the computer-generated people that appeared, cheering the combat taking place in the arena. With the magic of Hollywood, filmmakers also showed how they could virtually take us back to the glorious past of Rome at the time of Marcus Aurelius. Pillars of marble and stone. Imperial flags and banners flapping in a majestic breeze. Gladiators engaged in mortal combat. The grandeur and splendor of the empire near its zenith.

Where do the ideas for our stories come from? Every story comes from the mind of imagination, a limitless wellspring of possibility.

The story of Maximus, like the story of William Wallace in *Braveheart*, resonated with me; those kinds of stories always had. There was something about losing love and then being compelled to fight for it in the most magnificent of ways that appealed to me, even if this appeal was unspoken. To take on empires, or overthrow the yoke of slavery at the cost of your life. I cried watching those movies, without fail. That was the feeling of love I *felt* inside me but could never fully realize. If you'd asked me at the time why those movies called to me, I'm not certain I could have told you. That was just how I saw love. It sounds impractical beloved, but how could I fail to recognize that feeling when it was so plainly there?

Jesus was immediately a part of the story in the early drafts I wrote, but only in the most remote sense of the word. I believed he had died and come back to life. I just didn't appreciate the fact that he had done it for me. That concept felt incredibly foreign to me, if for no other reason than I felt that all my relationships, no matter how noble they might have been, had come up short.

Love that demanded exceptional, unreasonable greatness. That was the love on display in *Gladiator, Braveheart,* and scores of other movies like *Dances with Wolves* and *Last of the Mohicans.* The love I felt from those movies enflamed my belief in some unbelievable love on my horizon. That kind of love was within me, alive and well, though it seemingly lacked direction.

Seeing you alive elicited in me a feeling I wanted more of, a feeling I wanted to understand as wholly and as deeply as I could. Seeing you alive astonished me. If ever there was a Siren's Song I was meant to hear, I heard its first notes most clearly on April 4, 2020.

To this day, I believe the picture I saw that day was just the second picture of you I'd seen. I was still reeling from the end of my last relationship, and had taken to Instagram in search of beautiful women to follow as a means of bandaging my wounded pride. It was altogether pathetic. Each woman elicited a different kind of feeling. Each had their own way of representing themselves. Some appealed to a man's baser instincts. Some offered humor blended with an intellectual approach. Others shined in so many ways, from spiritual to good-natured.

The first picture I remember was you showing off your ridiculously sculpted abs, with a map of the world painted on the wall behind you.

Your eyes…even today when I see your eyes, I know I am looking into eternity. Two years ago, it was like I'd been struck by lightning.

Your face was so familiar to me. It was a face I'd somehow seen all my life. It's hard to be romantic talking about comic books, but you looked like virtually every woman I saw in comics growing up. I don't even know how that was possible. They all looked different, not just their costumes, but their faces. Jean Grey did not look like Black Widow. Captain Marvel did not look like the Scarlet Witch. And yet…there you were.

That's why you were so unbelievable. A living, breathing sculpture. I have never seen such harmony between someone's nature, intelligence, and beauty. It was like the earth had become a woman.

Seeing you a few days after my Judgment Day, I celebrated like I'd just won the lottery, not realizing that I still very much had a minimum wage mindset. I felt like a beggar. If you've ever seen the movie *Return of the King* from the *Lord of the Rings* series, I was Gollum. When he finally gets the Ring of Power near the end of the movie, he's being consumed by the lake of fire underneath Mt. Doom. That was the beginning of my pandemic.

Did I know, like Maximus, I would face my own fears? Could I imagine, like William Wallace, how I would falter? There was no way I could have known the strength I would need to call on, nor from where I would find it.

So many fears. So many questions. So much doubt. The price of being human.

Now, I see just how small I was looking. For nearly six months after I saw you on that day, I was delirious. I couldn't get over the fact that you were *real*, nor could I comprehend how you so clearly expressed the beauty inside you with your physical appearance. Like you were a marriage between human and nature. I would look at your posts and stories with such wonder. Never mind what it said about me. What it said about me would take me more than a year to begin to face. That was where Jesus came into the picture, as if to say, *you want to be worthy of my Mother? You must come through Me.*

No one comes to the Father except through Me. That includes the Father. To become a Christian, Jesus' Father must become a man.

I was so unprepared.

There was the euphoria, and then there was the fear.

There was also my first, *real* sense of identity. *That* was horrifying before it ever began to feel beautiful. To feel fun.

To feel free.

Did you know me? Had you been waiting for me to find myself? What else could that spark of intelligence in your eyes be, if not divine wisdom? Your mind, as sculpted as your physique. That was what I saw in your posts. A perfectly sculpted mind.

Seeing you drove me to the Bible. I have read more from that book these last two years than in all the years that preceded them combined. I have spent days, weeks, months in research.

It never dawned on me why the Jewish people adopted as their symbol The Star of David; only recently have I made the connection that the symbol is also the fourth chakra in the chakra system. The heart chakra. It never occurred to me to look at what Judaism, Christianity, and Islam shared, or the idea that the story of eternal love might somehow be intertwined in their stories, a golden thread meant to be unraveled by three souls.

King David, Jesus Christ, and the Virgin Mary.

Perhaps the scariest idea is to come out of religious thought that Jesus' Father is unknowable. Some being of pure light sitting on a throne somewhere. That was the cartoon pamphlets I remember as a kid; a throne with someone sitting on it, with nothing but light radiating from the being's upper body.

Jesus' Father would have to be quite the storyteller.

First Father. First King. First Son.

Can there be a Romance the world can believe in? What will happen when the world understands the true meaning of the Love of God?

The story of Jesus' Father *must* be explainable. Not only that, but it must also explain human history; why has there been such conflict and so much war?

Most importantly, the story of Jesus' Father must provide a concept of eternal love that everyone can believe in. A Heaven that doesn't allow for everyone is not one I want to belong to.

It is my hope that, with this brief narrative as precursor, I have provided you a view of the journey we are to undertake together.

Now, my beloved, I will share with you the story of how I became Thor.

THE SPANIARD I
AFTERLIFE—181 AD

When you surrender to a woman all apprehension of who you claim to be, and reveal your soul, she'll tell you exactly who you are.

Your name was Mariah.

The first time I saw you, I saw a woman clothed in the sun. The black dress you wore only seemed to brighten the wheat that swayed in golden, hushing waves around where you stood.

I was entranced. You were the answer before I knew the question.

I remember the first time I said your name. *Mariah.* A name had never tasted so delightful on my tongue, even after you told me what it meant.

Bitter.

You said I would remember it for a long time. I remember thinking, *of that…I have no doubt.* I was taken. It would only be after your death that I came to understand what exactly it was you intended to convey with your words.

When I fulfilled my pledge to Marcus, and returned power to the people of Rome, I believed myself free from my debts, and sought to join you in the afterlife. Paradise seemed but a few steps from me.

I could not know the role I was to play in shaping human history for generations to come; how could I reconcile myself to understanding that my consciousness was War, the second horsemen of the apocalypse, loosed upon the earth because of Jesus' death and resurrection?

Without a belief in something greater than ourselves, we are but shadows and dust. I believed I would see you again. You and Samuel, our son. I believed then, in the dusty grit of the Colosseum, that my journey in the afterlife began in a field of wheat, ripe for the harvest. As far as the eye could see, golden wheat. In the distance, I could see a cart path. It was in that direction that I began to look for the two of you.

The wheat is like walking through a memory. War. The legions. Germania.

In Germania, we used to hear of witches.

They were just rumors at first. Our scouts at the outposts would tell of spine-chilling cries emanating from the dark. Not the bellows of a man, nor the shrieks of an animal. I didn't understand the language, but the first time I heard these cries, their voices sounded demonic and defiant. There was something primal in their nature. What was true of them was also true of the land. You could feel it in the forests. Hear its echo in the towering, jagged trees. The air turned into something hostile, as if the edge of where empire met frontier were subject to some unseeable inferno, the war between the light and what I perceived to be the dark. Between knowledge and ignorance, order and nature. You could sense the crackle of oppressive energy.

These witches emboldened their men to fight like beasts. Prior to battle, we could hear them loosen their tongues. Feral. Savage. Whatever gods they believed in, they invoked them to fight on their behalf.

Sometimes the women fought alongside the barbarians. On at least one occasion, one of them had blinded themselves in one eye as a means of channeling their gods. I saw her in combat, saw the fresh blood dripping from underneath the wrapping she'd dressed over her wound. It was startling; these people loved their freedom. It was an intelligent and altogether ferocious type of warfare, one that harnessed the powers of the earth herself.

The second battle against the Marcomanni, a powerful tribe that ruled a large area north of the Danube, I watched in awe, and with some measure of admiration, the way a single warrior stood in front of the line of barbarian skirmishers, stirring them into a turbulent frenzy.

She spoke with such ferocity as she paced back and forth; her stride was that of some great commander. Across the battlefield, every eye, Roman and barbarian, was transfixed by her presence. Though the distance between us was not inconsiderable, I could see clearly, she held a chalice in one hand, and some kind of plant in the other. As she paced across the front of the line, her bellows echoed off the trees. As she finished, she ate from the plant she held, and took a drink from the cup.

This roused the barbarians intensely. At the battle's end we were victorious, but our losses had been significant.

Marcus didn't like fighting them. The "problem of Germania." as he called it, had plagued Rome for generations. Caesar Augustus, the "first man" and first emperor of Rome, sought to subdue the region by capturing the sons of the tribal chieftains and "Romanizing" them; Roman men of high standing adopted these sons, raising them as their own. The Germanic tribes recognized no central government and thus, were infinitely more challenging to subdue. The thinking was to breed the primitive tribalism out of them by civilizing the tribal heirs, and then installing them as chieftains loyal to the empire. In 9 AD, one of these sons, Arminius had been his Roman name, betrayed his Roman "father" and led the united tribes of Germania against the Roman empire in the woods of the Teutoburg Forest. The result?

Three Roman legions destroyed. A startling snakebite to the nascent empire. By the time Marcus became emperor in 161, fifteen emperors had tried to solve the problem of Germania, using whatever means were available—treaties, diplomacy, conflict. He enjoyed four years of peace as emperor before "the problem" would occupy his faculties for the remainder of his life.

I was there alongside him for much of that time; the hammer of might against the anvil of his vision.

I only knew life as a soldier. Whatever my life had been before the legion was lost on me as I made my way through the ranks. I learned everything I could about warfare.

I believed in Rome, without fully understanding what it was. It seemed the light of the world emanated from this great city, though I had never set foot inside its walls. The closer I got to Marcus, the more I realized…the light that I saw in him was the Rome I believed in. That light would die the day he did and I, I would be banished from its rays.

Every leader must choose where to focus their energy and efforts. The domestic affairs of empire, Marcus knew, were important. He also knew, expanding the empire meant solving the problems on its frontiers. Many peoples were easily subdued, at least for a time, falling easily under the yoke of Roman rule. They fought with a limited understanding of warfare, and only to preserve the free-spirited, natural way of life they knew. Romans had learned from our Greek ancestors the art of war. What we lacked in Greek culture, we made up for in our skill for conquest, expansion, and governance.

Marcus knew his legacy would be the sword.

History is a series of convulsions Maximus, he would say, sitting comfortably atop his horse. *One moment, it exhales a man like Augustus. A sublime man. A man of vision. He had a dream of what civilization could be; he took the lessons from his adopted father Julius Caesar, and breathed that dream to life with his words and deeds. He brought about a kind of peace previously unseen in human history.*

I cherished our moments together. He was extraordinary, not only for how he saw the potential of what could be, but how he kept himself in check.

Another moment, he continued, inhaling a wisp of his long, white hair into the corner of his mouth, *history vomits and spits out a Caligula. Here was a man who saw the greatness of Rome and sought to consume it inside himself. A devil of a man; incest with his sisters. A demigod. One man shines a light from within, the other seeks to devour it, for he finds so little of the light in him. His mind knows only darkness.*

As a soldier, my mind was honed to razor-sharpness in support of the empire; loyalty to the emperor was a must. I felt myself fortunate to serve under one bound by such practicalities.

Why have I been driven to do the things I have, Maximus? We believe ourselves to be the forebearers of some great knowledge, infinitely smarter than the barbarians before us. Barbarians who, for all their backwardness, all their crude ideas, elude our subjugations and in doing so, prove themselves wiser. And yet, every problem must have a solution. The obstacle becomes the path.

With that, he turned to me and smiled. He waited until my eyes met his, though I did not immediately discern the reason for such a gesture.

I had never been afforded the confidences of a man like Marcus. That only served to deepen my loyalty to him, if such a thing were possible, and underscored the steadfastness by which I executed his vision.

How did I become a General?

Many saw the emperor as a god, clothed as a man. Watching how the campaigns aged him, I knew Marcus wasn't a god. I didn't worship him. It wasn't just that he was the emperor...like Augustus, Marcus was a man of foresight. He saw what could be. I did not pretend to understand the emperors so consumed by the idea of power, they used it to devour themselves, or lurch the empire into such a precarious state of affairs as to warrant assassination. There was good in Marcus. I saw it in the same way I felt the good in you.

The voice of an emperor carried such weight, such impact, and the separation of knowledge between the working class and the imperial was much greater. Most Roman citizens could not read. Those that could, got their information from the acta, carved in stone around the city. Others relied on the orators, or secondhand knowledge.

Marcus was brilliant. I gravitated towards him. I listened when he spoke, absorbing his words and their meaning. That, and my abilities on the battlefield, led to my quick ascension through the ranks. I respected his intelligence, admired his resilience in how he carried the burden of being emperor. I understood what he intended to do, what he saw as possible. He spoke with such profound clarity; he said it, and it was so. I could imagine little else outside the grand purpose to which we marched. And then I saw you.

The first moment I saw you in that field, I knew I was home. How easily I succumbed to your spell.

Believing in eternity takes time and yet, I knew instantly…whatever fire you had lit in my chest would burn eternally, such was the intensity I felt in the moment when our eyes met. I would need an eternity to try and understand all that you were to me.

Before battle, I would encourage my men. *Elysium. Paradise. Imagine where you wish to be, and it shall be so.*

From the moment I first saw you, I knew my heaven would always have you in it. I would find a way. No matter what it took.

Seek and ye shall find. Ask, and it shall be given.

The story of our romance is familiar to you; I share these thoughts now in fond reflection.

As it is my beginning, in my journey back home to you, I shall now endeavor to share with you the man I became since the last time you saw me alive. Since I wasted little of our life together sharing stories of my soldiering, it makes sense to start there.

War, in its simplest form, is a matter of opposing forces, each seeking to impose its will on the other. What is true in man versus man is equally true with army versus army, and nation versus nation.

It is also true of God versus Man.

The individual fighter is made through training and experience in the field. As he sharpens his mind, he sharpens his sword. A weapon is only as useful as the mind that wields it. In time, the soldier who advances is the one who possesses enough intellect to "see" the battle; they have a sense of how the terrain guides the battle, like water flowing through a valley. This enhanced sight leads to success; success leads to victory. Victory, to advancement. Advancement of objectives, of vision. Advancement of purpose. Progress.

Ascending the ranks, a commander can direct his forces to disrupt what the enemy leader is attempting to do. In time, the great commanders visualize the battle *before* it has taken place. They do so repeatedly. They look at the land and imagine the clashing of opposing armies. They begin to put themselves in the mind of their enemy.

What is he thinking? Why is he fighting this war? What does he seek to achieve?

With study and focus, a commander can discern his opponent's aims and how they hope to achieve them.

What is critical is that the commander *must* be engaged. War has an edge to it. That man willing to get closest to the edge has the greatest chance of dictating the terms of the battle. Only in the rarest of circumstances does a battle go according to plan, which is why active engagement is essential to victory. Hope is not a course of action.

The commander must direct his efforts at what he believes is the critical place and do so when he believes it is the critical time.

The simple life of a soldier brings with it the clearest illuminations. What a common man indulges in is, for the legionnaire, an extravagance. There is a purity in soldiering, a stark clarity in war.

I was equipped with a clarity few men possessed. Most were tied up in the physical pleasures of life. Drink. Women. Gambling. I searched for something deeper. I saw warfare as essential to the advancement of wisdom over a world shrouded in uncivilized darkness.

When I was on campaign, I appreciated a warm fire. A hot meal. Dry weather. Watching the sunrise through the thick nest of German trees.

Prior to battle, I would rub dirt into my hands. As much as my men believed I did it to better grip my sword, the feeling of it as I clenched my fingers made me think of you.

The hints of gold in your brown hair. How you liked to walk barefoot in the garden. The fullness of your laugh. The way you didn't care if your hands were caked black with the rich soil. The way I made you blush just with the silence in my eyes and admiration in my smile. Feeling the earth, I felt you.

Conflict has a spirit to it. Opposing forces.

The side with momentum *knows* it has the momentum, even if this knowledge isn't spoken. It isn't even thought. It's an energy. A feeling.

It enflames resolve. It guides a man to channel an inner strength. Shields are carried higher. Blows from a sword are struck with greater certainty and urgency. That strength is anchored with the virtues by which the war is being waged.

I felt that strength drain from my body when I came to our estate in Trujillo, already exhausted from my escape from Commodus, and found you and our son, Samuel, hanged at the gate.

THE FIRST LETTER OF THUNDER

War was a game we played as kids. It started in kindergarten. Most every kid in the neighborhood had a toy gun of some kind. It was 1974.

My brother and I were lucky. One day, our dad brought home the wooden frames of old M1 Garands used during World War Two; the Marine Corps was finally getting rid of them. They were made of sturdy wood, and still had the metal ringlets that held the sling. The butt stocks of each had a metal latch and cover. Once we were able to pry them open, we found the cleaning gear inside the Marines used to maintain their weapons.

They were, by far, the coolest "toy" guns in history. We became the envy of every kid on the block.

We played other games too. War was rarely played when girls were present, mostly because none of them had guns. On those occasions, hide-and-go-seek, red rover, or some version of tag would suffice.

The rules of war were simple. Two teams, each as evenly matched as possible, attempting to defeat the other on the field of battle. Before the shooting started, it was important to declare what kind of weapon you had. While it may look like a regular toy pistol or rifle, we all had active imaginations and would allow either of those to be something awesome, like a bazooka or machine gun. This was important whenever there was a debate over whether someone got "shot."

When that happened, an immediate cease-fire would be called, and the gang of kids would huddle together to hear the evidence. We wanted to resume hostilities as quickly as possible, and hearing all the facts laid out by both sides was crucial, as it could ultimately turn the tide of the war.

I'd like to think that everyone had a sense of who was winning and who was losing, but we were kids. Everyone felt like they were winning.

We played in the neighborhood, oblivious if the war drifted into strangers' yards. Kids were running around, crouching down behind cars or one would peer from around the corner of a nearby house, looking for signs of the enemy.

Sometimes, there would be no movement. Silence.

Your heart would leap up into your throat, your pulse pounding against your temples.

Seconds stretched into hours.

Then, a shot.

"*Bam!*"

There may have been one or two of us who had a weapon that made noise on its own at the squeeze of a trigger. In most cases, you had to shout every time you fired a shot. That was one of the drawbacks of having the wooden M1 frames; we shouted *Bang!* a lot.

It was fun. War was on tv, whether it was news from the Vietnam War, old western shows featuring the likes of John Wayne or Clint Eastwood, the silliness of *Hogan's Heroes,* or other movies or shows about World War Two.

War was a game.

The First Letter of David

We were all gods once. Can you imagine it? An infinite number of eternal beings. The Bible calls it the fall from grace.

A rebellion in heaven. A great red Dragon. Satan. A woman, pregnant with child. But how does that rebellion start? Directed energy. Frequency. Purpose.

A single thought. The thought that gives birth to matter.

Picture an hourglass, filled with sand.

Each grain, an immortal soul. One by one, they pass through the eye of the hour-glass. They fall to earth.

Life starts over. Simple. Elementary. Even billions of years ago, quantum physics existed. Energy can neither be created nor destroyed; it can only be transformed. The quantum was as real then as it is today.... in many ways, more so than today.

The earth was young. Free. Rambunctious. She was caretaker to blind life scurrying over her surface.

Imagine the tickle...billions upon billions of little microbes, all interacting with a most curious universe. A drop of life floating in an ocean of stars and galaxies. That's what the earth is.

Souls are made in heaven. To become flesh, we came to earth. Material. Matter.

As life grows, the universe grows. In time, life produces vision. The Cambrian explosion.

To give vision, the universe must lose something. The universe must go blind. Faith in what we do not see.

Creatures begin to see. Life and nature develop a relationship with one another.

Evolutionary harmony. And yet, the scales must always be rocked off balance a bit. Earthquakes. Floods. Meteors. Intelligence.

Simple creatures give way to more complex ones. Animals. Mammals.

Apes. Cro-Magnon. Neanderthal.

Man.

As the hourglass fills with the souls of the fallen, there are multitudes of gods emptying from heaven down to earth.

Then, a council of the gods.

Finally, the idea that there is only one God. In a sense, the top half of the hourglass is empty. It is easy to suggest "God" is the top half of the hourglass, sitting on his throne in Judgment. Blind. Empty yet full. Everything and nothing. But all the grains of sand are in the bottom.

"God" has one purpose. Make all things new. Enter, Jesus.

That may be the easiest way to conceive of heaven and earth.

A great red dragon. A woman who gives birth to a son who will rule heaven with an iron scepter. And, where is the child's father in all this?

I'm getting ahead of myself. Perhaps it's best if I start from my beginning.

The Second Letter of David

My earliest childhood memory is running naked outside immediately after being dried off from a bath I have just taken. I am perhaps two years old. It is warm, either spring or summer, 1971. My hair is dirty blond, and incredibly curly. I am baby-pudgy, with the soft, innocent skin of someone so young.

I bounce down the sidewalk as only a child filled with such bliss can. Neighbors are mowing their yards, some are playing in front of their houses with their kids; I distinctly remember the presence of people, which made my celebration of life even more joyous.

Two-thirds of the way down the sidewalk, I stop and let out a shrill scream of pleasure. My hands fly up along my face in childish glee, my fingers spread wide.

What's most enjoyable to me about reliving this memory is my ability to see myself celebrating from outside myself. I found that much enjoyment in the moment.

There is such power in a moment.

My mother and father come from simple enough beginnings. Father grew up in a small town in Iowa. Born in 1939, he witnessed firsthand the spectacle of American splendor as our country entered the global scene in such fine fashion, defeating the Japanese and helping to win the war in Europe against fascism. Though I never asked him about it, I can only imagine the sense of awe he must have felt as a little boy, sitting with his parents, listening to the radio squawk about the advances the Allies were making in both theaters until the victory of 1945. What stirrings of the imagination did those radio reports awaken in my father's impressionable six-year-old mind?

Dad's family was stoic; my grandfather on this side chewed his words with a thick, Iowa drawl as they came out of his mouth. He was a deliberate man, with deep lines in his skin, like worn leather, from all the time he'd spent in the midwestern sun. He rarely joked, and lived with a mind set on the way things should be. Dad had two younger brothers, both who served in the Navy during Vietnam. Three boys growing up in a Cornbelt town the size of a postage stamp, all left with a deep impression of what America could be for the world.

Going to Iowa from the East coast never failed to be an adventure. It often meant at least one overnight stay in a motel, which in turn meant a swimming pool if it was summertime. Iowa was fascinating; there was so much open land. Driving with the windows down, dad always implored us to breathe in that "fresh country air" that usually smelled of cow manure.

Dad enlisted in the Marines in 1959, and met my mom that same year. She was born outside Pittsburgh, Pennsylvania in 1941. Her Hungarian family was quite large, and had settled in the hills surrounding the Steel City. You could feel the Old Country in that side of the family when we went to visit them. Some of it was the furniture, or the faded, black-and-white family photographs from Europe.

Mom's family was LOUD. Much of it was all the Hungarian being spoken, and the unique aromas wafting from the kitchen of my grandmother or great-grandmother, depending on whose house was hosting our get-togethers. If ever I learned the definition of "cackle" it was listening to the roars of laughter that frequently erupted from the kitchen during these trips. While I never learned more than four words of Hungarian, I did pick up on some of the smells. Nothing smelled so tantalizing as when my great-grandmother was making her special chicken soup. It might cook for hours. It was one of the big *hope-for's* on a visit to Pennsylvania.

There were lots of women on mom's side of the family. Gatherings at my great-grandparents' house sounded of wild, raucous laughter from the kitchen, while the men drank whiskey at the dining room table, talking about serious things, like the war or the recession.

My dad wasn't a big drinker, but going to Pittsburgh usually meant he'd be having more than a few shots with my great-uncle, a barrel-chested man who spoke with a thick Hungarian accent. He'd help lead his family out of Hungary when the Russians arrived and, despite his modest means, had a unique understanding of the world, and of life. He'd bribed and killed border guards to bring his family across the Atlantic.

Mom was a nurse when my parents met. Sometime after my brother and I came along, and we started moving every few years, she gave up on her nursing career and spent a fair amount of time working retail near the various bases where we were stationed.

My childhood was pleasant enough, even with the dark scenes of which I now share.

The voice in my head…my imaginary friend when I was just a kid? I knew it was Jesus. I can't tell you how I knew. I just *knew*. He told me things that were brilliant, even though I was too young to understand the full weight of their meaning.

I remember him telling me about living forever. About a kingdom, and the glory to come. I don't know if I was old enough to take it for granted…I just know, I always loved hearing him talk.

He warned me of dangers to come. I don't remember exactly what he said…I just knew he said I didn't need to worry.

At night, while lying in bed waiting for sleep to overtake me, I would rub my blanket against my scalp, then use my fingers to create little bolts of static electricity. The tiny crackles were fascinating, and the "pops" of blue light felt like they were lighting up my whole room.

Even as a five-year-old, I was thinking about romance. I can remember balling up my blanket and pretending it was a girl from my kindergarten class. I would say whatever kinds of things five-year-old's thought were romantic, and kiss my blanket. Larry, my eight-year-old brother would walk by my closed door, stop, and giggle at what I was saying.

I remember my first kiss; in kindergarten, a girl named Mimi knocked me through the cardboard wall of the castle we were playing in. Cardboard bricks were tumbling everywhere. She landed on top of me, gave me a little kid grin, and kissed me on the lips.

I had a vivid imagination. Though I liked playing games with my family, I was oddly selective about who I wanted to play with outside that circle. I couldn't say why. I would just get quiet, particular after the incident with the hammer.

As a family, we would often play badminton, when the weather was nice, have game night, or watch our favorite TV shows together. During this age, Larry and I would draw "plans" with pen and paper for defeating our dad during our frequent wrestling matches with him. We probably watched a little too much Bugs Bunny. During the summers, we would manage one trip to the beach, usually Ocean City, Maryland. There, besides basking in the sun and exhausting ourselves in the sea, we'd make plenty of time for different kinds of board games. We would indulge with saltwater taffy, or snow cones, and take long strolls along the boardwalk, imploring our parents to give us their spare change, that we might spend it at the arcade. Life was always good at the beach.

When I was two, and shrieking with glee in my birthday suit, I really did have the sense of being outside myself, in the most beautiful of ways. Even today, that memory feels vibrant and colorful.

My next out-of-body experience would bring with it an altogether different sensation.

It was the mid-seventies. I was five or six.

We lived just outside the University of Maryland in a town called Hyattsville. It was the only time growing up that we lived among the civilian population here in the United States; the rest of the time was spent on military bases.

A military base is a self-contained city. It has all the municipal functions of a regular town or city; police and fire, sanitation. There are grocery stores and fast-food places. There are recreation centers and movie theaters.

I didn't realize it at the time, but I grew up among a culture of men whose chief function in life was to defend their country and one another, sacrificing themselves if necessary. When my dad had people over to the house for get-togethers, they were in the same line of work; they were Marines. Even my parents' close-knit friends were Marine officers my father had known over the course of his military career. If we had guests that weren't family, they were foreign officers visiting the U.S. from another country. They talked about their "business" all the time.

I grew up among a tribe of warriors. What does that mean?

Growing up in the military and then joining the military here in the US, I realized...people in the military spend the bulk of their time focusing outside of America. The world is viewed through the lens of potential hot spots; figuratively speaking, your back is turned to your country. You stand on the wall, looking out.

Safety isn't measured by where you go on a military base. There are no "seedy" parts of base. People just feel safe. House doors aren't always locked. As often as not, the same is true with cars, or used to be. Everyone recognizes themselves as part of something bigger. Each person on the base is part of a family. Each family has someone on active duty, or someone who serves in some capacity of supporting the base. Each of those individuals is a part of a unit or organization. Each organization comes together to create larger organizations, and so on. They come from all different walks of life. All races, all religions.

There was no visible fence where we lived in Maryland. No barrier that separated "us" from "them." I still remember our address; 7303 Wells Blvd. We were the only military family in our neighborhood.

Living "off-base" was cool. People's parents dressed differently.

On a base, you have a definite sense of boundaries or areas that are very distinct. The first boundary is the fence or gate that defines the perimeter of the base. If you are inside the perimeter, you are thought of as being "on-base." If you are outside, you are "off-base."

Hyattsville, Maryland was just a town that connected in some way or shape to other nearby towns.

A base is organized so that where the Marines work is separate, to some extent, from where they live. If you are a single, enlisted Marine (read "young"), you are very likely living in a barracks or sharing space with another young single Marine, and live very close to where you work. You have access to food, a gym, and other forms of entertainment that are available on-base. If you want to go off-base, you're going to need a car. Some Marines can afford them, some can't. That's why a buddy system is important.

From there, the "housing area" is distant from where the single Marines live and where most Marines go to "work." Housing is assigned by rank, and people of the same rank are grouped together in common housing areas. The houses are cookie-cutter in their appearance, but each occupant can create their own personal feel with decorations and lawncare.

Off-base in Maryland, we lived in an area that we could afford. I remember my parents borrowed money from their parents for the down payment on the house. All the houses looked different. One of our neighbors a few doors up from us had a nice house. It was an elegant, white two-story house with an iron gate surrounding the perimeter. It felt like it was twice the size of ours, with an expansive yard and a gazebo.

Our house was small by comparison, one-story with an attic. Shrubs bordered the sidewalk leading up to the front door. Over the four years we lived in that house, my brother and I alternated between sharing one of the three bedrooms in the house, allowing the third to be turned into a playroom. The rest of the time, we had separate rooms. The back yard was bigger than the house, with an elevated tier where my dad set up the badminton net. There was a cement patio. In the back right corner of the yard was an old tree; jagged roots cascaded down the soft slope. The earth between the roots was bare...I remember how much I enjoyed playing with my plastic toy soldiers in the soft dirt back there.

One of my first memories from living in Maryland is my brother and I coming down with the flu. It seemed like we were sick for days, with trash cans placed beside the door in every room in case we got sick.

It was hard to appreciate the similarities of people off-base because everyone was different. That included my two best friends, Joan and Danny.

Joan was a redhead. I remember that because she was the first person I ever met with red hair. We went to kindergarten together, and I always enjoyed going to her house, which was just a few doors up the street from ours, just past the big white place. Her house had a basement, which was the domain of Joan and her two older brothers, Eric and Paul. Paul was the same age as Larry. The fun we had with Joan and her brothers was always good, clean fun.

She and I would often turn the downstairs toilet into a jacuzzi for her Barbie and my G.I. Joe dolls. Sometimes we would bake, or spend the afternoon watching cartoons...she was awesome. Joan was good-natured, and the first girl I ever liked.

And then there was Danny. Danny also had two older brothers, Matt and David. Like Paul, Matt was the same age as Larry. David might have been twelve, roughly the same age as Eric. Looking back on him now, he seemed like a full-grown man.

Spending time with Danny was always fun. He had a wicked sense of humor. One of our favorite pastimes was playing with plastic soldiers in his back yard. I can only imagine we picked up on the idea from one of our older brothers, but we fell in love with snagging a bottle of hairspray from his mom's bathroom and grabbing a lighter from the kitchen. Lighting toy soldiers on fire was the first way we taught ourselves about the consequences of war. Watching toy soldiers melt was weirdly humorous, even if it meant we were mauling our toys beyond repair in the process. Then again, little plastic soldiers were cheap.

I did say we were six, right?

But Danny had a different side to him. Sometimes, he would get angry. Really angry. Hulk-angry. It was exceptional. It was the kind of anger where one or sometimes both of his brothers would have to intervene to restrain him. No one else our age was like Danny in that regard.

We called him a spaz. It was hard to know what was going to set him off.

During the incident leading up to my second out-of-body experience, there was no indication that anything bad was going to happen. How could there have been? Real trouble is what you don't see coming.

The seventies were a crazy time. When I look at parents with their kids today, NO way are parents letting their six- and nine-year-old's roam free in the neighborhood unsupervised, the way we did. I took my first hit of a cigarette when I was six or seven, courtesy of an eight-year-old who rode the same bus as me.

On this occasion, there were five of us; Danny and his two older brothers, and Larry and I. It's hard to go back to the exact details of what happened and the circumstances immediately leading up to it. I remember we were playing in a stranger's backyard. Like I said, the seventies were a little crazy.

There was lots of bamboo forming a nice natural screen at the edge of the yard. It was cool; I hadn't seen bamboo before. I have no idea whose house it was. Frankly, it didn't matter. We were little terrors.

There was also a workbench of some kind. There were tools in the backyard, as if someone had been working on a doorframe or something. I'm sure I saw the hammer but didn't pay any attention to it.

It was getting close to supper time, and David indicated it was time to go.

Danny didn't like that. He was having fun, and the idea of closing it down before he had used up all his fun did not go over well. He went into a fit. Everything happened so fast after that.

The kind of anger Danny was able to muster, and the speed at which it arose in him, always got your attention. In this case, he had gone nuclear. His eyes bulged, and his face filled up like a jug of Kool-Aid.

The last thing I remember is seeing Danny pick up the hammer, his eyes wild with rage.

I heard Matt scream, "RUN!" I bolted, the way a gazelle might when a lion breaks from the brush. I was sprinting towards the front of the house.

There is a flash of bamboo to my right and then, darkness.

The hammer struck me cleanly in the back of the head. Danny had thrown it with all the might an enraged little boy could. I was knocked unconscious.

Loki could not have landed a better blow.

Then, the weirdest thing happened. I don't remember how much time past, but I saw Danny's oldest brother, David, carrying my body down to their house. Whereas my post-bath celebration had been filled with brilliant color and joy, the view I had here was dark and dreary. I was behind him by a good fifteen feet as he carried me. I had the strange sense that I was moving as they moved, but could get no closer than I was.

At six, I had no idea what an out-of-body experience was.

After a time, I regained consciousness. I was home, bandaged, and in our living room.

Danny's mother brought him by to see me after I got home from the hospital that night. His eyes were saucers. He'd been crying. He gave me a coloring book. It was based on a popular kids show at the time called, *Land of the Lost*.

And that was it. Our friendship was back on. Bygones were bygones.

Except for me, that wasn't it. A kind of darkness settled over me the remainder of our time in Maryland. If there was a mood in the country at the time, with all the raw emotions the war in Vietnam had stirred up in people, I didn't understand it, but I definitely sensed it.

I had trouble falling asleep. I was unable to avoid bad dreams. On one occasion, I dreamt I was being chased by a giant. I ran up a hill and hid in a hollowed-out log. Undeterred, the giant found me atop the hill and kicked the log, sending both the log and I rolling down the hill.

I rolled in my bed with enough momentum to roll over the protective railing of the top bunk and fell. My head smacked against the stepstool I normally used to climb into bed. The commotion woke my parents. Another trip to the ER. Another head wound. More stitches. I wasn't yet seven.

My brother bought KISS albums. Even as little kids, we had heard the band's name stood for Knights in Satan's Service. I was leery, but I also implicitly trusted Larry. With these grown men wearing strange makeup, and album covers with titles like *Destroyer* and *Love Gun*, I got exposed to Rock n' Roll early.

We read *Conan the Barbarian* and *Vampirella* magazines; ultimately, we switched to comic books because, unlike the magazines, the comics were in color.

Perhaps the strangest recollection I have from our time in Maryland was the day I felt the cold sweep over me.

I was playing in our front yard by myself. It was Fall. I was quite content playing alone; the temperature outside felt calm and pleasant. The day was overcast; I remember the clouds being like a pale colorless curtain across some grand stage. And then, I felt coldness, as if the world had become just a little bit greyer. There was no sudden gust of wind, no cold front sweeping in. It just felt...cold. I remember pausing in my play; that was how palpable, how all-encompassing the feeling was. It was an unsettling trickle of fear; I felt it embrace me, the way a long-sleeve shirt feels after you put it on.

There was a brief stage where I was afraid to sleep by myself. There were images in my mind I could not make go away. In one, the silhouette of a man appears at the far end of a corridor. Suddenly, like a camera zooming in, the dark figure draws close until he is right in front of me.

In another, the entire vision of my mind's eye is blocked by a giant thumb. I see nothing but the enormous spirals of this thumbprint. I was thankful for my brother in those moments, and that fact that we stilled shared a room.

And then there was the time Danny dug up his parents' entire front yard.

It was after the hammer incident, and may have been near the time when we were getting ready to move to my dad's next duty station.

It wasn't like he was digging to plant a garden or make a small trench. He had turned their yard into a maze, with the trench as deep as two feet in some places. When you're seven, that's deep.

Danny and his brother Matt stood outside their front door on the porch, Danny with a shovel in his hand. Their once beautiful green lawn was now a series of broken trench lines and dead ends. Danny threatened to kick my ass if I entered the yard.

I don't remember what provoked this sudden, dramatic twist in our friendship, I only knew that, after that, we were no longer friends.

And finally, there was the cross burnt in our front yard.

There were a pair of teenagers who lived a few doors down from Danny. I never recall seeing their parents, but the kids had a kind of wild look to them. They said they were witches. Back in the mid-seventies, you'd see kids in the woods wearing Halloween masks in the Spring. When teenagers said they were witches, you believed them.

We had made our annual summer trek to Ocean City, Maryland. Though we weren't exactly poor, the military didn't pay great. We could usually only afford one vacation like that each year. Otherwise if we were traveling, it meant we were visiting family and staying with them.

The mid-seventies were a particularly fun time to travel to the beach. The film *Jaws* came out in 1975, and every kid floating on a raft had to grapple with the not completely unhinged fear that a shark was going to come from under them and gobble them up. Granted, the odds of a twenty-five-foot shark attacking you in five feet of water were pretty slim, but who rationalizes that kind of stuff when you're a kid?

I loved the ocean. There was something so enchanting about the sea; the fear of a shark attack in the briny waters of the Atlantic added a thrill, at least for a few summers after the movie came out. Tan skin. Hair that lightened. I would spend what felt like hours in the waves.

My parents and brother used to make fun of me in the most playful of ways. Back in Hyattsville, I'd fallen in love with two of the lifeguards at our pool. The younger woman was named Peach. Peach had sun-kissed skin, the faintest freckles, blue eyes, and short, golden hair. She might have been late teens or early twenties. And then there was Kathy.

Kathy was married. She had short brown hair, blue eyes, and the most amazing smile. Sometimes during swim break, when kids had to get out of the pool, she would invite me into the water with her and hold me as I kicked my legs. I couldn't swim.

During our trips from Hyattsville to the beach, my family would sing, in unison, "We're going to the beach, beach, beach...it'll be a peach, peach, peach." Larry would tease me incessantly about puppy love.

I had NO idea how strong a dose of love I'd been blessed with. I fell in love easily. Was that a crime? Didn't everybody? Girls were amazing and, with an unspoken confidence, I knew there was someone magical out there for me.

We came home from the beach our last summer in Maryland, rested and tanned, and there, in the middle of our yard, someone had planted a two-foot cross in our lawn, and set it on fire. The now-blackened cross was haloed by a ring of charred grass.

The FBI came to our house. I don't remember what came of it. Later in life, I thought of the two teenagers who lived up the street near Danny. Witches.

The hits I'd taken to the head had meant one thing that I only learned to appreciate recently...I slowly started losing my ability to hear myself think. It was like there was a delay growing between my thoughts and my ability to speak. An echo between thought and action. As I grew up, my confidence in who I was would diminish. That was when Jesus and I began to separate from one another.

He had been my companion...the voice in my head, whenever I was alone, or in preparation for bed. We had the most wonderful conversations. We think of a child's imaginary friend as something fanciful, when it has always been so much more.

We must be like children to enter the kingdom.

The First Letter of the Pandemic

You are a science teacher. You teach young children, from what I can tell. I'm guessing you don't spend time with them talking about the quantum realm. Maybe, at least you've introduced them to the Avengers?

Nikola Tesla once stated that all matter is energy vibrating at a certain frequency. In the time since his remark, scientists have deduced that the atom is comprised of ninety-nine percent space, and the universe is one hundred percent comprised of atoms. That means, we're surrounded by stuff that is mostly made of space. That "fluffiness" also applies to us as humans. This flies in the face of the classic Newtonian model of physics, and the idea that everything is solid, and separate from everything else.

When most people think of quantum physics, I suspect they think of the concept as applying to the world outside of them. Separation. Newtonian physics.

But we are quantum beings. In recent years, the theory has arisen that we may be living in a simulation; quantum physics is *that* baffling to people.

The easiest way to explain quantum physics is this: nothing exists until it is observed. Further, there is a relationship between observer and observed. How we observe something, no pun intended, matters. How then, does a quantum being observe itself?

Men are conscious animals. Some behave like brutes. Afraid to awaken something inside themselves, they do their best to shut off the voice of compassion that all are born with. Men are most blinded by the Light of the Cross. That's how powerful the sacrifice of Jesus was.

Men favor strength. That strength hammered the world into being. Conquest. War. The world became real. Physical. Hard. Material. Men develop from the outside-in.

Women develop from the inside-out. They are spiritual. They embody the soul of the Earth. The Divine Feminine. The Vessel of Life. The Ark.

And then what happened? We learned. When we give power to women, women are in tune with the blind side of the universe. The spiritual. Call it witchcraft. Magic. Harmony. Nature. The esoteric. Women's intuition is a global needle for the Divine. It is the unified voice of the earth, and it grows stronger every day.

And what is that needle pointing towards?

Equally as important, in a quantum world, what separates the needle from what it's pointing to?

It is such a singularity of focus, it just barely defies existence.

It is the living moment. Presence without thought.

There is the famous two-slit light experiment, which has shown us that light responds to being observed; it can be particle or wave. It just depends on what the observer is looking for; if the observer is looking for a wave, they see a wave. When they're looking for a particle, the particle appears. Light, responding to a conscious being. The universe, responding to consciousness.

Finally, there is Dr. Emoto's famous water experiment, in which he had people contemplate various emotional states while staring at glasses of water. He had two different groups. When he looked at the water crystals of the subjects who were feeling positive emotions like love, joy, and happiness, the water crystals were ornate and beautiful, like brilliant snowflakes. Conversely, when he looked at the water crystals of the subjects who were feeling negative emotions like anger, rage, and jealousy, the crystals were stained and malformed, with dark blemishes. Same water source. Different observations. Different realities.

Being that you are a teacher, on many levels, I will not delve too much further into these subjects, all of which are commonly known among the science community, and easily accessible on YouTube.

Assuming Tesla is right, then each human on the planet is vibrating at a certain frequency. What guides that frequency? Thought. Mood. Temperament. Where we put our focus. What we ultimately believe.

Someone who surrounds themselves with negative people, performs negative actions, and broods on dark thoughts vibrates at a different frequency than does someone who surrounds themselves with uplifting companions, performs positive actions, and reflects on goodness and beauty. The former, it stands to reason, views the world as Newtonian, even if this concept isn't consciously articulated: separation, scarcity. Finite resources…a lack of resourcefulness. The latter, as quantum: interconnectedness. Abundance. Limitless possibility.

To take the idea further, we all experience Time differently. For someone who has put absolute faith in something greater than themselves and sees change as necessary for growth, Time must feel quite delicious, particularly when we seek to spend our time in the service of others.

Conversely, someone who believes that we live and then we die, only to fade out of existence, will view Time very differently. Time may be hoarded.

As conscious beings, we emit these frequencies, and receive them. This shouldn't come as a surprise, as there is information traveling all around us, all the time. The world is more interconnected than ever before; we can share information globally at speeds that are unprecedented. Everything is wireless these days, and we can watch movies, videos, or stream live conversations with people from anywhere. In one sense, we take for granted that our phones are these powerful transmitters and receivers while, in another, we don't think of our minds in the same way, even as most of us can rationalize that thoughts are things.

What we focus on, we become. In other words, we tune ourselves to a certain frequency. What we focus on is up to us, unless we surrender our focus to someone else, or something else.

And yet, if we are all vibrating atoms made of 99.9% space what, then, is directing our consciousness, and what in turn is responding to our focus?

These points demonstrate the underlying principle of quantum nonlocality, which is the idea that two objects can be aware of one another's state, even when separated by large distances. Said differently, nonlocality intimates there is no separation between anything because everything that exists has its origins in a quantum state. It only waits to be observed.

It is not too far a stretch to say that Tesla's energy-frequency-vibration idea and nonlocality applies to the phenomena known as the butterfly effect, where a butterfly flaps its wings in Kansas, and a typhoon stirs in the South Pacific. The definition of quantum entanglement is when two particles link together in a certain way no matter how far apart they are in space.

Can quantum entanglement be romantic?

With these ideas as backdrop, perhaps the easiest way to explain the trajectory of my life leading up to the events that preceded the pandemic was that I was out of tune. By this I mean, I lacked *real* focus. My mind was a corridor through which there passed a near-incessant amount of traffic. If it wasn't a song I'd recently heard, there was the noise of to-do's, reminders of things I hadn't yet done or, I would replay conversations over in my mind, analyzing why they had turned out the way they did. Simply stated, I was scattered.

It was, by necessity, the diffusion of my awareness to the greatest degree I could manage. I lived outside myself. I people-watched. I searched outside myself for something that would bring me back to me. A key to the prison of my mind. A key to unlocking my heart.

The first reported case of the coronavirus is believed to have sprung up in November of 2019.

For twelve years, I'd lived in a bustling little suburb called Cary, North Carolina, just outside the capital city of Raleigh. It was the longest I'd ever lived in one place.

The end of my last relationship was like a hot iron resting on my psyche. It consumed my waking moments with a rawness I could not avoid. Four years earlier, we had planned to buy a house together in a whirlwind romance that saw me write her a poem a day for more than six months. Most days, it was two or three poems. That was the strength of my determination in seeking to subdue whatever this thing called love was inside of me.

I was a walking wreck of tangled emotions.

By the summer of 2016, less than a year into the relationship, I was trying to make my escape. At the last minute, I had backed out of putting my name down on what was to have been a joint mortgage, throwing the relationship into a tailspin. That summer would be agonizing, as I resisted the temptations of abandoning the relationship as I'd done so many times in the past. As ingrained as these patterns had become, as restlessly as I searched for an answer to this unquenchable thirst for love I finally began to understand: *I was the problem.*

To an outsider, it would be easy to say I had commitment issues. The truth is, I had no idea why my ambitions for love were so grandiose; I just knew that I was *compelled* to seek something within myself for which, after decades of searching, I could find no easy answer.

While I successfully broke this most destructive of patterns that summer, and returned to the relationship, the damage had been done. The on-again, off-again nature of my suddenly tenuous commitment threw the stability of the relationship wildly off-track. While we were together, and despite my best efforts to heal it without ever directly accounting for it, the wound I had created would fester for the next three years with steadfast resiliency. We both desperately tried to return to the fleeting glimpse of beauty the relationship had flashed at its beginning, but with each passing month, by begrudgingly slow degrees, the necessity of its end became clear. Finally, it became too much.

By November 2019, I felt like an exposed nerve-ending. My ex quickly moved on. Our last hurrah together had been our annual Halloween extravaganza. I loved Halloween. Our house was ridiculous. I spent my free time making custom props to decorate the front yard. In a rather odd twist of fate, I shed my annual pattern of dressing up in a scary costume that year, and instead bought a wig, a robe, pajamas, a stuffed belly, and a replica of Mjolnir. That year, I went as Fat Thor.

Despite a few dates, I was too off-balance to pick up the pieces of my life. I needed time to get clear on who I was and what I really wanted. Additionally, I had convinced a handful of my friends to run a thirty-two-mile Spartan ultra-beast obstacle race. For more than a year, we'd been focused on training for the race. By the time October rolled around, knowing the relationship was near its end, the ultra-beast had become a burden. I just wanted it to be over. As the end of November neared, I did my best to concentrate on the race, and not the gaping crater that had been my life.

This unyielding quest for love had driven me to make what most would see as poor choices. While I didn't put my name on the mortgage, we shared the bills. She had paid the for the house, I paid the utilities, cable, and other bills. I wasn't thinking about the tax benefit of being a homeowner. I was trying to get love right.

I never imagined God might have a romantic side. That, more than anything else, is why I started looking for love without God. After multiple failed marriages, I began to believe God had failed when it came to love. I naively thought, I needed to create it on my own.

When the relationship ended, I was without a home. In an embarrassing and altogether familiar refrain from my past divorces, I moved in with my mom. Besides my clothes, all I had was a bedroom set, some holiday decorations,and a handful of framed art, and some comic books.

My mother, now in her late seventies, welcomed me, as any mother would.

While I felt ashamed and more than a little embarrassed, I knew I could use this time to continue to dig out from all the self-sabotage I'd done to myself over the years. I was committed to enjoying time with my mom. The pandemic was little more than a buzz in the news.

When you really believe in a higher power, then you begin to understand that everything does indeed happen for a reason. That explains Sara.

At the time, I couldn't say why we hit it off. Chalk it up to energy. I was drawn to the strength she possessed.

Sara was nearly twenty years younger than me. Like me, she was an instructor at our gym. Slim and fit, with powerful, muscular legs. When she wasn't teaching up-tempo fitness classes, Sara's main job was as an environmental attorney for a French environmental company.

Married and without kids, Sara was wildly quirky. Born and raised in North Carolina, she lacked a southern accent, but had a keen sense of humor and a kindness that called to mind the best aspirations of southern hospitality. She was incredibly smart and enjoyed guiding conversations towards the amusement and benefit of all, often with outrageous results.

She had formed the Saturday Strolling Club with one of her friends, Meghan. As the name of the club suggests, they met every Saturday and walked for two hours or more, diligently covering as much as seven miles on some occasions. Sometimes they'd walk around the local Target shopping center, replete with a nice greenway along the perimeter of the complex. On other occasions, they would meet at one of the nearby parks, and hit the trails. They were co-presidents of the club. They were the club's only members. The club had bylaws. Outrageous.

One day, I ran into Sara and Meghan as I was leaving the gym. I asked about joining the walking club and was met with a bout of unrestrained laughter. Sara laughed with a loud, boisterous laugh that felt over the top, but it genuinely reflected her outlook on life. At best, Sara informed me, I might receive a guest pass. She went onto say even the pass would require a full background check, blood sample, and the completion of an application. I laughed at the ridiculousness of the application process.

A few days later, I received an application via email for my guest pass to the WWC. In my desire for connection, I pricked my finger and signed my application with the slightest trace of blood. Sara didn't believe me, and stated that there was no visible trace on the paperwork.

Despite this speculation about the integrity of my application, it was accepted. I got my guest pass.

Sara and I grew closer quickly; occasionally we would get together during the work week for lunch. She sympathized with my emotional state following my breakup, and showed me the greatest compassion. At the same time, she didn't allow me to wallow in self-pity.

The Spartan race came and went; it was eleven hours in temperatures that bordered on freezing, accompanied by a steady drizzle that increased as the day wore on. The course was muddy and wet. Halfway through the race, I wanted to quit. My emotional state was still so fragile, and the less-than-ideal conditions of the race exacerbated my mood. But I got some food in me, took a small swig of whiskey, and finished the second lap under cover of darkness.

The following week, on Thanksgiving Day, I went to one of Sara's classes outside of Raleigh. I was clothed with such an untethered despondency, such an untethered despondency, my first holiday post-breakup. I felt radioactive.

After class, seeing me in such a state, she hugged me in the parking lot. We stayed like that for more than an hour. I had held such high aspirations for hope, had poured so much of myself into the last relationship, and yet felt like I'd come up empty. I was so vacant.

I didn't know what was coming.

I couldn't explain it, but I was reluctant to get too close to Sara. Love, for me, was a dare-to-be-great calling; I found myself attracted to women who weren't always happy in their present situations. I know it sounds childish, and on the outside, I must have looked like a monster. She didn't seem unhappy, and yet I couldn't understand where her compassion for me came from, and why it persisted.

I once told her that I wanted to pull away, that I did not want to flirt with torpedoing someone else's marriage. She said no with such a frightful urgency, I was completely caught off guard. I did not know it at the time, but Sara was the first Valkyrie I would ever meet.

Over the month of December, we were both traveling. She and Jim were heading to South America for a vacation in the Galapagos. I was traveling to Central America for work.

We'd gotten into the habit of texting throughout the day, and she became such a tremendous source of comfort, and a wonderful friend. During our travels, we each intermittently experienced periods of spotty reception. Not all of our texts were getting through. The result was a very confusing text conversation that suggested we were drifting apart.

I was heartbroken, and felt like I was on stormy seas about to capsize. Yes, I had friends I could rely on, but Sara was providing me emotional support that I wouldn't receive and didn't expect from my guy friends. With the strange text conversation going on between us, I couldn't understand what had happened to our friendship. My emotional state was so fractured.

They arrived back home a few days before I did. When I landed in Miami, and resumed texting with her, the texts came across as very reserved. Finally, wanting to understand what had happened, I called her. It was then we discovered that texts had dropped out of one another's conversations. It was silly and dramatic, and brought back the greatest sense of joy for both of us. We spent the better part of the holidays together.

★★★

It was January of 2020. In the same way I successfully resisted getting back into a relationship right away, despite several promising opportunities, I now withstood the inclination to buy a house and furnish it in some odd attempt to get "back on track" with where I saw my friends, all happily married, in their lives.

I had finished my second book, *The Lighthouse Keeper*, and had hired a Los Angeles-based PR firm, Conscious Living, to help me with the marketing. Besides getting me booked on podcasts, Conscious Living was going to offer me the opportunity to write magazine articles. In a very real sense, I wanted to focus on promoting the book prior to its launch at the end of March and, at the same time, dive into my next book with the working title, *Being*. Buying a house could wait.

My friendship with Sara and her husband, Jim, had deepened. I was now regularly visiting them on weekends. Jim, not yet thirty, was clean cut with an amazing heart. He was soft-spoken and good natured, and showed complete trust and confidence in my friendship with Sara. I liked him immediately.

As the New Year progressed, we ventured down to my family's beach condo on the quaint jewel of the Southern Outer Banks, Emerald Isle. There, we would play games, watch movies, and enjoy what little of the beach we could manage, given the cold temperatures. My weekend visits, which usually included dinner, and watching movies, evolved into sleepovers in their basement guest room. At the same time, I got more comfortable vaping cannabis.

I had steered clear of marijuana most of my life; it was an odd bit of guidance I'd taken away from my religious upbringing; drugs were bad and for some reason, marijuana was near the top of the list. It didn't matter that it came from nature, had been around nearly five thousand years, and was known to have medicinal properties. I only first tried it in my late forties when co-workers encouraged me to indulge while we were at a Dreamforce conference in San Francisco. My first reaction was, it made me vividly more aware of my surroundings, and a little chatty.

Early in 2019, while running Spartan races, a friend from Arizona shared some. It was legal there, and its popularity was growing as its medicinal value became more understood and accepted. My friend had a prescription, and mentioned it helped him recover after races. He provided me with a tin of low-dose chocolate coffee beans, and I started taking them after we ran.

I can vividly remember sitting across from my friend Hector at the American Airlines lounge in LAX after a Spartan race south of Los Angeles in late January 2020. Hector, a Colombian-born chiropractor, had such an easygoing demeanor. We'd started hanging out in August of 2018, and our friendship had grown in the time since, bound up in the camaraderie of the Spartan races. We'd both taken a coffee bean and looked at each other as if we were telepathically speaking to one another. It was the two of us, and Shepherd. Shep hailed from Jersey, but had moved to North Carolina years earlier. A successful executive vice president for a pharmaceutical company, Shep ran his company's logistics and, as a result, racked up tons of miles on American Airlines. Whenever we traveled together, it was fascinating to see the service Shep got when we landed. There would be a golfcart there, ready to take us to our next flight. On more than one occasion, we walked off the plane and went down onto the tarmac, where an SUV would drive us to our next gate. Traveling with Shep was fun.

Shep didn't indulge in the beans, which somehow made Hector and I nervous. At the same time, we giggled like kids, holding the silliest and most obvious of secrets. Shep tolerated us. He knew, if we got ourselves kicked out of the lounge for being too boisterous, Hector and I would be the only two leaving. Shep had earned his status in the executive lounge; Hector and I were riding on his coattails.

Of course, I liked getting high. Long an opponent of drug use, my time as a yoga instructor had softened my stance. The older I got, and the more widespread the legalization of marijuana became, I knew it could be a vehicle for enlightenment. Lots of artists and musicians cite how mind expanding plant medicine could be.

I had no idea what the effects of marijuana would have on my pineal gland. I had no idea how much expanding my mind was about to do.

Flying back from Los Angeles was enjoyable. Being high also helped me cope with the loss I still felt from the relationship, but there was something I didn't fully grasp. The plant medicine I'd long decried as a detriment to society was doing something else for me. It was beginning to unblock a lifetime of a most spiritual post-traumatic stress disorder.

Back home in North Carolina, I was feeling a little cavalier. I'd come clean with my family and those who meant the most to me on my infidelities. It had been grueling, devastating work that had stretched out over two years. I had held onto this shame for such a long time, unsure of how it would ever be released. I was so hellbent on finding whatever was at the core of my love, I never bothered to look in the most obvious of places—Jesus.

I was off-balance most days. There was the pain of releasing all the guilt and shame I carried with me for decades, and there was this crazy sense of optimism. I loved the feeling the optimism provided, and certainly understood there was a cause and effect between the two; despite feeling like I'd trampled love as best I could, love hadn't given up on me.

When I was a kid, my brother and I used to watch *Star Trek*. Captain Kirk and Spock, and their bold mission to seek out new life and new civilizations.

In the show, they would teleport from the starship *Enterprise* down to the surface of the planets they were orbiting. I wasn't old enough to question the validity of special effects back then. Usually, teleporting only took a matter of seconds.

I did not know it at the time, but for the next twenty-four months, I would feel like that. Like I was teleporting between two worlds—one where I believed Jesus had died on the cross, and another where I didn't. I would spend the next two years struggling to bring the universes of Faith and Doubt together by removing all Doubt from my mind.

That was going to be my pandemic.

When I received the email to enter a crowdfunding book contest beginning in February, I was feeling good about myself. Was my Faith strong? Hardly. I knew a weight had been lifted from my shoulders by coming clean about my infidelities, but hadn't the slightest comprehension of just how sizeable a burden I still carried.

With *The Lighthouse Keeper* coming out in just under two months, feeling slightly off-kilter after still being single since late October, and only the vaguest sense of what my third book was going to be about, the idea of entering a book contest in February made complete sense. It would force me to stay busy, keep me preoccupied, and focused on making 2020 the best year of my life.

I was excited by the ideas I was discovering with *Being*.

No one had any idea the pandemic was going to forever change things.

No one had any idea what the pandemic really was.

THE SPANIARD II

Trujillo. All my life, I grew up believing that was where I was from. I considered myself a Roman; Spain had been under Roman control for nearly four hundred years by the time I was born. I did not sense that there had been something before Rome. I did not appreciate that the advance of civilization meant the consumption of the old to produce something new.

That was a lesson I would learn as the commander of the Northern Armies.

That was a lesson I would teach as the second horseman of the apocalypse.

I was War. The Savior of Rome.

While I was alive, this identity, with all its consequence and promise, was unknown to me.

I died at your feet, and the feet of our son. My Fall from Grace.

After the murder of Marcus at the hands of his son, Commodus, there was little recourse afforded me. Marcus had entrusted me to restore power back to the people as the guardian and protector of a Rome I had never seen. Unable to swear loyalty to this false emperor, I was taken to be dispatched. I managed to eliminate my assassins, and made haste for our home, knowing with dreaded certainty the grave danger you and Samuel now faced. I was too late.

Seeing your charred, lifeless bodies swaying in an infernal breeze was more than I could bear. My mind snapped shut. Silence.

When I awoke, I was enslaved. Gone were the hillsides drenched in green, the favorable trees lining the roads, and the familiar sense of all that had been right and beautiful about our home.

In their place, the angry hot breath of the African desert landscape.

Beyond the wounds received during my escape, I was starving, dehydrated, and nearly unable to cope with the rending of my heart. It had been destroyed and felt irrecoverable. Everything I once possessed, gone.

Though I did not know at the time, my history was being erased from the annals of Rome. There would be no record of a general, favored by the true emperor Marcus Aurelius, who returned power to the people. My legacy would be snuffed from history, an echo, shattered across eternity. It hardly mattered. I was completely outside myself, with no sense of how to get back to the goodness I had once felt inside myself. I ached at my own consciousness, eager to divorce myself from such inescapable anguish.

It was not to be. Instead, I found myself driven by my remorse. I had failed you, my love. Our love was unfinished...of this, I was certain. Though my grasp on it was exceedingly tenuous, I clung to the belief that you were not lost to me. It was barely a speck of dust, so small was the thought. I fumbled for it with a hopelessness that frequently surrendered to the darkest despairs. I was numb.

I had commanded armies. Had seen the triumph of knowledge forced onto the savage mind, bringing order to what had been feral. Conquest always looks oppressive to the conquered, but there was *good* in the light Rome promised. That Marcus had promised.

Now, what was I? A wretch, possessed of an elite mind, a mind that had served as an instrument of enlightenment, bringing order to chaos. All my talents, all my skills and knowledge, reduced to the most primitive form of servitude. Death as entertainment.

I was to become a gladiator.

Marcus had once told me of a tribe of people on the southeastern outskirts of the empire's border who had nailed their god to a tree.

He had called them Christians.

He did not divulge much more; they had shown up in Rome more than a century before, and their numbers had continued to grow under Rome's liberal religious policies. He did express wonder at how such a story might influence the world to come.

Can you imagine that, Maximus? he had said with genuine wonder; he spoke with such eloquence. His emotion stretched the words, filling them with his life and breath. He inspired such awe. As was often the case, he did not wait for an answer before continuing. *We sacrifice to our gods, celebrate them at parties. Theirs was the sacrifice. Astonishing.*

There were a few men in the legions who had heard these stories, and been converted to follow this unusual faith. During a particularly unfavorable dry spell while on campaign in Germania, some of these men had prayed to their god. As they prayed, the rains came, offering relief to the entire army.

Marcus said it was a miracle of this God called the Christ.

Are you familiar with history? To some extent, we are all. We each have our own history of our lives. It is the story we tell ourselves. I hope you will find my rendering to be something familiar.

Thousands of years ago, a god-king named Xerxes descended on the city-states of ancient Greece to conquer and enslave its peoples. His army was massive, numbering in the hundreds of thousands. The vanguard of his army was an elite force known as the Immortals.

Some three hundred Spartans, led by King Leonidas, rallied several other hundred Greeks and made a stand at the Hot Gates in Thermopylae. Eventually, Leonidas and the Spartans were overcome, but what they did gave the Athenians enough time to rally the Greek States to turn back the evil tide of Xerxes. Not an empire or subject to one, Greece became a nation.

The Spartans were part of the tribe of Abraham, father of all nations.

Rome took the lessons learned from Greece, and expanded them. While Rome did not fully entertain nor explore art to the degree the Greeks had, it eagerly adopted the notions of governance and conquest, turning each into its own kind of artform. Whereas Xerxes wanted to enslave the world and bring people of all nations to heel, Rome, through the fits and starts of different emperors, sought to give the world knowledge as the price of submission. Advancement under force of will. By many degrees, this notion of advancement would shape western civilization. In my time as a gladiator, I could not comprehend how the imprint of Christianity would imbue civilization's advance with the indelible ink of the word of God, or the role I was to play in its writings, even in the afterlife.

I would hear the story of Christ in greater detail for the first time in the vast remoteness of southern Algeria.

In all my travels with the legions, I had never ventured this far south, never enjoyed foods, meager though a slave's portions might be, that showered my taste buds with such tantalizing flavors. Foods that enflamed my tongue, or seduced my mind with their smells. Foods that found their life amid such seeming austerity. Lands drained of moisture, like some great fire had charred the earth, so immense were the stretches where the landscape was dominated by an absence of any meaningful foliage. For a time, we traveled through tremendous, ancient gullies, flanked on either side by enormous walls of sunbaked rock and earth. Their height was fantastic.

While the wounds I had suffered at the hands of Commodus after his failed attempt to end my life had healed, I still nursed the despair inside me and, despite my inability to subdue the fascination such foreign lands held, welcomed their appearance with a hostility born out of resentment. As we continued our journeys, we were greeted by gently rolling oceans of whispering sand dunes, sharing secrets on the breeze that only the earth understood. Eventually, we made our way to a village. The cacophony of human commerce reminded me of the markets you and I frequented when I was home from campaign. At the same time, there were marvels I'd only previously heard stories of, or seen expressed in rudimentary etchings. Camels. Hyaenas. Lions.

The first time I saw a lion, I gushed with admiration. What a powerfully beautiful, majestic creature.

I watched as it paced back and forth within the confines of its wooden prison, bits of straw dangling haphazardly from its mane. This one was not yet underfed. That would not happen until it was thrown into the arena, when its hunger would serve to spark its primal instinct for survival. The result would be a focused, unhesitating killer.

It had such golden eyes, with only an obsidian pinprick for a pupil. *Like a woman in black, clothed in the sun.*

Even though I was a good distance from it, I felt the labor of its breath. Its golden coat strained against the powerful muscles and sinews underneath.

The Romans had crucified the King of the Jews, and He came back to life.

That was how I would hear of Christianity the second time. Another moment in time.

It was as we pulled into the village, jostled about in our caged cart by the uneven, ill-tempered roads. We were passing through the market, filled with meats and fruits of all kinds. Loud chatter from traders, vying to unload their wares.

Some commotion to our front brought the cart to a halt. It was there, I saw and marveled at the lion.

Separated by some length, and further ahead along the rows of merchants to our left, a man stood, speaking to a small group of people gathered around him. In one hand, he held a small cross fixed atop a staff. With his free hand, he was motioning to his listeners. There was too much noise to clearly make out what he was saying.

"Believers in the Christ," the slave next to me, whose name I did not know, said with a nudge, pointing to the man. He had been recently sold into his enslavement, and still reeked of olive oil; he might have been a farmer in his free life. "The God who returned from the dead. Killed during the reign of Tiberius."

"He was killed by the Romans?" I asked with mild curiosity.

The slave nodded, then paused. He gazed at the man with the cross. "Some say he was killed by his Father."

There were all kinds of wild stories then. It was a different time. The minds of men were less constrained, less bound to the idea of a material world. People were not distracted. True, Rome and the advance of knowledge demanded a kind of governance that increasingly relied less on the gods and more on the reasons of men, and progress on the ideas of economy and commerce, of relations with other peoples, but the idea of a single god for the world was nowhere close to being realized.

This story of Christ didn't feel wild. It felt raw. Romans had held banquets for the gods for generations, and the Twelve Great gods had been influenced by Greek mythology and were deemed to be couples or lovers. Romans feasted as if the gods themselves were in attendance.

A story of a Father sacrificing a Son stabbed at my consciousness, though I could not then explain why.

This part of the world felt beguiling and ancient, and that such a story would be born in lands on the fringes of the empire was unsurprising. The people here were colorful and exotic, like the animals from this region. They were cloaked in a restlessness that never ventured beyond festering agitation into open revolt, but the tension snaked beneath the surface of everyday life.

The best legions were not dispatched this far away from the empire. The soldiers I saw, while adequate, were far from elite; poorly maintained uniforms and weapons in need of upkeep spoke as silence evidence to their poor discipline. It was only a matter of time before soldiers garrisoned to watch over a village or province, lacking the urgency of purpose found in mortal combat, succumb to the tedium found in such garrisons.

As a military man, I had heard of the Jewish rebellion a hundred years before though, given its distance from Rome and marginal impact on the daily activities to which I directed much of my focus, paid it little mind.

Emperors of Rome were the closest things to gods on the earth, such was the sweeping scale of power at their fingertips. Though I allowed myself little introspection on such matters, I knew they were just men. That a man like Augustus should set civilization on its journey with such virtue and superior intent was fascinating. The initial vision of what Rome could be was indeed, beautiful.

When a man like Marcus Aurelius, someone gifted with such a profundity of knowledge about the order and structure of things, issued a command, it was absolutely understood. There was no question of how much effort would be put to it, in the hopes that it might be accomplished. It *would* be accomplished, *must* be, and whatever resources were necessary to see it carried out would be found and utilized. Disobedience was out of the question. Failure, incomprehensible.

I understood how the weight of civilization's advance had aged him, had seen it as one season blended with the next, and any hopes of a swift reconciliation with the Germanic tribes faded, as the months gave way to years. The difference between knowledge and ignorance was more easily understood at the time. There was the order, structure, and promise of Rome. And there was an unflinching desire to preserve a way of life as it had always been; to live in communion with the earth instead of building on top of it. But how could man advance if he did not conquer the earth? I hope this clearly speaks to how passionately and how seriously I pursued my endeavors.

I was to liberate Rome. And I did. There was a single consequence the details of which, like so many things back then, I was blind to. Though I was considered by many to be a master strategist, it was in this endeavor where I failed to see the bigger picture.

Each of our lives has its own unique reality.

My first death came when I found you and Samuel, dead. With this, I was quickly and easily removed from known history; my life became little more than fiction.

But what we do in life echoes through eternity.

I believed I entered the afterlife after killing Commodus in the

Colosseum. As I now write these letters beloved, I appreciate my journey through hell began the moment I realized I'd lost you.

Before our battle, when Commodus asked me to embrace him as a brother, I did. He was the emperor. And then, I killed my brother, just as Cain slew Abel. The awakening of War.

★★★

There was a door. Rustic and weathered, it beckoned me to push on its handle. I was so certain you and Samuel were on the other side of it.

When I passed through its inviting portal, and immediately found myself greeted by the alluring warmth from its interior, I found myself among golden grains of wheat, ripe for the harvest. I believed I was close to home, so inviting were the smells, so reassuring, the sense of familiarity. I felt my chest swell with the expectation of our reunion, so confident was I that I might quickly find the two of you among the fields. There was a flash. An image.

I see you and Samuel, standing on a hillside, just off a cart path. Your dress is tan, like a lioness. You shield your eyes from the sun, looking in my direction. Samuel stands in front of you. Your other hand rests on his shoulder. You lift your hand from his shoulder. He starts forward. Then, the image is gone.

The cart path I had seen in the distance vanishes in the blink of an eye.

How long have I been here? In a fragment of consciousness, it feels like a flicker, the briefest point at which we might recognize we are observer in the act of observation and yet, I was immediately overcome with a sense of incomprehensibly immense amounts of time, slipping through my fingers, like heads of wheat, budding into life only to rot into withering decay countless times, over and over.

So much time has passed. The memory is like a trick of the light. In one moment, I feel the door's welcoming embrace. In the next, I am keenly aware that I passed through that door eons ago. Were I able to turn to look for the door behind me, I know it would not be found. Looking ahead, I believe I will see you, and Samuel, but you are not there.

They say a man who falls asleep in the snow is like a frog tossed in water that is slowly brought to a boil; neither is aware that the feeling coming over them is death. Who knows what the frog feels?

It feels like I am falling asleep in the snow. Winter in Germania. There is a flash of a lion.

Samuel.

It is not an unpleasant feeling at all. The cold is gentle in numbing my senses.

The fields of wheat are blue, shrouded in moonlight, yet there is no moon.

My hands graze over their spikes. They are cold and do not return my caress. What is the point in moving on? *The snow always beckons.* It is a disquieting breathe from somewhere behind me, pulling me down. Pulling me back.

The moonless blue light feels heavy. The wheat waves in every direction, a dizzying, ever-shifting sea. Where is the road? Where, my path?

Sometimes, it feels as if there is no wheat. In the most elemental sense, I feel there is no me.

There is what feels like a source of light, but it is ever behind me. Always behind me. No matter where I turn, the light directs me forward and away from it. I am unable to turn back and look towards it. I am unable to turn back.

Into the darkness. Darkness becomes my path. It is *the* path; it is the most curious horizon between the earth and sky. A pinprick of absolute black, where my sense of gravity is my truest measure for navigation, and the only thing I can discern as the faintest hint of an orientation. I am the point of a needle, fumbling further into the black before me. The air becomes colder. The light behind me, less bright.

I feel neither the presence of time nor its absence. Dreams.

I must be dreaming. I will awaken at dawn.

You *will* be there, smiling and waiting for my eyes to open. Your smile. That knowing smile, the perfect lines of your mouth, a precious mix of curiosity and mischief. You smiled like a cat.

The smell of you after a night's sleep. I relax.

No. You will not be there.

I remember, and feel the frigid pain in the cold's snowy embrace, cutting through my consciousness like a frosted blade. I regain my senses.

You are *there*. Somewhere, in the dark. Alert again, I wade further into the black.

Samuel. The last time we spoke, you said something about Samuel. What did you say?

I search my mind for answers and, finding none, resume wandering away from the light. If I have ears to hear, there is the faintest sense of ringing.

The Third Letter of David

After Maryland, we had just one year in Virginia before we moved to Okinawa.

I couldn't say how, but our time in Maryland had changed me. In 4th grade in Virginia, I first became acquainted with the idea of solitude.

After saying goodbye to Joan, I felt what I can only describe as anguish. Danny and I had been friends, but I'm not sure we said goodbye to one another when I left, especially not after the "maze in the yard" incident, and I didn't miss him like I did Joan.

Leaving Joan was my first real sense of loss. We visited them once or twice while we lived in Virginia, but it wasn't the same. It was hard to appreciate that we might never see each other again, let alone that my best friend was now going to become a memory.

From this, I would learn a punishing lesson. I would eagerly make friends, or try to, and then keep them at arm's length, knowing the separation that loomed with my dad's next relocation. We would be moving again in a year. I couldn't consciously express it, but I didn't want to get hurt again like leaving Joan behind had made me feel.

As a result, I favored playing on my own, though usually within the physical presence of someone else. It was an uncanny observation Larry once made while talking with mom.

"David likes to play alone." She had said.

"No mom," Larry replied, "He likes to play alone with others nearby."

He wasn't wrong.

Fourth Grade in Quantico, Virginia was forgettable. My teacher yelled at me on more than a few occasions because I hadn't done my homework, the girl I liked only had eyes for someone else, and the year felt like a dizzying mess knowing that we were soon going to be moving to the other side of the world.

One of the more curious memories I have from this time deals with two little girls who "kidnapped" me. The school I went to was Ashurst Elementary School aboard the Marine Corps Base at Quantico, Virginia. The school sat atop a hill up the street from where we lived; the hill, adorned with a thin nestle of trees, sloped down to the left of our neighborhood. On the other side of it, another neighborhood.

The girl I liked lived in the far neighborhood. One Saturday, I went near the school to the hill, where I planned to sit and look down on the other neighborhood, lost in romantic feelings. It was silly.

When I got to a spot in the trees that gave me a good view of her neighborhood, I was met by two older girls. I was only nine or ten; while they were teenagers. The girls tied me up and had me sit with them. They had set up a little picnic setup, except they told me to drink the potion they had concocted.

I wasn't scared. I didn't feel threatened. It was just so strange. They freed my hands, and I drank whatever it was they had prepared. After that, I went home.

I found something of a reprieve when we moved overseas.

Our time on Okinawa blessed me with one of the best friendships of my life. Jason was like a brother to me. He was a year younger than me and a grade behind me, but it didn't matter. We arrived on the island at roughly the same time, in the summer of 1979, and became the best of friends.

Living on Okinawa introduced me to the power of typhoons. Our first summer there, a major storm slammed into the island. Ferocious winds tore at the trees, and enormous waves slammed against the sea walls near the hotel we lived in while we waited for houses to become available. And then the next morning, the skies were calm.

Jason and I went outside. We were in the eye of the storm, surrounded by a fortress of clouds. As the afternoon progressed, the trailing edge of the storm hit us, and the sky once again erupted with fierce winds and roiling seas. Luckily, those storms were few and far between. After several months living in the hotel, we moved off-base for a short while, and then were assigned a house on-base.

Our dads didn't work together, but it didn't matter. Our families got along great, we ended up living next to one another, and when Jason and I weren't exploring off-base, we'd usually hang out at his place. After school, we had one American television channel; the other two we could tune into were Japanese. We might watch those if they had cartoons.

Only one American television station meant watching the soap opera *General Hospital*, or watching *Star Wars* on Betamax. I'm sure the drama of *General Hospital* influenced my romanticism a little; they certainly weren't dealing with issues ten- and eleven-year-olds found themselves facing every day…but who didn't love Luke and Laura? I don't know that we paid too much attention to the storylines beyond their romance; it was just something to watch after school on the days when we didn't have soccer practice. We watched *Star Wars* all the time and literally memorized the lines of our favorite characters, acting out the movie to one another as the action on the tv unfolded. Jason was Obi-Wan and Luke; I was Darth Vader and Han Solo.

When we weren't playing video games on the early precursors to today's PlayStation and Xboxes, we were reading comics, drawing, or traveling what felt like long distances, on-base or off.

Okinawa was incredible. Turquoise waters surrounded the island, and there was abundant coral and fish life. I had never seen water so clear, or fish so bright and abundant.

I'd also never experienced humidity quite like Okinawa. It was muggy all the time. We landed at Naha International Airport on a June night in 1979 just after ten-thirty, and I remember in the time it took us to walk from the plane to the terminal, about fifty meters, my shirt was drenched with sweat.

As a result of the magnificent weather, we played a ton outdoors. There were open fields behind our house, which afforded a great view of the northeast corner of the fence-line that separated off-base from on-base.

Living on-base in a foreign land felt incredibly different. You were aware, seemingly always, that you were a foreigner living in *someone else's* country. The feeling was inescapable. Every time you looked off base, the Okinawan buses, unique taxis, and merchant trucks, were a constant reminder: you were not in America.

Going out into town was always a unique experience. The air smelled different; it might be from foods being cooked nearby, or from the semi-open sewer system, which ran alongside the road. There were few signs written in English. As ten- and eleven-year-olds, we rarely saw other American kids when we were off-base. It was like we were the only ones who elected to climb over the barbed wire fence to explore.

Okinawan candies and toys were the best; so beautifully crafted compared to the assembly-line feel of American toys. Felix gum, named after Felix the Cat, was like something out of *Willie Wonka and the Chocolate Factory*. It was the chewiest gum I ever had, and the flavor lasted for hours. We interacted with the local Okinawans only in the most remote sense of the word.

The people were so different. Most Okinawans were comparatively short in stature. There were few blonds. All the kids our age wore uniforms to school. The only person I remember who spoke English was the owner of Frank's Toy Shop. Frank's had the best toys on the island. It was a fifteen- or twenty-minute drive from where we lived, but if I wasn't buying comics, playing spaced invaders out in town, I was saving up my money to buy toys from Frank's.

While I felt like a kid at heart, another part of me noticed the rituals and customs of the Okinawans. The Oban festival, in which they honor their dead, comes to mind. During the festival they beat drums at night. Listening on our side of the military fence, I couldn't help but admire the sound, and appreciated I was hearing something few Americans ever would. We introduced our festivals to them too.

After six months living in temporary housing on Camp Kuwae, we had to move to a small apartment off-base for a few months before our military housing was ready. The four of us lived in a small, four hundred square foot apartment. My brother and I slept on fold-out futon mattresses. During this short stay off base, we celebrated Halloween by going to Okinawans homes dressed in our costumes, expecting candy. Mostly, they just gave us Japanese yen.

Their use of incense fascinated me, and their temples were so very different from American churches. Sometimes when we were off base, we could be traveling through small spots of jungle, and would run across tombs buried into hills on the island. There, we might find figures of Buddha, or teacups a loved one had set there to honor their ancestors.

While on the island, my dad made sure we had several opportunities to visit the Philippines and South Korea. In the Philippines, I'll never forget seeing how poor some of the families were that lived outside of Clark Air Force Base. They bathed in muddy water and lived in shanties made up of corrugated aluminum. Still, they had the biggest smiles, and seemed genuinely happy.

Seoul, South Korea was the biggest city I'd spent any reasonable amount of time in by that point of my life. It was spectacular. So many high rises, and there was a real urban energy, with buses, taxis, cars, and cyclists all scurrying about their roads. I was so grateful for those experiences, though unaware at the time of just how much an impression they'd made on me.

On one trip to Seoul, we stayed underneath a discotheque. Between the pounding of the dancers above us and our dad's snoring, Larry and I struggled to get to sleep.

My friendship with Jason flourished. We both liked comic books, and had different favorite characters. Jason was a big fan of Spiderman, while I had become fascinated with Wolverine. While Spiderman was good-natured, Wolverine had a berserker rage to him that fascinated me.

Jason was a great friend.

After three fun years, I left Okinawa as a thirteen-year-old. We had hoped our families might get stationed together, but it wasn't going to be. His family was relocating to Northern Virginia, while we were going a base on the coast of North Carolina, Camp Lejeune.

When we made it back to the states, I would begin to fully embrace my teen angst, and slowly started to move away from my understanding of and faith in God.

The Second Letter of the Pandemic

As March arrived, news of the pandemic was simmering, and life was happening at normal speed. By the end of the month, most of the world would be shut down. The last day of March, I would experience my Judgment Day.

March was to be a busy month. To end February, I had ventured up to Buffalo, New York to run another Spartan race with Shep and Hector. It would be our last one for more than a year.

The second weekend in March, Sara held a birthday party for Jim, who was finally turning thirty. I was spending more and more time with them, and grew increasingly grateful for their friendship.

The Monday after the party, I was heading to a Mastermind Retreat with Jack Canfield in Santa Barbara, California and the following weekend would be in Florida for a John Maxwell conference on public speaking.

Jack was the author behind the wildly successful *Chicken Soup for the Soul* series of books, having sold more than 500 million copies of his books worldwide. Jack was a legend.

The idea behind a mastermind is, bring like-minded people together to learn from someone who has had tremendous success in a particular field so that all may benefit and grow. It's like condensing decades into days. This Mastermind would take place March 17-19 at Jack's home in Santa Barbara.

I had signed up for the Mastermind in November of 2019, and had initially planned to get Jack's take on *The Lighthouse Keeper*, but with my third book, *Being*, occupying an increasing amount of my attention, in the winter I elected to focus on my newest book idea instead.

The idea for *Being* had come to me just as my relationship was crashing down around me in October. It was born out of our fascination with social media, and how constantly people were checking their smartphones. Back then, on average, people were checking their phones eighty-five times a day. I was as guilty as everyone else. Sometimes I would check my phone for no reason. I hadn't received any kind of alert or notification; I would just randomly pull my phone out of my pocket and stare at the screen. Standing in line at Starbucks or Chipotle, everyone had their heads down, staring at their phones.

Being was meant to ask and hopefully answer the question, *to what end? Why* were people becoming addicted to their smartphones? Yes, there was the dopamine hit of getting likes and followers…but where was it all headed?

Preparing the video for the crowdfunding contest had given me plenty of time to wrap my arms around the idea at the core of the book. I'd spent two hours shooting and reshooting the three-minute video that I ended up submitting as my application to the contest.

In the video, I observed there is a relationship between what we do and who we are. One is constantly shaping the other. If we focus on doing, without a sense of who we're becoming in the pursuit of our actions well, it seems like that's where people get stuck. On the other hand, if we have an idea of who we want to be, or become, then that vision of ourselves will define and refine our actions towards the accomplishment of realizing that vision. That was the premise for the book.

The shadow of the pandemic spread quickly in March. With reports of people getting sick all over the world, it was amazing to see how rapidly things changed. At the Fortune 500 company where I worked, we took the drastic steps of moving everyone working in offices to work from home. All the while, we continued to provide twenty-four-hour support to our global customers.

I remember being on a work call during the middle of the month. Someone on the call said they couldn't wait until things got back to normal. The pandemic felt anything but normal. If anything, it had awakened in me my combat instincts from my time in the Marines.

"Don't say that," I interjected. "This is normal, right now."

The way everyone got quiet on the call, I could tell I struck a nerve. People were looking for the comfort of the familiar. They wanted reassurance that things were going to be alright.

I went onto explain about how I'd spent the first twenty-two Christmases of my life in the traditional setting of how most Americans celebrate the holiday. There were the wonderful smells of Christmas trees and wreaths. There might be snow, and the air was crisp. The leaves had all fallen. Decorations adorned front yards and homes. Gifts under the tree. Stockings hung by the chimney. Santa.

My twenty-third Christmas was spent in Mogadishu, Somalia, just a degree or two off the equator. I was with the 15th Marine Expeditionary Unit, which had served as the landing force for Operation RESTORE HOPE. We landed on December 9, 1992.

Mogadishu was the hottest place I'd ever been. You could feel the heat move around you in ripples when you were sitting still; it was like being in a jacuzzi of hot air. When the breeze came from the ocean, we could smell the sea; most of the time however, we smelled the refuse and dead animals in the sprawling trash dump a few hundred yards southwest of our position. Our artillery unit was camped at the southern end of the single runway at Mogadishu's international airport.

For a Christmas tree for the Marines of our artillery battery, I'd cut up the cardboard box our meals were packed in and turned it into the branches of a Christmas tree. I'd taken spare tent poles to serve as the tree trunk, then stuck the cardboard branches on the poles. For decorations, I took glow-stick chem lights, snapped them, and hung them from the ends of the cardboard limbs. The meals from the box es were the "presents" for the Marines under the tree. One of my fellow Marines cut out a star, cut open an orange chem stick, and poured it on the star, then stuck it on top of our makeshift tree. Christmas 1992.

As I shared the story with my colleagues on the video call, it seemed to set people's minds at ease. Things weren't going to be normal anytime soon, and that was okay. It just meant, learning to live a little differently. To become resilient in the face of change. To awaken to a richer quality of life; the thin, immaculate line between love and courage.

In a matter of just ten days, we moved our entire workforce of more than seventy thousand employees from their assigned offices and cubes to working from home. In some cases, countries had to change their policies on the fly for our employees or contractors to accommodate this global shift. It was breathtaking how quickly things moved.

The Mastermind with Jack was still on. When I left for LAX the third week in March, only six of the seventeen people who had originally signed up were now attending. The rest were unwilling to make the trip because of the pandemic.

The Boeing 757 that took us from Charlotte, NC to Los Angeles could hold two hundred and eighty passengers. There were just thirty people on the plane. I was one of a handful wearing a mask.

Arriving in Los Angeles felt surreal. It also felt a little daring.

Besides the airport being nearly empty, there was no traffic on the historically famous and normally congested Los Angeles freeways. What could have easily been a three-hour trip up the coast to Santa Barbara was completed in just ninety minutes. The Mastermind was scheduled to start the next day on Tuesday. With just six of us now attending, we would get more time with Jack and the people he regularly worked with. It was exciting. Little did I know that the next day, more changes awaited us.

As we met in the hotel lobby early the next morning, Steve Harrison, the host and marketing genius who had aided Jack in promoting his books, informed us that due to the fact that Jack was high-risk for COVID, we would not be meeting at Jack's house as originally planned. His planning team had found a nearby hotel. We would be shuttled to the hotel and connect with Jack via video conferencing.

That approach lasted for a little more than two hours, before the Mayor of Santa Barbara banned public gatherings in hotels. Steve huddled with his team to come up with a new plan on the fly.

Ever resourceful, Steve and his team decided we would continue the mastermind at Patty Aubrey's house. Patty was Jack's longtime friend, and the president of his company.

All this added to the surrealness of the week, which somehow became more exciting with each break from the original plan.

Patty was incredibly kind and accommodating. Her home was beautiful and sat on top of a hill well removed from the city, with a lovely view of a valley to the west. Her living room became our cozy, makeshift conference center, with Jack on a big screen on the far end of the room. Each of the six attendees would spend approximately forty-five minutes in the "hot seat" where we would have a chance to discuss our ideas for our book, program, or both. Jack and the others gathered would ask questions or offer suggestions. My time in the hotseat would be on Wednesday.

I'm sure by this time, I'd seen the first picture of you. It had likely happened in the weeks leading up to the Mastermind. You weren't on my mind everyday just yet. Well, that isn't fair to say. You have been on my mind my entire life. Up to this point, I just hadn't seen God's love expressed with such perfection. That would come in April.

When it was my turn in the hot seat, I was eager to jump right in and talk about *Being*, but Steve wanted to know about *The Lighthouse Keeper*. Part of me didn't want to waste time on the book. It was slated to launch in a few weeks, though I didn't appreciate how the pandemic was going to dampen its release. Besides, *Being* felt magical.

Being honest with myself, as painful as it had been, it had also been liberating. I was seeing with a clarity I hadn't previously known, and genuinely believed that freeing myself of the weight I'd been carrying for so long would yield the greatest love I'd ever known. How could it not? I'd finally started taking ownership of my own life, which meant owning my body, mind, *and* spirit.

That had come at a cost. I'd lost friendships. My daughter, increasingly frustrated by my inaccessibility and failed relationships, had grown distant. I was keenly aware of this, yet love was demanding I stop looking at my faults from the past, and start focusing on the promise of the future. I shared enough about my second book to provide context on why, despite the impending sense of isolation the pandemic was providing, I elected to make the journey to attend the Mastermind. Being real with others felt good. Being real with myself felt even better.

I covered *The Lighthouse Keeper* in a few minutes. Doing so made sense; I was happy with how it had turned out and shared how finding my purpose in 2017 had begun to alter the trajectory of my life. I went on to explain how I had written my ex-fiancée two or three poems every day for six months, when we first started seeing each other.

I remember Patty saying with a bit of a sarcastic surprise, "That's sustainable."

"I know," I replied with a sigh, "It's crazy."

It *had* been crazy. It had also been my determination to break whatever protective coating I'd built around my heart. I *wanted* a lasting love. *Wanted* unflinching fidelity. Now, I *finally* felt like I was making progress in realizing that love, after fifty years.

After doing all the painful work of recognizing my self-destructive behavior, I was excited for a destination I didn't yet clearly see. I was convinced it was out there, I felt it, regardless of the pandemic.

Explaining *The Lighthouse Keeper* and the flare-up and eventual burnout of my last relationship was a natural segue into discussing *Being*. The book had begun occupying more and more of my attention, as I now found myself with the headspace to apply real focus to its contents. I was tuning into my own self.

If there was anything, however, that truly began to open my mind to the possibility of you being real, it was my reading of Dr. Joe Dispenza. I'd started reading him in the weeks leading up to the Mastermind. His most recent book, *Becoming Supernatural*, was fascinating.

Dr. Joe had spent years working on researching and seeking a deeper understanding of the quantum field. He had taken Tesla's ideas that all matter is energy vibrating at a certain frequency to the next level. In *Becoming Supernatural*, he explained how it all worked.

As Dr. Joe explained it, the quantum field was an inverse reality to our own. Where we experience time through space...if I am three miles away from you and want to see you, it will take me *time* to close the *distance* between where you are and where I am...the quantum field was different.

The quantum field was infinite time *and* space. There was no separation between the two. Endless possibilities. All of this, through the power of the mind. It made sense. A science for the imagination. A deeper understanding of the law of attraction.

By this point, my love, I hadn't yet considered the idea of the perfect mind, and certainly hadn't discovered the poem, *Thunder: Perfect Mind*.

A huge part of my excitement and interest in the quantum field was born out of the Avengers' movies from Marvel Studios. Marvel had done such an incredible job in entwining more than twenty movies into a seat-of-your-pants climax with *Avengers: Endgame* in 2019. The quantum realm, as they called it in the films, had played such a pivotal role in their storytelling.

I had dabbled with quantum physics over the past few years. At first, it was a difficult concept to understand, but through researching and understanding various experiments on the subject, I slowly began to embrace how quantum physics connects everything to well, everything.

In the Newtonian model of physics, physical objects are separate and distinct from one another. In quantum physics, reality is a kind of mesh since everything is quantum, including humans. Growing up, I applied my understanding of physics to the things around me; I didn't appreciate that whatever was true of my environment was also true of me. I was quantum...so what was my consciousness?

Divinity.

Dr. Joe had guided meditations he performed at his workshops. Many of those meditations were available on his website. When I returned from my trip, I was committed to downloading some of them to give them a try.

At the Mastermind, I mentioned that I'd been reading Dr. Joe, and how his ability to connect the scientific to the field of infinite possibility had already begun to radically alter my thinking. In my journaling, as I focused on designing my life for the next few years, I'd started incorporating some of his teachings into my planning.

Jack listened intently while I spoke. Others asked questions.

One of the key comments Jack made to me was to suggest I connect with the CEO of Ford. The Law of Attraction. The eight-cylinder engine. Accomplished not solely through engineering, but through the power of faith, focus, and perseverance. As I was wrapping up my closing comments, Jack said the most peculiar thing.

"You've got a year."

I was stumped. "Uhh, Okay."

What did *that* even mean? I was the next-to-last person to sit in the hot-seat. None of the other attendees had been given anything quite so cryptic in terms of feedback.

I'd never met Jack before. On what grounds did he make his comment? What could he possibly know about me that I did not know about myself? Nor was that the only odd thing Jack had shared with me.

The day prior, while we were on a break, I had lingered in the living room while everyone else had gone into the kitchen for lunch. Jack was still on video, and I began talking about *Becoming Supernatural*. As the conversation continued, Jack shared that while on a trip in Costa Rice, he'd undergone a past-life regression and discovered he'd been a Roman soldier. It was a cool story. It never dawned on me that he might have known me in a past life.

When my time in the hot-seat came to an end, we elected to take a break. Everyone headed to the kitchen but Patty, who went over to the screen to speak with Jack in as private a setting as possible. I don't know how I knew, but she asked him about the comment he'd made to me…about having a year. I didn't hear Jack's reply, but when Patty turned to face me, her face was awestruck. Whatever he told her had freaked her out.

The final day of the three-day Mastermind was spent filming professional interviews with Jack, which each of us could use as promotional materials on our website. When that day concluded, we all wished one another well with our programs and books, and said our goodbyes.

The next day, I took another near-empty flight home to North Carolina.

The John Maxwell event I was to have attended that weekend had been canceled due to the pandemic. I was disappointed, but quickly shifted my focus to the opportunity in front of me; I could now begin honest work on writing *Being*.

That weekend, I churned out twenty-seven pages and called it chapter one. I was elated. While I had hoped to follow up *The Lighthouse Keeper* with another fiction story, and perhaps even a sequel, I was inspired by how quickly *Being* had taken shape, and the direction it promised to take me.

Back home, our gym had closed its doors and a small number of us had taken to meeting in a nearby park to workout. Sean, the personal trainer who had coordinated our Spartan training program, loaded up his Ford Explorer every day with as much boot camp gym equipment his SUV could hold, and shuttled it to the park. Of Irish descent, Sean was a fair-skinned redhead who drove us to push ourselves at every workout. At the park, we would help him set up equipment before turning our attention to the workout for the day. Working out during the pandemic was a lifeline that was desperately needed.

Working from home felt fun, and a little refreshing. After spending years going into the office (when I wasn't traveling for work), working from home brought with it some relief. I started to get a better picture of what my work was, and how much of the day I needed to spend doing it. The early months of the pandemic made me realize that, for a lot of people, time spent at work isn't always focused on work. Working from home was creating some efficiencies which, in time, would lead to greater productivity.

I wasn't working on *Being* during the week, though it was constantly percolating in my mind. The crowdfunding contest that began in February wrapped up and *Being* had drawn interest from nearly twenty publishers. I was looking forward to the last weekend in March to progress the writing beyond chapter one and get to the heart of what *Being* was about. Instead, that weekend I did something completely unexpected.

I set aside the pages I'd banged out on the keyboard of my Mac, grabbed two pens and a notebook, and started writing a conversation between two voices.

The connection between hand, pen, and paper was electrifying. If *Being* was going to come to life, I was going to do it the old-fashioned way. I was going to write it by hand.

The first draft took me about six hours. At the end, I had a little more than a hundred pages. It was a cerebral text conversation between two voices. One voice represented unconditional love…being. The other, conditional love…doing.

Where I placed words on the page mattered. Upper left, higher value of words. The further the words went to the right, less value. Words in the lower right corner were lesser ideas or small thoughts. Some pages had sentences with both voices. Other pages had only a single voice, and there might only be a few lines of conversation on any given page. Empty pages denoted the passage of time.

What surprised me most about the writing was, the unconditional love voice started as masculine early on. Then, with the introduction of the second voice, something changed. The unconditional love voice became divine. Feminine. The voice of conditional love became the voice of man.

The unconditional voice was both inquisitive and sensitive. The conditional voice was proud of the labor it took to be a man. Doing stuff was cool. The harder the challenge, the more it forced man to think. To shift to something greater. To expand beyond the limits of what they believed was possible, and to envision a greater future.

The first person I had read it was my mom. It took her about twenty minutes and she said it was very heavy reading. She was tired and needed a break. She was right.

The story was a simple conversation, but the ideas being explored were significant. I had the rough sense I was teaching myself something that I'd always known. Since getting back from California, I'd spent my Friday and Saturday nights at Jim and Sara's, eating dinner and watching movies. I was also vaping more regularly.

Sara had invited me to come live with them. She was adamant about it. I enjoyed their friendship so much, but felt living with people at this stage of my life was a little weird, and somehow beneath my station. Still, it was inviting. I was open to considering it. With no end to the pandemic in sight, why not make life an adventure?

The following week, Judgment Day.

Tuesday, March 31, 2020 was not unusual in any meaningful way. I did my work. I may have gone running with Hector after I finished working for the day. I had already done a couple of Dr. Joe's meditations.

They were intense. Much different from meditations I'd previously done. While most people think of meditation of something that's subdued and calm, and you're motionless, Dr. Joe was directing the listener to contract the muscles from the glutes up through the upper body, pulling your energy and awareness from your root chakra, up through the chakra chain and ending with your awareness focused on the top of your head, or crown chakra.

He had specific meditations focused on accessing the quantum field, by pulling their awareness from their body, or reconditioning the body to a new mind. Intense.

As pre-work for one of these meditations, I'd thought very clearly about who I wanted to be…the version of me I saw in the future. I listed traits and attributes I wanted to embody, and how I would conduct myself. I thought about the kind of woman I hoped to attract into my life, the kind of father I wanted to be to my daughter. The kind of friend. I wrote all this down in a journal.

As I settled in for the evening, I was eager to perform the meditation that pulled the awareness out of the body and into the quantum field. With the world changing so quickly, with the fascinating trip to see Jack and his odd comments to me, life felt exciting.

Normally, I would be ashamed to share this, but dosing with plant medicine had opened my pineal gland, or third eye. I was open to experiences I previously wouldn't have allowed myself to consider. I had shifted from a fixed mindset to a growth mindset, unaware of just how much growth the next few years would demand from me.

After several rounds of intense breathing and body-clenching while simultaneously pulling my awareness toward the crown of my head, like a tadpole wiggling free from its embryonic shell, my awareness broke free from my body. With my eyes closed, I knew my body was still there, knew I was sitting in the corner chair of my small bedroom in my mom's home. I also knew I was quantum.

Some part of me listened to whatever Dr. Joe was saying. Once the separation from the body had been achieved, there may have simply been ambient music for a time. I wasn't thinking. I was in receive mode.

That was when my Judgment Day began.

The easiest way to think of it is like a USB thumb drive had been plugged into my mind. There weren't scenes from my childhood. I didn't relive moments of joy or disappointment, there was no one telling me I should have zigged when I zagged, or turned left when I should have gone right. There was no one on a throne, rendering a verdict.

There were black and white patterns of light. They weren't blinding, as I wasn't really seeing them. I was feeling them. That it was my Judgment Day was instantly understood, and without fear or doubt of any kind. It was simply a transmission of information I was receiving. It was the most beautiful awakening of my spirit.

In it, themes and patterns in my life were highlighted and ad- dressed, without any sort of subvocalization. It was a reader's digest version of my life, playing out decades of missteps when it came to my career and most importantly, when it came to love, all in a matter of minutes. Their meaning was clearly communicated and just as easily understood, all in real-time and again, with no subvocalizing of any kind.

The total meditation lasted an hour.

When it ended, I was there, in the chair, in my bedroom. The evening sky had gone dark. I felt wonder. Excitement. Peace.

The next night, fascinated by the spaces that were opening in my mind, I attempted the meditation again. This time, the results were slightly different.

There was no Judgment Day, part two. Frankly, I wasn't sure what I was expecting.

In this meditation, I more easily extracted my awareness from my physical body. How to explain what transpired?

It was like I was looking down on myself meditating from inside an upside-down basket; there was a distinct sense of isolation. What- ever part of me was "in" the basket, it felt very compressed. I could not clearly see myself, but sensed the connection between being in the chair and looking down on myself being in the chair. Then, a voice asked a question:

David?

It wasn't my voice. It was His. There was a vague image of my name written in a dim kind of light, surrounded by an oval shape in the same faded light.

In hindsight, I'd hope the meditation would provide me with

more direction on the path I needed to take. Instead, I was left with more questions.

As the weekend approached, I had no idea just how radically my world was about to change, and certainly had no idea that I'd come across the origin of my identity, in the shell of the first thought in human existence.

The Fourth Letter of David

I do not mean to paint my life as full of suffering. I laughed. I had friends, and shared wonderful, tender moments with them. Like most people, I had good moments and bad.

The brightest spot in my youth was spent under the plentiful sunny days on the island of Okinawa.

When I returned to the United States, it would not take me long to appreciate the teenager I had become on that tiny island was ill-suited to the environment of high school on the coast of North Carolina in the early and mid-eighties.

I loved video games, comic books, and dungeons and dragons, none of which were worth much in the ever-shifting landscape of high school popularity. Video games were seen as a waste of time and money, comic books were for little kids, and Dungeons and Dragons was simply uncool.

As a result, because of a natural desire to fit in, I began compartmentalizing my life. I didn't care that comic books had become childish. I loved the stories, and spent my weekends going to local comic shops in Jacksonville, the town just outside the Marine Corps base Camp Lejeune, looking for back issues to fill in gaps in my collections. Video games were the most socially acceptable with my friends, and whenever we went to the mall, I would spend my spare change playing *Galaga* or *Ms. PacMan* while my friends ate Chic-fil-A. D&D was hard to give up, only because, more than any other hobby at the time, it called for the most imagination in playing. My imagination was a bit over-sized.

Trying to be cool was a hard proposition to come by. On one hand, I entered high school as a freshman when Larry was a senior, and the president of his class. He was well-liked, popular, and highly regarded. I was none of those things.

I was a skinny kid with big ears who wore baggy clothes. I was Larry's little brother.

On the other hand, I was creative. I had boundless energy and ideas. I loved fiction writing, and was rewarded by receiving national recognition for a short story I wrote. My poetry won contests.

When it came to love, I felt like someone displaced in time. I would read Keats, Yeats, and Wordsworth and be fascinated with and wrecked by their poems about love. John Keats' *"La Belle Dame sans Merci"* ruined me. I read that poem over and over, haunted by how it called to me.

To my friends I feel certain, I was a gentle buffoon. I was Duckie Dale from the eighties film *Pretty in Pink*. When the movie originally came out, a large group of friends went to see it. I was busy the day they went. When we next saw one another the following week in school, the verdict was unanimous—I was Duckie.

The truth hurts. After seeing the movie, I knew they were right. I *was* Duckie and didn't want to be, which somehow made it more pitiful that I was.

If high school popularity were a card game, I'd been given the wrong set of cards and the wrong instructions. I was playing a different game. I made up for it by becoming something of a class clown. I would flirt with insensitive subjects, or cross the line of decency on occasion, seeking the edge of appropriateness and then pushing past it. And while my drinking became more prominent as I went through high school, I steered clear of other drugs.

Much of this stemmed from the proximity I still felt towards God. I didn't judge my classmates for their actions. My sense of it was, God was going the way of Santa Claus and the Easter Bunny, a fairytale from childhood that it was time to outgrow. At the most, it seemed

God was saved for church on Sundays. I was attempting to navigate the concessions that seemed necessary to survive high school while staying true to the part of me that was tied up in my fascination with video games and comics. I loved my imagination.

Even then, the idea that God's love was involved with romantic love seemed remote, if not impossible. I knew people got married in churches. Going to church brought up lots of feelings; romance was not on the list. Church mostly felt like a solemn affair.

As a result, I turned inward. While I was disappointed at so often not being invited to weekend parties, I also didn't understand them. Drinking to excess and then waiting for stupid or outrageous things to happen didn't make sense to me at the time. That would come in college.

My inward journey led me to look for companionship with lonesome characters from fiction, like *Tarzan*. Reading Edgar Rice Burroughs' stories of Tarzan spoke to me on such a deep, heartfelt level. The split between the ease and beautiful life lived in the wild and the necessity of interacting with human society. The paperback versions of the books had artwork by Neal Adams who, along with John Byrne, had been one of the great comic artists I was first exposed to.

I lacked the faculties and patience to fully grasp the agonized beauty and power of eighteen-year-old Mary Shelley's *Frankenstein,* but the depths of the creature's torn existence pierced my soul. I still remember watching the black and white *Frankenstein* movie at my grandmother's house in Pennsylvania, operating with the misconception that it was the creature who was the film's monster. At various points throughout my life, I've owned copies of the novel, with artwork by Berni Wrightson. His ink work is spectacular. Why did the creature's pain call to me so poignantly?

In high school, I began to write a follow-on story to *Frankenstein.* In my story the creature, unable to die, lived on into the present day. Living life among vagrants in dilapidated warehouses dotted along a bleak pier-side, the creature yearned for the answer to the endless song of love that sustained its essence. This wasn't a homework assignment; it was something inside me, wanting to be expressed.

Though I collected the classic horror stories such as Bram Stoker's *Dracula* and Victor Hugo's *The Hunchback of Notre Dame*, I was often intimidated by the maturity of the writing and thickness of the books. At no point in my life did I conceive that the blow to the back of my head I had received as a young boy had in anyway affected my ability to learn.

I just found comics easier to read. They generally ran less than thirty pages and had pictures to aid in the storytelling. That was my happy place.

I was a bit of a slob. My dad would jokingly observe that I was Pig Pen from the Charlie Brown and the *Peanuts* cartoons. *Wherever you go, a mess seems to follow*, he would say, unable to restrain the smile that blossomed on his face. My dad was as tidy as they came. I would have hundreds of comics sprawled across my bedroom floor. There was barely any room to walk; I had to receive my laundered clothes from my mom in the doorway and then tiptoe like I was walking through a minefield to dump the load of clothes on my bed.

Outside of English, school was distracting. I struggled with math, and our physics teacher, keenly aware that, of the fifteen or twenty people in his class, only one or two were understanding half of what he taught, opted to have us play charades a few times every semester. History was interesting, but I daydreamed so much.

It was as a teenager that I first started to appreciate the differences between DC and Marvel comics. DC characters like Superman, Wonder Woman, and Batman were paragons of unyielding virtue. The cities they lived in were universal and quintessentially American cities. Metropolis. Gotham. Central City. Their characters seemed morally flawless and incorruptible.

Marvel's characters were flawed. Besides Wolverine's drinking and smoking and Tony Stark's alcoholism, Moon Knight had multiple personalities. The Hulk had anger issues. Peter Parker was trying to live a normal teenage life while also fighting super villains. They lived in cities like New York City and Los Angeles.

Even with the books scattered across the floor in their plastic bags, I knew where every issue was. If I was trying to answer a question I'd been pondering, I automatically knew where on the floor to look. Though the books were in no discernible order, they were organized in my mind.

My social skills were stunted by my lack of confidence which, in turn, was born out of my lack of identity. When I was with my friends, I was a poor reflection of their coolness. My head was too stuck in the clouds, wondering about love and romance. Weren't poets supposed to suffer?

That was not a great approach to dating in high school.

Because I didn't know how to "fit in" I brooded on weekends. Sometimes, I would spend my weekends attempting to meditate.

Part of my exposure to eastern philosophy in Japan had gotten me interested in Shambhala, a mythical city said to exist somewhere between the Gobi Desert and the Himalayan mountains. I read a book that described in detail how to clear one's mind of any thoughts. That was my first understanding of meditation. From there, the book said, with an empty mind, after a time, a thought would appear. I didn't stick with meditation for long back then.

Frustrated by my inability to replicate the success and normalcy I saw other kids achieve, I threw myself into the tortured emotions of hard-rock.

With my early exposure to KISS, the Beatles, and the Rolling Stones, the edgier music resonated with me more so than the social commentary of REM, or the feel-good vibes of INXS.

My first rock concert was Ozzy Osbourne in 1984. Hard rock was amazing. I loved the straining guitars of Judas Priest, and the galloping tempo of Iron Maiden. If there was one band that I thought of as "my" band during that time in my life however, it was Motley Crue.

They had an album called *Shout at the Devil*.

I hesitated in buying the record. The pentagram on the cover enflamed my Christian sensibilities, but when I heard the bass player, Nikki Sixx, explain how the title of the album and symbol were about standing up to authority, that was all I needed.

I couldn't say what it was about their music, or their makeup and outfits. Their music sounded raw and full of pain, even as it attempted to talk up the perceived glory of the rock 'n' roll lifestyle. I was hooked. I'd buy magazines with them in it just to cut out their pictures and put them up on my walls.

Hard rock was angry. It was easy for me to relate.

At the height of my self-induced misery, I asked my parents to let me stay at the only high school I'd known, so that I might graduate with my friends. The summer before my senior year, my dad received orders to move to a base in Georgia. By the time I was a junior, I was a little more accepting of myself, and more accepted by my friends and classmates.

The thought of leaving for my last year of high school and starting over in a new environment was gut-wrenching, particularly with my fragile confidence and sense of self. My parents relented, and I stayed with family friends, whose children had already graduated school.

I was grateful that I could graduate with my friends, and didn't know how sorely I would miss my parents' everyday presence in my life. Going into my senior year, it brought a new strain to our relationship.

I was the rebel in our family. My brother once confided to mom that he couldn't understand why I always disobeyed our dad, knowing that it would result in me being punished. With the pain and resentment I'd nurtured from our moves, I antagonized my dad and what I perceived as his need to assert authority over my life. After I joined the Marines, I would come to appreciate; he was trying to add structure to an unstructured life.

Without a car and absent the proximity of my parents, my drinking increased. I lurched back and forth between joy and misery. There was a pier close to where I lived, overlooking the New River. In my despondency, I would venture out to the pier Friday nights alone, a bottle of Jim Beam in hand, and drink while listening to rock 'n' roll mix tapes. There, I would sing songs to the shallow waters, doing my best not to fall into the water. I enjoyed my concerts, even though I was the only one in attendance.

Besides Motley Crue, it was incredible to me how popular the Devil had become in hard rock. Bands like Dio had album covers with the devil holding one end of a broken chain while on the other, a priest was bound, unable to swim in deep waters. Ozzy supposedly bit the head off a bat and was the self-proclaimed Prince of Darkness. Iron Maiden sang about *The Number of the Beast*.

Today, we've concluded that "666" refers to the atomic structure of carbon; six protons, six electrons, and six neutrons. We are carbon-based lifeforms. How did the folks who wrote the Bible know about carbon atoms back when it was written?

It would take me decades to appreciate just how right Nikki Sixx had been. In the eighties at the time, there was a pronounced effort from our Congress here in the US to take action against the "devil's music" by censoring lyrics, or putting warning labels on albums. At the same time, many politicians and even religious figures were in the news for taking bribes, or having affairs with their secretaries. Rock stars flaunted their misdeeds while the politicians and priests tried to cover theirs up. The two sides were pointing fingers at one another, both with credible claims to make.

The eighties also made great gains in jarring people loose from the idea that God existed. With priests being accused of crimes, and scientists boldly asserting the known universe was explainable without the need for a Creator, America turned to making money and enjoying the security and stability provided by the generations that preceded them. As I prepared to head to college, I was ready to grow up. To me, at least in some sense, that meant putting my belief in God behind me.

A PRAYER FOR THE DARKNESS

How was I to find you?

I knew you were out there, and that Jesus was safe with you.

I knew only darkness, having surrendered myself to the Light.

My mind grew so dim. I began to doubt myself.

Not knowing what else to do, I began to search for love in the black.

I prayed to the darkness, give me at least a little light to go by. Anything. The near-imperceptible flicker of love.

There must be a light in the darkness for me, for darkness is nothing without the faintest ray of light.

For so long, I thought I would never find you. I agonized within the fragile framework of a mortal existence from which I saw no relief. I wrecked this life with all the strength I could muster, hammering away at my relationships, searching for one thing; a light that might pierce the darkness that concealed my identity. Even in my anger, in my frustration at the destruction I had wrought, I began to understand the purpose of love.

A moment can be microscopic. A second is something we only pay attention to when we realize the power of a second.

The second I saw you, I knew you. I did not know how, or why. I had no conceivable notion of how powerful the love of an Eternal Son could be. I knew victory over the Cross had been realized, but could not grasp its full magnitude.

Not as a man.

Over the course of my journey, I felt so small when I saw you. Your power. Your wisdom. The Mother of Our Son. How my heart raced in the moments when I considered writing something to you.

What I saw in you was simply a reflection of how far I had to go. I could not dare imagine that I was somehow responsible for your beauty, yet what are my letters to you if not a reflection of the beauty you have awakened within me?

I prayed to God, looking for you, and not Jesus. My Original Sin. I needed to find you to get back to Our Son, and need Our Son to get back to You.

That is the story of how far away earth fell from heaven, that is the length of my darkness.

BOOK TWO

Faith:
I, the Storm

The Second Love Letter

It's hard to say when I first fell in love with superheroes.

In the early seventies, Spiderman had a cartoon on in the mornings before school. If we were lucky, we might get to watch it.

In the afternoon, Batman and Robin lit up the television screen with live-action, bright costumes, and silly dialogue. "Come along chum," Batman would say, and then Robin would reply with something like, "Gosh Batman, those criminals sure did punch hard." Silly, but we watched without fail.

The weekends had *Super Friends*. Simply drawn, that cartoon was my first exposure to Superman on Saturday mornings. It was hard to appreciate how strong he was. There was also Wonder Woman, Aquaman, Batman, the Flash, and a few others. The stories were easy enough to follow. Mainly, Larry and I were thrilled to be watching TV while our parents slept in.

I wish I could remember what the first comic book I ever picked up was. It might have been my brother's. He liked a book called the *Fantastic Four*. He also liked *The Avengers*.

Something about their stories appealed to me. The drama was of an extreme nature, and the stories were unlike traditional horror stories. Back then, Frankenstein and Dracula movies competed for our attention on the few television stations we had. The superhero cartoons led me to the comics. Realizing these stories continued month after month drew me in. The first book I really remember collecting was *The Invaders*.

The *Invaders* was a Marvel Comic. It would take me years to fully embrace the difference between DC and Marvel, but *The Invaders* combined three things I was fascinated with: superheroes, monsters, and war.

The Invaders followed Captain America, his sidekick Bucky, two human torches, and this guy called the Submariner. The Submariner was the King of Atlantis, wore green speedos, had wings on his ankles, and pointy ears. These Invaders were facing off against the Nazis in war-torn Europe. When they weren't battling directly with Hitler's goons, there was a host of supernatural characters to fight with. There was a nazified Frankenstein's monster, and a vampire disguised as a German baron. There was even a Golem, a creature formed out of a lifeless substance like dust, earth, or clay. They are brought to life by ritual incantations and Hebrew letters.

My love affair with comics would catch fire when we moved to Okinawa.

While on this tiny island south of the mainland, I discovered Tony Stark. Iron Man. I also discovered the Uncanny X-Men.

Living on a subtropical island in the middle of the Pacific as a kid was a sweet deal. One of the biggest drawbacks, however, was the distinct absence of a local comic book shop. That meant whenever our family went to the Post Exchange, the shopping center for military families on base, I'd always make a run to the magazine stand or the comic rack to see what new comics had come out. It was that, or mail ordering comics from the States, and that could take months.

I'd gotten interested in *The Invaders*, not realizing that shortly after we moved to Okinawa, the comic's story arc would end, and they stopped the series. In the DC Universe, I liked the Flash. He was the fastest man alive, and I had a couple of comic books where he and Superman raced one another. I even remember a giant-sized comic that had Superman fighting Spiderman...the first time I can recall Marvel and DC teaming up.

Iron Man was wild because he had grown-up problems. Marvel

wrote a story called *Demon in a Bottle*. Tony Stark was battling alcoholism. And then, there were the X-Men.

What attracted me to the X-Men was the art. It was incredible. John Byrne and Terry Austin, the artist and inker, respectively. Their artwork was like nothing else. And the stories were epic.

This guy Chris Claremont had dreamed up this brilliant storyline, the Dark Phoenix saga. Without going into painstaking detail, he had taken one of the original characters, Jean Grey, and turned her into the force of nature called the Phoenix. She was powerful enough to feed off entire planets, but managed to keep her powers in check… for a time.

The X-Men were so completely different. Unlike the open acceptance of Superman, Batman, and the others in the world of DC, the X-Men were shunned by society. They were mutants. They looked different, and possessed the strangest powers, everyone was unique. They were international. A Russian metal man, a German blue demon-elf, a Canadian buzzsaw named Wolverine. An African goddess. They were mutants; humans who acquired extraordinary gifts and powers through the mutation of their cells.

Wolverine loved Jean, but Jean was with Scott, or Cyclops. Wolverine cursed. He drank. Smoked. He was constantly brooding. He was phenomenal, and their relationship fed my romantic angst.

And then, there was Jean. She was spectacular. I knew they were comic book characters but as an eleven-year-old, these stories were my world. Jean loved Scott, was a little intimidated but also slightly attracted to Wolverine, and was trying to understand this hunger that was growing within her. Eventually, the darkness won.

When she became the Dark Phoenix, the comic book world exploded. That storyline transformed comic books. Today, some of those books are worth ridiculous amounts of money. I fell in love.

Jean became consumed with hunger; she would fly through space and drain the energy from entire planets. She was like a living, breathing death star.

The movies never quite did that story justice, but it didn't matter. To me, that was love on a cosmic scale.

For reasons unknown to me at the time, that was the kind of love I was going to spend my entire life searching for.

THE SECOND LETTER OF THUNDER

At some point, as all boys do, we outgrew playing war and running wild in the streets. The wooden rifle frames that we cherished as kids were thrown away, and I moved onto playing wargames with my dad.

He didn't talk about his job much, or his time in Vietnam. Not when I was young. He would save those conversations for when I was a Marine.

He used to purchase WWII model kits and, when he wasn't taking care of our yard or the garden, would spend his weekends putting them together. He went to such painstaking detail to paint them as accurately as possible. The models were small, and I would watch with fascination as he used a toothpick, a drop of white paint on its tip, to fill in the eyes of a model soldier he had in his hand. Eventually, he got interested in board games. They were from a company called Avalon Hill, and they were all focused on warfare.

Two of my favorites were also two of the more beginner level games. The first was called *Tactics II*. *Tactics II* wasn't based on a historical battle, it was just a generic map full of different types of terrain, mapped out on little hexagons. Each hexagon on the map represented a unit of movement. If a unit could move twelve turns, it could move twelve hexes, provided the hexes did not have mountains or river symbols on them. Each military unit was represented by a small half-inch square. The face of the square would have a symbol for a particular type of military unit on it. It could be an infantry unit, mechanized infantry, or armor. Each unit had three numbers, an attack number, a defense number, and a movement number. Armor units might have strong attack and high movement numbers. Infantry, would have smaller numbers all the way around.

Any game might have anywhere from thirty to a hundred of these little units per side. I was too young to play the more complex games. Besides *Tactics II*, the other one I liked to play was *Afrika Korps*.

Afrika Korps pitted the Nazis against the British along the northern coast of Africa. The scenarios and the battles depicted in the game were historically accurate, and reflected the units present during that portion of World War Two.

I was also too young to understand what the Nazis had represented during the war. I just knew they were the bad guys.

Afrika Korps was dominated by desert. Irregular mountain ranges dominated the board, which meant, if one side decided to drive through the desert instead of relying on the main roads, the movement could be slow. That, or you followed the valleys in between the mountains, which could give away to the opposing player your intentions.

There were two key cities that comprised the campaign; Benghazi and Tobruk, both in modern day Libya. In the game we played, the British had to hold the cities, and keep the Germans at bay long enough for reinforcements to arrive. For the Nazis, they wanted to seize the cities and destroy the opposing force.

I never beat my dad playing these games. Ever. Never beat him in basketball. As I got older and grew stronger, I would try and push him around on the court. He would push back, harder. I would later learn of the losses he'd suffered in Vietnam, and the weight those losses occupied in his life. I'd only seen him cry three times in my entire life; once when his mom died. The other two were recounting Marines lost in the war.

My dad, this idealistic kid from Iowa, discovered firsthand how hard the world can punch. That was why he never cut me any slack.

In the games, each turn represented a month, with the game starting sometime in 1942. First, the British player would go, complete all their moves, place reinforcements on the board if they were getting any, and resolve any attacks. The German player would repeat the process; that concluded one month.

The idea was to maneuver enough of your forces against as few of the enemy forces as possible to gain the greatest numerical superiority. Six-to-one odds were more favorable than one-to-six. Different terrain might reward the defender or penalize the attacker, or the situation might be reversed.

I can't say I fully understood the game's objective. I just knew I wanted to obliterate my dad's army off the board. And one time, I came close.

Normally, I could never get very far. If I were the British, I would lose the cities and most of my forces in just a few turns. When I was the Nazis, I could never get the odds in my favor to take either city. On those occasions, my father would slowly eat away at my forces until I was forced to retreat, which was as good as surrender. There was one occasion where I came close. Closer than I'd ever been before.

By this time, I was in college. We'd played the games regularly until I became a teenager in high school. In college, on my way into the Marines, the games ignited in me a new interest; I had some context on how to focus on the outcomes I wanted to achieve. I understood more clearly how I might use my forces more effectively. I was beginning to understand waging war on a broader scale, and to view different units as instruments of war. On this occasion, we pulled out *Afrika Korps*. I was the Nazis.

To start the game, I was given the seemingly insurmountable task of removing my father's forces from the two cities. There had been enough separation in time from my struggles when I was younger that I was not concerned with my failures of the past. It wasn't going to be easy, but with attention to detail, and a little luck, I could be victorious.

My father had "stacked" his units in both cities, each of which consisted of two or three hexes. Defenders in cities were given a defensive advantage, which played into their overall defensive strength.

As wisely as I could, I divided my forces. I first focused on the westernmost city, Benghazi, keeping as much of my firepower with this larger army. The rest of my forces pushed to the east, to prevent my father from attempting to reinforce the city under siege.

I did not face good odds, but after several turns, Benghazi fell. I was thrilled. While I had lost some of my units, an impressive amount of armor and mechanized infantry remained. I kept a small garrison in the city, while the rest of my forces advanced towards Tobruk.

My father was surprised by my victory but remained focused. By this point, he had been a Marine for twenty-eight years. I had studied rudimentary tactics in a class.

Tobruk proved harder and my victory, more costly, but ultimately the city fell.

My father could not hide his surprise now, and seemed pleased that I had already accomplished more than I ever had when we had played this game.

I felt victory in my grasp, my chest swelled with the anticipation of a feeling I'd yet to experience. His forces were on the run towards the east, and reinforcements were months away. Emboldened by the swiftness of my victories, I eagerly pursued him into the desert. There, I would find my undoing.

Military men have several sayings that have passed down from generation to generation. One is, *Amateurs talk tactics. Professionals talk logistics.*

As I followed my father's retreat into the desert, he used his turn to divide his forces into three separate groups, each separated by at least one hex and each in the mountains. Another defensive advantage. This meant, while they could not combine their strength to attack me, I could not, in isolation, attack any single force without having to commit some of my attack to one of the adjacent forces. I did not see the trap he had lured me into until it was too late.

My attacks were ineffectual, and I was unable to eliminate or repel any of his forces. With his next turn, he maneuvered two of his units behind mine, effectively cutting off my supplies. If I could not break his blockade within a few turns, my army would run out of fuel and ammunition.

I had stretched my forces too thin, and had committed too much of my army to destroying his, without securing my supply lines. After multiple failed attempts to break through his defenses, my army literally ran out of gas. The game was over.

THE SPANIARD III

These fields are filled with my memories, as if each head of wheat is a second of time. Some, I sense more clearly than others. Wherever I am, it is still cold, and while the chaff is brittle, I do not feel its pain, even as the grains of wheat fall silently beneath my hands.

There are moments where I still sense the lush plentifulness of our home in Spain. I can smell the jasmine, can hear Argento and Scatto teasing Samuel with playful neighs and whinnies. He is just a boy, only four or five. I see you from the courtyard. You are in the garden, thoughtfully selecting herbs for the night's supper. I am in a trance.

And Samuel. When he was born, you told me his name meant *God has heard*. From what well of knowledge you drew such wonderful sips of wisdom, I never understood. I simply appreciated they were there.

There feels like a flicker of light in the dark. A pleasant memory caresses my soul.

When you were pregnant with Samuel, I would put honey on your stomach and kiss it. Watching his life grow inside you….

One God.

As I began my journey in search of you and Samuel, I did not know Jesus' crucifixion had broken open the first four seals as described in the Book of Revelation. The Wrath of God.

Conquest...the advancement of Christianity across modernity. The Christ moving through Time and Space for an inevitable confrontation with the Antichrist. The spreading of salvation at the cost of brother killing brother.

The inevitable Fall of Rome. The Dark Ages. The Crusades. The Spanish Inquisition.

The conquest of the New World.

So many gods fell before the Cross. Greek Gods. Roman. The Norse Gods. The Gods of the Native American tribes, and those of the Mayans, and Aztecs.

Famine...disparity of consumption. The parched earth in forgotten lands providing only meager supplies of food, forcing people to move near fresh water supplies. Water designs so much of how we live. The wealthy threw away food, while those less fortunate begged for scraps from their table.

Death.

That was the real war in heaven. The war to tame the earth, with men's hearts opened to their darkest desires. Rome was a symbol. The great city. State. Empire. Nation.

Over the march of history, every country's rise to prominence under the banner of Christianity was ferried by the notion that *their* people would be responsible for bringing about heaven on earth. France. England. Germany. America.

When the triumph of a new form of government, or new idea that might bring heaven and earth together, reached its zenith without the promised reconciliation, people began to lose faith.

This knowledge fell to me with what passed for time on my journey. While I learned its meaning at the tapestry of history unraveled, I did not consciously take part in its untangling.

What did it mean to me?

It meant there was a necessary nobility to be explored in bringing an enemy to heel. While I was alive, I operated with no such understanding as to the grand unfolding of conflict as the recipe for bringing heaven down to earth.

Did I relish in killing? No. I reasoned that every foe felled by my sword brought me closer to the fruition of Marcus' vision; the eradication of ignorance was the cause of my endeavors. Every successful campaign led me one step closer to home. To you.

That kind of virtue possesses a man. With absolute clarity of purpose, my heart burst into something greater. I became a man consumed by a lion. The center of my forehead burned like a gilded eye from the great cat—blazing light centered around a blackened pupil. It lit in golden hues at the center of my brow with a most glorious decree; that all might see the Light.

War *was* a Truth.

War. The nexus of hell was forged in the heart of what would become Germany. That was where Christ defeated Thor, a pagan god. The god of the common man.

It was there, in the heart of Europe, that the Darkness of Man would finally begin to give way to the Light of God.

★ ★ ★

In a war, usually there are clear outcomes. When that is true, a decisive and quick victory is preferred. An army does not posture to the delight of the crowd. There are instances where feints or withdrawals may be necessary to extend the length of a campaign, but these ruses serve a military purpose. While both an army and a gladiator fight for the emperor, their reasons for doing so could not be more different.

In the legions, we fought for the glory of Rome, focused on the nobility of our purpose. We fought for one another. For the emperor. For our wives and families back home, wherever that might be. We faced an external enemy.

A gladiator fights for the emperor because there is no other choice. Good ones make it from the desert outposts all the way to Rome. The best might win their freedom. Death or freedom.

The greatest know a truth: those in the crowd live under the deepest illusion. It is the illusion of safety in numbers. The mob pulses in waves, it gasps with every sword strike, and shrieks in mental ecstasy with every parried blow. The distraction of watching someone else live and die is but a momentary respite from the battle each of us must face.

Before battle, whether with the legions or in the pits, I thought of you. I no longer allowed myself to say your name, and chose instead to live in its brittle embrace. Bitter. I was possessed by a narrowness of focus. The needlepoint at the center of my forehead; death to all who stood in my way.

I feel the weight of the sword in my hand.

Balanced. Even as my hand becomes an extension of the sword, there is no tension. Only balance.

If I am with shield, I carry it loosely. I invite the opening. The first few who accept it serve as apt teachers for those that follow.

The Spaniard carries his shield low. They learn.

Men don't want to die, and a gladiator must hone his craft. Compared with the mayhem often found on the battlefield, gladiatorial games afford a level of focus to combat that allows for scheming and even deception. They are, after all, games. It is not enough that men fight one another to the death; the games demand intrigue. Variety. Excitement and anticipation. Historical reference.

The gates open.

War is not an embittering enterprise when it is undertaken with the highest virtue in mind. Salvation for the oppressed. Salvation for all.

Marcus knew what he was doing. I knew Rome, the Rome Marcus lived with, was the light, though I had never set foot in Rome proper during my time as General of the northern armies.

I would enter Rome as a slave.

The mob roars like a voracious beast.

In the small arenas in Africa and elsewhere—the pits, I called them—it was often taxing. Contrary to popular misconception, the pits were filled with slaves. There was so much churn and bustle. Everyone wanted to get to Rome once the gladiatorial games returned. As a slave, the first time I killed a man I did not know then that I was getting closer to you. I knew only that the grandstanding gladiators had never fought a veteran of combat like me. I was to be a devastating and decisive teacher.

How could I have known? The wound felt fresh for so many years. The very idea...that taking a life would bring me closer to you?

It was a ridiculous proposition. I had knelt at the feet of where you and our son had been hanged, your bodies charred into hideous ornaments.

The decorations of my tragedy.

My opponent stands before me. Mace at the ready, his face hidden beneath a helmet.

Even that moment's reflection is enough to relive the profound agony by which I measured each waking second. There seemed no medicine for the fracture I felt inside, as if my heart had been torn from my chest, while physically I was left intact.

But hunger brings about a strange occurrence in the minds of men. While I wasted away physically, content for a time to deteriorate into whatever pitiful state might afford the greatest solitude, something behind the wound where my heart had been wrestled for my attention. There *must* be an answer. That was when I turned my focus outward.

Why could we be made to suffer if not to overcome our sorrows?

The obstacle becomes the path.

Once we had settled in the next village that promised glory, awaiting the next round of gladiator games, I did my best to extinguish the blazing fires of my remorse. After a time, content with the simmering embers left behind, my appetite returned, and I found my strength. It was born from the most fanciful thought, something that only comes to me now with a settled moment of reflection.

I once told you I never worried about saying goodbye to you when I left home, because I knew I would see you again.

And in that thought, a spark.

That spark provided illumination to a strangest resolve. For the first time in my existence, I was beyond the hallowed boundaries of what I believed Rome to be. Outside the light, looking in. My disillusionment was complete. Instantly, I understood the purpose behind Marcus' final message to me; the light of the empire was fading.

That a son would kill his father in the pursuit of near limitless power only deepened the hues of my resolve. I prayed to whatever gods might hear me. Neither hearing nor sensing their response, I committed to praying to you and Samuel, that you might guide me on my path, and allow my every breath to bring me closer to the two of you.

The closer one got to Rome proper, the better the quality of fighter in the pits. Gladiators with numerous victories. Reputations.

Identities.

It was distasteful, killing men for sport. For the amusement of the mob. Filling someone's pockets with money while men and sometimes women fought for their survival.

Historic battles reenacted. The *new* glory of Rome. Deplorable.

The first time I found myself in the arena, I understood the meaning of the word slavery; a life expended for the amusement or benefit of another.

But a mind trained to handle a sword illuminates the most brilliant episodes of concentration. The greatest benefit of growing up in the rank and file of the legions was the discipline by which we fought.

The phalanx is incredibly effective against the rambunctious mind of the barbarian; its uniformity allows each legionnaire the opportunity to study their enemy, who initially fixates on the need or desire to disrupt the integrity of the formation. It is quite the same as rats looking for an exit from a sinking ship. As swords, axes, or hammers smash against the aligned shields, each legionnaire studies the movements of their intended assailant.

Those who did not serve in the military that find themselves in the pits fought for the glory of living to fight again. Those who succeeded became regarded as something worthy. Those who didn't died to the roar and amusement of the crowd.

The survivors licked their wounds and, emboldened by their successes, were rewarded for their resilience. Armor was acquired and worn like a badge of honor, each piece unique and somehow given to ceremony. Extravagant headpieces, some made from animals were worn as decoration. Stories were told. The greats hoped to be legend. All sought freedom.

I found it all sickening, which only reinforced my desires to dispatch my foes with an urgency that matched my revulsion. Combat was an instrument for enlightenment. Death as entertainment reeked of negligence and an internal indulgence of self-aggrandizing.

Commodus.

Marcus had done away with the games. My disgust with the affair only sharpened my determination to learn the tricks of this new trade to which I had been enlisted, such was the discipline of a mind honed to erode resistance. Despite my misgivings, my appetite on the matters within my control subdued my anger and disgust, and I focused my mind on mastering these "games."

In real combat, something that resembles the gladiatorial games might best be likened to a skirmish, a "spontaneous" encounter with a few opponents in open ground. Without the safety and fortitude of the phalanx, single combat is assessed by energy. Intrinsically, the seasoned fighter understands the symphony of each weapon. Some weapons are one-handed; others, heavy and awkward enough to require two. An axe is both for slashing and butting. Most can be thrown.

A sword is a piercing and slashing weapon. While its flattened sides are useful, they are also the weakest point. A flattened sword becomes the poor man's dagger; a broken blade, and the advantage of reach is immediately surrendered.

And then there is the hammer. The hammer is an awkward instrument. Small hammers, while useful in close quarters, are hardly suitable for a prolonged engagement. Better left with the blacksmith.

A long hammer poses an intimidating challenge; a man must first be large enough to lift it. Using it in combat is an altogether different matter.

Some hammers might be metal balls with spikes protruding from them; others could be a block the size of a calf's head.

Armed combat of this nature is a dance, a tale of two symphonies if you will.

Sword on sword is common. In the fray, there is no thinking. There is not time to think. There is only being. That is why training is so vital. A disciplined unit is one that stays alive, and discipline comes down to the focus, urgency, and resilience of each individual soldier. That responsibility falls to the commander.

This kind of combat is man most closely aligned to his primal nature, which is why an unerring moral compass is so essential.

In a sword versus axe encounter, the axe has the advantage in that the axe-wielder's efforts to parry the sword may result in their opponent being inadvertently struck by the axe-head. The advantage is with the imbalance of the axe.

Encounters with a hammer-bearer require a different strategy. The hammer bearer must think faster than his opponents; it requires time and energy to create the momentum and begin the dance of the hammer.

If swarming the hammer-wielder is not possible, the advantage is with the swordsman so long as the hammer is not swinging as the encounter begins. If that is true, the swordsman's agility is used to their advantage to close the distance and use the hammer's unwieldiness against it.

A good berserker anticipates the dance and starts their swing early.

A great berserker is a savage conductor of the most devastating orchestra. They are usually enormous beasts, towering over their opponents and wreaking havoc in punishing orbits that range anywhere from six to ten feet.

The best will dance, stepping deep into fantastic, swooping lunges, decimating men with uncanny precision and fluidness. They see the battle unfolding on the most visceral terms, sensing the nearest threat seconds before it manifests. They are nearly impossible to subdue up close, and often require a team of archers. Even in these instances however, they are possessed of a spirit that can best be described as otherworldly.

Swordsman, eager to engage and accustomed to the equality of smaller weapons often find themselves inside the arc of the hammer;

they rush to closing distance through habit. That is why it is best to swarm the berserker, most particularly in the absence of archers.

There were few berserkers with hammers in the pits.

The killing of a gladiator brings about an artificial artistry; killing for sport. Some play to the crowd, feeding off the mob's lust for blood. Few champions tortured their foes.

That first appearance in a pit, I knew what the caged lion felt like. My anger seethed behind my eyes; instinctively, I channeled my inner thoughts, closing my mind from fear. My routine was the same; dust my hands dry, leaving the grains of sand to add texture to my grip, to feel with unerring precision of the hilt in my hand. Wait for the gates to open.

There is an image of you. It is but a flicker in the mind's eye. Some days, it's easier to see then others. You are wearing all black, your olive skin soaked in sunlight. The wheat around you rustles; you are a black vessel on a sea of gold. Your smile. The look on your face. Whatever I receive from that flicker, I send back to you in silent prayer.

From there, instinct takes over. There is no thought. There is no crowd. My opponents are currents of expectation and hesitation. Angles, balance, and the eyes tell a man's fortune in combat.

Gladiators are curious creatures; those who have advanced through a succession of victories use the gimmickry of it all to their advantage. An opponent who trembles at the sight of a man wearing a bull's head for armor has already lost.

It is best to kill those poor souls quickly; they are seething with fear which, at any moment, can flip into fury. Their unpredictability can be a danger if left unaddressed.

At the same time, the seasoned gladiators are encumbered by their costumes. Heavy headpieces or irregular armor became limitations in the space where speed and dexterity matter.

The closer one got to Rome, I learned, the better the quality of armor for the empire's champions.

Under the armor, behind whatever weapon yielded, a man is still a man. Survival as a motivation for living is a poor man's guide; it leads you to the same place again and again. To truly live, a man must have purpose.

What does it take to build heaven?

That was my promise to you, my love. Did I call it something else? Was it Elysium? That I would find you and together, we would build heaven on earth. It was my whispered prayer to you, every night I was away.

Like a bolt of lightning, the last words you ever spoke to me ripple across my consciousness. I do not catch all the thought as it passes.

Remember Samuel.

God has heard.

You knew, knew there would be loss.

How was I to find you?

Marcus. Something about Marcus.

He had once chided me. When he decided something, it was executed. On military matters, he wanted to hear my voice, even if my words might be contradictory to his proposals. I recognized my duty to the empire necessitated speaking out when my military mind sensed something out of place. It was rare of us to disagree. He was a brilliant man.

You must remember who you are, Maximus. Always remember who you are.

Marcus. Samuel. And the one called the Christ.

How would I understand loss, virtue, even destiny, had my life not taken the surreal course that it had.

For a time, there was so much darkness. I thought the light lost to me. I couldn't quite see it, but felt it on my periphery; I could never bring it into focus. It was a most deserted and vacant sense of orientation.

I was without any sort of joy, so occupied were my dim faculties with the disorientation I felt in my feeble attempts at advance. My limited sense of balance, of equilibrium, would afford me the illusion of forward progress. And then, it felt as if I were liquid being sucked downward and back. It was like I was a stew, being supped by some colossal giant.

This would be followed by a brief sense of stillness, and the process would begin anew; move forward, pulled back, balance.

I did not know if I was standing still; I was without a destination, except the unnerving dreariness of looking for the light that eluded my vision.

In my despair, I do not want to think of you, do not want to tarnish the rapture I felt in your arms, not even with the residue of a negative thought. And yet, you were inescapable. *Bitter.*

Instead, I do my best to think of Samuel. His messy hair. The warmth and innocence in his eyes. Just like his mother's.

Samuel was a good son. *I shall defend this land until your return father!* He would shout as I trotted off to war, a branch plucked from a nearby tree serving as his sword.

He was so insightful, full of awe. He saw the world with wonderful imagination, and was such a perfect blend of his mother's kindness and my devotion.

On campaign, when I had moments to myself, I reflected on how intelligent he was. How he would sit next to me or, when young, simply invite himself onto my lap, resting his head against my chest. Once there, he wanted to know what life was like as a soldier. Of what it meant to fight. To command. To hear of the world that existed outside our estate.

He asked of the emperor, and whether he would like our family.

When I think of Samuel now, I understand just how much our relationship had shaped my path.

My purpose was to fulfill Destiny.

The Third Love Letter

There is a poem called *Thunder: Perfect Mind*. Originally believed to be from Egypt, it was written sometime before 350 AD.

It is the voice of a female divinity, uniting all that is opposite. She is daughter to her husband and sister to her father. She is shameless and ashamed. She is war and peace.

A perfect mind. Then, thunder.

You are a teacher by trade. You are the greatest teacher I have ever known.

Imagine it. The Virgin Mary is told she will give birth to the Son of David.

I have so many questions. What did you feel? What emotions welled up inside you, knowing what your Son would bring to the world? What did you think of me? Did you know of Isaiah's prophecy over the tribulations Jesus would face?

How close did you feel to heaven, after he rose?

I may have created our Son, but it was you who brought Him to life. You carried this knowledge. You carried Him. What did you say to Him in utero? How did your love influence and shape His character?

More than two thousand years have passed in the time since those events occurred. My questions must be burdensome, asking you to go back so far.

I have, quite literally, been searching for you as long as I have been alive.

How was I to find you? No one else believed. Even my Christian friends didn't believe there were two people destined to be together. It would be a long time before I ever thought to look for Jesus' Mother.

By April 4th, I had started writing an early version of this story. It was virtually dust; a simple, one-hundred-page outline consisting of less than six thousand words. It was like a handwritten text conversation between two, and then three voices.

It was a delightful writing experience. When I took a break to check my phone, I had zero expectations. Well, at the very least, I hoped what I saw would make me feel good.

I have never considered what it would mean to see a flawless profile. Sculptors can capture beauty in so many unique ways. You had the precision and focus of a statue, as if someone had sculpted you.

The slight break in your lips, the hint of a smile. The wisp of hair caressing your cheek and flirting with the corner of your mouth. The perfect ratios; your ears, your eyes, nose, and mouth. The incredible slope of your neck. It was a profile created with sacred geometry.

The black dress, opaque and yet somehow highlighting the strength and power of your physique. The sea of blazing wheat surrounding you. The hint of weather in the grey clouds swirling in the distance.

With what had happened a few days prior, I was ready to go wherever the intelligence behind your beauty was going to take me.

One of the places it led me was to Frankenstein's monster. That story, with all its haunted imagery and macabre subject matter, reflected the strange sense of abandonment I nourished for much of my mortal life. I found solitude with the creature, so lonely and curious about its own creation.

That the story was written by a teenage woman named Mary comes to me as no surprise at all. That her inspiration for the story sprang from rumors born two centuries before her about a man performing experiments in a castle in Germany on corpses, and attempting to reanimate them using electricity? Art imitates life. The art of seeing you stirred within me the most sublime feelings of joy I had ever known.

How I marveled at that picture of you. I took a screenshot of it, doing my best to memorize the lines of your face. The way your hair rebelled, I could feel the strength of the wind that blew from behind you, could hear the whispered chatter from the waves of wheat. My speculation managed the most wonderful foothold as I ascended the heights of the beauty this picture afforded me; I wondered…*what were you thinking?* With one arm raised to the side of your head, you were looking for something, someone, in the distance.

I call that picture, *Love Looks to the West.*

What spark of genius shown from within those eyes. What made your smile so certain of itself? Your caption for the post was perfect: *Freedom is priceless.*

Little did I know, I was now face to face with the Darkest Phoenix; on April 4th, I had seen the first memory in human history.

The Fifth Letter of David

Despite the reality that I was very clearly moving away from God, I felt like I was fitting in more with people around me by the time I got to college.

I went into my four years of college wildly confident that love was virtually around every corner. I carried with me an invisible, magical slipper, and was convinced the foot that matched it was somewhere out there. Being so young and naïve to the ways of the world, I had no real sense of how I might find that foot, and the woman to whom it belonged.

Penn State was huge. I had spent a fair amount of time with my relatives outside Pittsburgh, but Penn State was a very different experience. It was a small town built around a massive university campus that was, quite literally, in the geographic center of Pennsylvania. College was a blast.

Penn State had been one of two schools I had applied to. After years spent growing up on military bases, I had no idea how big the world really was, even after living three years in Japan. Lacking a real sense of purpose and the confidence to try my luck as a writer, I chose Penn State because it was close to family, I liked football, and my brother was already there. I didn't know who I would be at a big university like that; having my brother there, I assumed, would make that easier. I would quickly be proven wrong.

The fraternity Larry belonged to was an eyesore called Sigma Tau Gamma, and the house address was 329 East Beaver Avenue. State College had such a college feel to it. Our fraternity was full of ROTC candidates, people who had already committed to serving their country. In many ways, our dilapidated house reflected that. It was like the house in the movie *Animal House*, except we didn't have any cars on the lawn. People stayed away.

The house was fantastic and strange. Fantastic because it was so care-free. Larry was president when I got there. As the son of a Marine, it was like he brought creditability to the chaos. People loved him. There were all these other ROTC midshipmen, few if any of whom had parents in the military, and they all looked up to my brother.

Larry and I had grown increasingly distant, and our relationship bordered on antagonistic. That became evident in college, when we rarely spent time together.

Our fraternity was strange too, in that most people in college didn't think about losing their friends in war, or hearing their buddies were injured or killed during a training exercise. We lived with that possibility every day. We looked at the world through the lens of academia, the college experiences of football games, tailgates, and parties. We also looked at it through the lens of threat levels, hostile states, and global hot spots.

Where would America lend its might next? Where might it be needed?

In places like Pennsylvania, it sometimes felt like we lived among the echoes of the Vietnam War, the war when this once great nation was defeated by a much smaller one.

Since World War II, America had won what most would consider as a stalemate in the Korean War. After that, a clear loss with Vietnam. In the time since, we'd lost more than two hundred Marines in Beirut. It wasn't clear to me, but now I suspect that, before Desert Storm, people didn't hold the military in high regard. I remember hearing stories of people who'd committed minor crimes being told, go to jail or join the military.

There were a handful of brothers in the fraternity who weren't in ROTC. They balanced out the rest of us.

That same year, I knew I was truly beginning to separate away from God. As I found myself slipping into the herd mindset of reckless drinking, I met with a Naval officer from the ROTC unit assigned to the university, and asked him to pray with me.

When we prayed, I felt nothing. I heard nothing. Within me, if I were expecting a signal from the other end of my connection with God, there was only silence. I took that as a sign; I was on my own.

I was in the ROTC program, but had selected the Navy over the Marines.

The truth was, I had grown resentful of moving all the time, and blamed my father and the Marines. I believed that my best friend from Okinawa should have been so throughout high school, that we might share the rites of passage afforded during those magical years. When we ended up moving to different states after our time in Japan, and I struggled to find a group of friends who readily shared my interests, I was of an age to undercut my father, and did so with striking regularity. It would take me a long time before I realized, my dad was doing the best he could.

I set about creating distance between us as a form of punishment, not appreciating that I was the one being punished, by my own hand. I had missed their support and love my senior year of high school, and blamed them, even though I was the one who had pleaded to stay in North Carolina. I pushed his buttons as only a second son could. Larry was so like him in confidence, composure, and purpose. Still, he loved me. He was a good man. He believed in the America he'd known as a little boy. He had lived in that America...that was how he knew it still existed.

After struggling my first two semesters with the engineering classes required for the Navy, I instinctively tucked my tail between my legs and applied for the Marines. My brain wasn't wired for engineering back then. I knew the Marines required mental toughness. I thought I was a shoe-in. During my sophomore year, my application was declined.

My grades weren't great. I was in better shape than I'd been in high school, but not up to Marine Corps standards. I'd spent so much time focusing on my freedom while in college, I lost sight of my reason for being there. I drank excessively, with no sense of self-discipline. The denial of my application devastated me. It was my first real setback.

The day I received the news, I sat in my fraternity room with this tough Irish guy named Joe, and held back bitter tears while Guns N' Roses', *Patience* played over the speakers in my room. I was dismayed, foolishly thinking I deserved to be a Marine for all the time spent moving because of my dad.

I became obsessed with getting accepted into the institution I'd essentially been born into, with the intent of following the footsteps of my dad and brother in serving my country.

I stopped partying. I barely socialized. My college roommate Mike used to joke that I was like a robot; I'd walk to class like the greatest speed-walker the planet had ever seen, no stopping to chat up friends. Get to class. Do the assignment. Eat. Study. Go workout. Sleep. Repeat.

If there wasn't a party at the fraternity on weekends, people still found an excuse to drink. Undeterred, I would go to the far side of campus and play basketball in the recreation hall for hours, before returning after the parties had died down.

That was my life for the better part of nine months.

It worked. My fitness improved. I made the Dean's List. More than that, studying became easy for me. Throughout high school and my first year and a half in college, it was a challenge for me to pay attention; I would lose myself in my imagination. I drew sketches of Frankenstein and Batman. I'd always like to draw. It was an outlet for me.

I majored in English. Some of it was literature, but I focused on writing. I was still enamored with the romantic ache of history.

I'd wanted to be a writer since I got into comic books. There were such amazing adventures, and the artwork had dramatically improved from what superheroes looked like in the late seventies and early eighties. I drew, but it was painstaking, and I had trouble creating pictures freely...I needed to be looking at something, and usually ended up copying a cool pose from a comic. Creating scenes with words was a fun challenge.

College was my first exposure to real writing. My English professor didn't want me writing fantasy. He wanted me writing about real people and bringing those people to life. I wrote about how being heartless made men do ugly things.

After I did that, I understood how to bring stories to life.

Back then, I just assumed joining the Marines meant I'd put my childish ambition aside. Real writers wrote all the time. I wrote for homework. Being an English major for my undergrad was something like a swan song for my writing career; at least, that's how it felt at the time.

Going to Officer's Candidate School was the first real hard thing I ever did. There was so much pressure. I *felt* my father's rank. When your dad is a Colonel and veteran of the Vietnam War, people know him and they know you. The Marines working OCS always liked to know if any of the candidates had military parents. We didn't get special treatment. If anything, I felt like I was expected to live up to my family's name.

It is true the military breaks down the individual, and few do it more passionately than Marines. To have grown men bark orders at you with such a fierce intensity, commands every ounce of your attention.

On one hand, we were instilled with incredible fortitude and discipline. Marines demand one more drop of sweat, one more ounce of energy, one more step. Training is a well-orchestrated dance with chaos, where two questions weave around each candidates' psyche: 1) how much life do you have in you and 2) how much are you willing to fight for it?

On the other, we were expected to have a savage instinct close at hand, if we ever found ourselves in combat. We trained this with boxing, and with giant Q-tipped sticks that mimicked weapons. Candidates would run from opposite ends of an arena and confront one another wearing helmets and padding. The first candidate to score a good headshot or a piercing stab with their Q-tip was declared the victor.

OCS was extremely competitive; every few weeks, we evaluated the other twelve members of our squad on their leadership. The name of this activity was called "peer evals" but we used another name… spear evals. If someone wasn't performing up to standard, a bad spear eval could end their time at OCS.

The pressure to perform was extreme, and every moment of the day was scheduled. We awoke at 4 a.m., and would march to the chow hall by 4:30. There, the forty-five candidates in my platoon would all be fed within ten to fifteen minutes and be back outside, ready to begin the training day. From there, we usually went to a large field for our morning exercise. The day would end back in our barracks around 7:30, when we would be afforded thirty minutes before lights out to look at mail, talk with other candidates, or prepare for the next day. Every second or third night, I would be on fire watch for an hour, walking up and down our squad bay to maintain "good order and discipline" while everyone else slept. That daily routine repeated itself every day for six weeks, except for a few weekends where we were given a brief respite from the training program, and allowed to venture off-base. That meant splitting the cost for a motel room with a buddy from the platoon. We would eat junk food and watch tv for hours before falling asleep. I graduated OCS, said goodbye to the one significant girlfriend I had throughout college, and dove into my senior year. The relationship had lasted all of nine months and being at OCS made me appreciate a simple truth; she wasn't the one.

My last year of college was fantastic. My grades were great, I didn't need a ton of credits to pass, and I was old enough to drink. That made for a fun, carefree year.

I was also naïve and wildly immature. While home for Christmas break, I met a woman who was amazing. We dated for four months, and I was convinced I'd found my soulmate. When the relationship fell apart after an otherwise forgettable spring break trip, I was heartbroken. Finally, with graduation only weeks away and, knowing I would be in the Marines and training for the next six months, I just wanted to have fun.

Graduation came and went in a whirlwind. After a quick trip down to North Carolina to see my parents, I reported to Quantico, Virginia, and The Basic School, my next step in leading Marines in the operating forces. It was May 1991.

The fact that the world had recently witnessed the lightning-swift victory of the United States and its allies in OPERATION DESERT STORM bolstered the image of the military in the eyes of many Americans, or so it seemed. America felt good about itself, and rightfully so. We had expelled Saddam Hussein from Kuwait, as had been the purpose for the war in the first place. We didn't occupy Iraq, we just told them to go home. A just cause for a just war.

There were around two hundred officers, all men, in my Basic School class. Many, like me, were ROTC graduates. We also had our share of officers from the military academies, and a few officers who had previously been enlisted in the Marines before going to college and earning their commissions.

TBS offered a different kind of intensity from OCS. With two hundred men, there was plenty of bravado, and yet we all respected that everyone had gone through the same, grueling gauntlet of OCS. For training, we learned basic infantry tactics, spent days at a time in the field, patrolling the hilly woods of Northern Virginia, and took plenty of helicopter rides. There was plenty of homework.

I dated. Never anything serious, though I was always hopeful.

Training was incredible. We patrolled in the rain, and attacked fake towns hidden in the middle of the woods. We fired all kinds of weapons, and learned the basics of hand-to-hand combat. We learned tactics, like how to set up defensive fields of fire, and how to lay an ambush.

Our last big event at TBS was a ten-day "war" in the woods just before Thanksgiving in 1991. The war was cold. We learned what life without fire was like, and how bad things could get when it rained and the only shelter you had was a poncho and poncho liner. Even when it was nasty, we found humor.

It might be a joke; someone would make light of what we were all going through. When it was cold, and the rain was turning to ice, someone would say, "at least it's not snowing." It was silly, but true. Snow *would* have been worse. On other occasions, the response might be, *suck it up and drive on.*

After graduating TBS, I spent the holidays with my family, and then another six months in Oklahoma, undergoing artillery training with the Army. It was fascinating to see the difference in culture between the Army and the Marines. The Army officers didn't attend The Basic School or anything like it. They didn't get six months of training to become an officer. They went from college right to artillery. The relationship between the Army's enlisted and its officers felt very different than the relationship we had with our enlisted Marines, even in training.

My dad came out to Oklahoma once on business. We shared one of our first drinks together. It was one of the few times he shared with me his experiences in Vietnam. From there, I was headed to Hollywood. I was going to be a California Marine.

Southern California was a paradise, and the training I was doing in the Marines was mind-blowing. I was in the artillery. The King of Battle, real God of Thunder stuff. Artillery was loud, the concussion of the shells sounded like thunder.

Growing up in the military, you don't really appreciate how different your life is from the civilian world. You take for granted going to the beach on board a military base and watching fighter jets zoom overhead. It's commonplace to see Navy ships off the coast, and Marines coming ashore in landing craft, or helicopters carrying cargo flying overhead. That difference crystallized for me when I became a Marine.

In the military, everything is simplified to the greatest extent possible. Running shoes are known as "go-fasters." The floor is a "deck" which makes it easier to speak the same language when dealing with the Navy.

Ideas are distilled down to their bare essence. *See the hill, take the hill. Don't fire unless fired upon.*

The language is simple because warfare requires all your energy and focus.

We would only march as fast as the slowest Marine. No one gets left behind.

This simplicity is essential to ensure everyone is invested in their unit and their mission. In the Marines, it was mission accomplishment *first*; troop welfare, always.

The military is a fascinating world. In one sense, you are trained with the ultimate purpose of crippling or killing your enemy. A well-trained military is a strong deterrent to potential adversaries. You immerse yourself in the art of war.

In another sense, you are asked to uphold virtues like honor, courage, and commitment. These ideas are, at best, loosely adopted by society at large, if at all. And yet in the military, they are regarded as sacrosanct. Moral fiber as the basis for how one lived their life.

Our unit was going to deploy on Navy ships for six months in the Pacific. A global police officer, sailing their beat. In training leading up to the deployment, we would fast-rope out of helicopters in the middle of the night, go on small-boat raids off the coast of California, and shoot artillery.

We fired tons of artillery. I loved it. I thought my entire career was going to be nothing but training and deployments.

Artillery changed battles. Napoleon. The Germans at Verdun in WWI. Desert Storm.

It felt romantic; that was my interpretation of artillery compared to the grunts on the frontline. But, I didn't write.

I was too busy in my off time trying to figure out California women, and I had met someone back in North Carolina while visiting my parents. She was sweet, and I appreciated that, unlike me, she'd lived in the same small town her entire life.

Being a Marine was fun. It's hard to explain what it means to spend time with people day in and day out who are all bound by a common cause. I never told another Marine that I loved them...I probably would have gotten punched if I had, but I didn't have to. I knew at any moment, any one of them would risk their life for mine. And I would do the same for them. It was the one thing I was sure of while I was in the Marines. It may go by a different name, but that is a rare and deep form of love.

We left San Diego in October 1992. There were three ships as part of the 15th Marine Expeditionary Unit.

Ship life was magical. The ocean was such a grand, deep blue. During the days, Marines would clean their weapons. I taught some basic call-for-fire classes to the infantry company to which I was assigned.

While the sailors worked non-stop with the ship underway, we found ourselves as little more than passengers. We read books. We talked about life back in San Diego. There was plenty of time for reflection. It was like being on the outside of your life, looking in. I thought of all the things about life back in San Diego I wanted to change when I returned.

At night, all the young officers would congregate in one of the bigger rooms and watch movies on VHS. We might play cards in the dining room. We had a lot of time on our hands.

I don't remember how many sunrises I saw, but the sunsets were spectacular. There were always clouds in the sky, and the sun would light them up in brilliant splashes of orange and red one day. The next, there would be deep hues of purple mixed with gray clouds that threatened rain. Storms aboard ship were intense. This massive boat, with all these vehicles and marines and sailors on board would sway from side to side. If we were eating, you and your plate would slide to one side, then rock back to the other.

We stopped on Okinawa for a few hours. Our ship needed repairs, and the necessary part had been flown into Japan. From there, we steamed to Singapore.

Singapore was muggy. I remember being on the deck of the ship, anchored in the middle of the harbor, waiting for the junk barge to come and take us to shore. The sailors and Marines on deck watched in amazement as a sheet of rain moved towards us. In another instant, it was on us. The temperature dropped ten degrees and the monsoon pounded us in a furious downpour.

In two minutes, it was gone. The humidity returned, the sun broke through the clouds, and the temperature went back to stifling.

The time spent in Singapore was fantastic. I didn't do much drinking, but lost myself in the Chinese/Japanese gardens. The beauty of the gardens with their Japanese lanterns, calming waterfalls, and breathtaking greenery refreshed my spirit. I walked in the gardens for hours. From there, I headed to the zoo. I remember being close enough to a black panther that I could have easily reached through the thin enclosure bars and touched its back. I resisted the impulse, but loved how close I was able to get to the animal.

From Singapore, we were scheduled to go to Kuwait for a live-fire exercise. Instead, we were diverted to Somalia.

I never imagined I would take part in something like OPERATION RESTORE HOPE. The joint operation involved dozens of countries from around the world, and was focused on relieving Somalia from a devastating famine.

I was full of anxiety, and a little fear, the night before we landed.

There's no sleeping when you think you're about to meet one thousand armed Somalis...that was the intelligence we received the day prior to our landing. I, along with my shipmates, lay in our beds aboard the ship for four hours, feigning sleep and trying to rationalize what was about to happen.

It was a thought I could not reconcile: someone I didn't know, and had never met, might kill me. A bullet fired has no prejudices; it goes where it's told. I could hear the other men in my room wrestling with their thoughts and fears, tossing and turning in their cots.

Finally, at midnight, it was time to get up. We got dressed, went into the belly of the Navy ship to retrieve weapons and ammo, and then made our way to whatever mode of transportation was going to take us to shore. I was going ashore in an amphibious tractor, not unlike the ones Marines had used during World War II during the Pacific campaign against the Japanese. It was 3:30 in the morning when we finally splashed off the back of the ship in our tractors.

My unit's mission was to set up a roadblock outside Mogadishu International Airport, and confiscate weapons from people trying to enter the airfield. The artillery wasn't going to come ashore for a few days. We might have studied setting up roadblocks at TBS. Now, I was about to do it in a real-world situation with Marines I barely knew. Our Rules of Engagement stated that we could not shoot at someone unless they pointed a weapon at us first. The idea that we might be facing a thousand weapons pointing at us as we came ashore with most of the Marines huddled in the belly of the tractors was unsettling. Amphibious landings are hard, especially under the cover of darkness.

A full moon was setting into the heart of Africa. The city was almost pitch-black; there was virtually no electricity. It is difficult to convey the emotions I felt. We were Marines, we readily adapted to the unknown. With the moon reflecting off the waves, it also felt beautiful to me. And why wouldn't it? I have always been, and will always be, a romantic.

There was palpable tension. The tractors had some armor, and an automatic grenade launcher for protection. I sat in the command turret, with the gunner next to me, and the driver a little in front and between us, peering out his small window as he navigated us through the choppy waters towards the shore. I was the only Marine in my tractor exposed to the elements; the driver and gunner were in their respective seats, and protected by the armor of the vehicle. Behind me, seventeen Marines were scrunched together in the tractor's belly, ready to spill out as soon as we got to our destination. When we got within two hundred yards of shore, flashes of light erupted from the beach.

In training, we'd gotten close enough to bullets being fired in our general direction to learn what they sounded like when they whizzed past you. Besides the four engines of the tractors churning to shore and the sounds of the waves, there were no bullet sounds. We kept moving towards the beach, despite the increasing number of flashes. Still, no bullets. As we got closer, we understood why.

The beach was littered with film and television crews. The only "armed" people we saw as we came ashore were armed with cameras and microphones. It felt completely surreal. We made our way through the scattered journalists and camera crews, and arrived at our destination.

Somalia gave me my first real exposure to Islam. The first time I heard the *adhan*, the call to prayer, I didn't know what to make of it. The sound system over which it played was horrible...a really scratchy-sounding, glorified megaphone. Hearing it go out over the capital of Mogadishu was both haunting and mysterious. I didn't know who Allah was, but I instantly appreciated how seriously Muslims took their prayers.

I felt fortunate. Helping a nation that was starving felt like a noble cause, like a good use of the military. My dad had been in Vietnam for thirteen months. My brother had spent nearly a year in Kuwait supporting Desert Storm. I was involved with Somalia. I had done something, even though much of the rest of my military career would be a struggle between the life I thought I was supposed to live and the one that was calling to me to leave war behind me.

Still, I held out such hope for love. Every day, I felt an adventure, and romance and love were going to be at the heart of it. The girl from North Carolina wrote me while I was deployed.

We might get mail every two or three weeks. There was no internet at the time. No one had mobile phones capable to talking to satellites in space. Getting mail while deployed was a beautiful feeling.

Besides friends and family, we would have elementary school kids from across the country write to us. That only served to reinforce the idea that what we were doing mattered.

I wrote the girl back. It felt like it had big romance potential. By the time we returned to California in April of 1993, she made plans to come visit me with my parents. In the long weekend they came out, I didn't feel the same. She was still amazing, but I didn't understand how this smalltown North Carolina woman would fit into my San Diego Marine Corps life.

Around that same time I met Jill.

Jill's father was a Marine. I and two of my friends were renting Jill's dad's house in Oceanside, California, just south of the Marine Corps Base Camp Pendleton.

Jill came by one evening to drop off the garage door remote. We clicked instantly.

Looking back now, we were proud reflections of our fathers, it seemed. That was all it took, and we were off on a whirlwind romance.

We eloped nine months later. We basically did it on a dare.

I'd been out in the deserts of 29 Palms training with the Marines for three weeks. What I mistook for love was a wicked insecurity that led me to believe, the surest way to strengthen a relationship was marriage.

The day we were married, I remember coming home with a queasy feeling in my stomach. Several months later, we had a full-blown wedding. On our wedding day, I knew I'd made a terrible mistake, it was a feeling I couldn't avoid. I dismissed the feelings as post-wedding jitters. But that was my life…a new location every few years. At every new location, I was looking for a new version of me.

Love has always been my Achilles' Heel. Always.

I got married to Jill because I didn't know any better, and I some-how thought marriage would heal the insecurity I felt inside me. It didn't. We got married in a church, surrounded by family and friends.

My best friends were getting engaged. In the early 90s, adulting seemed easy. The Marine Corps life is anything but ordinary. I might be out in the field training for days or weeks at a time. At any minute, a call could come in, and I could be on a ship or a plane in days, even hours. One Labor Day weekend, I received a phone call, telling me to be prepared to go to Kuwait that Wednesday. Life in the military was unpredictable, and I certainly appreciated that, while on active duty, my life was not my own. With that understanding, with a sense that life could be so tenuous, who didn't want someone to come home to?

I had little experience in relationships, and was enjoying the adven-ture of being a Marine who already had a combat deployment under his belt at the tender age of 24. I wore my naivety like a headlamp.

Jill was an amazing woman. She was refined, and was the first person to teach me not to put red wine in the refrigerator. She enjoyed classic movies and classic music. I liked comic books, action movies, and Pearl Jam.

She had a sense of style. I wore what I could afford and what the Marine Corps deemed was "appropriate civilian attire" which always meant a belt, shoes with socks, and a collared shirt. I suspect we be-lieved each of us would complete the other. Looking back with two decades of maturing, I appreciated just how incomplete I was.

When it came to marriage, I thought getting married before God meant you'd miraculously be endowed with everything you needed for a successful marriage. I remember my mom trying to talk me out of it when we got engaged. But what could she have done?

I was twenty-four, had led Marines in combat, and figured mar-riage was the fairytale waiting to happen. Lots of my fellow officers got married and built beautiful relationships. It was a script most found easy to follow. Everyone seemed to blend into the standard approach of an officer and his wife. They started families. Went to soccer games. It was all very traditional.

I was frustrated because I knew I wasn't in the relationship I was looking for. I tried to give it my best. Now that I was in it, how long would be that be tolerated?

It turns out, about four and a half years.

Part of the challenge I faced when it came to relationships was, I always measured a relationship's potential based on how much time I had left at a duty station. If I met someone after just moving somewhere, great. That might give us to chance to get a relationship on solid ground before I was going to move again. Meeting someone with six months left before I would relocate was a tough sell. This was before instant messaging and communication happened as easily as it does now. None of this was helped by my very real lack of identity.

It was challenging enough to report to a new duty station and learn a new job. Trying to make a long-distance relationship work on the off chance that the other person was going to give up their livelihood *and* follow me wherever the Marine Corps sent me? It was more than I could manage, and much more than I expected anyone would reasonably agree to.

That gave me a very small window of comfort in which to get serious about someone and, when married to the understanding that my life was not my own, drove me to lunge at love with all my heart.

Jill and I moved across country within a few months of getting married, from the sunny coast of Southern California to the humid heat of South Carolina. In my new job of supervising the training of recruits to become Marines, I would be working twelve-hour days, Monday through Friday, and six hours on Saturday. The training was intense. Everyone moved with urgency.

On weekends, I was exhausted. I had little desire to do anything except sleep and watch movies. I was a terrible friend, lover, and husband.

We separated just over two years after moving across country, and less than three years of being married. The stress of work and my increasing dissatisfaction with the status of the relationship had me looking elsewhere, a cardinal sin in the Marines. Even friendships within the military are limited; you don't become friends with people who aren't close to the same grade as you. Relationships between male and female Marines come under extreme scrutiny.

I got too close to someone.

I remember seeing the proposed separation agreement and how callous I came across in the summary of dissatisfaction presented. That wasn't who I was. That wasn't who I wanted to be.

It was enough to get us back together. Our separation lasted a little less than six weeks.

After two and a half years in South Carolina we moved to Virginia, where I spent six months training in Quantico before traveling back across the U.S. to report for duty back in California. When you don't know how to really communicate with your partner, are in a career where, at any moment, you could be sent to some hot spot in the world, and don't have a keen sense of yourself, what's the best thing to do? Bring a beautiful daughter into the world.

The Third Letter of the Pandemic

In 2016, I'd taken my last real stab at trying to write a horror story. The book was going to be called *Belief*.

The premise behind *Belief* was that God, whoever or whatever that was, had died or fallen asleep at the proverbial wheel. It was this idea that there would be no Second Coming.

My protagonist was going to be a Lance Henriksen-like preacher with a checkered past and a bagful of doubt.

There were some moody ideas I wanted to explore, like everyone in the town started waking up at the same time, very early in the morning, well before sunrise. I wanted to entertain the idea of premonitions. The preacher kept having the same dream every night. That dream was going to be the end of the book, when angels came crashing to earth. Giant creatures with train-horns for voices, they would immediately begin waging war on smoldering demons that arose out of dark fiery pits that had opened in the earth. Watching all this in horror, the preacher realized that humans were nothing more than collateral damage in this unholy war.

Fittingly, Jesus was nowhere to be found in my writing. Without Jesus, it wasn't going to be much of a story; it reflected where I was with my own faith. I couldn't fathom that Jesus was the only path to salvation. Even with the slew of Christian related movies that had come out in recent years, movies like *Noah*, *Son of God*, and *Exodus*, so little of my attention was focused on Jesus.

By the time I began working on *Belief*, I had made what felt like every bad choice a man could make. I had judged people while overlooking my own deficiencies, had treated others poorly and then become indignant when I received the same treatment. It was during this tumultuous time in my life that I slowly began to awaken to the reality that I was looking for the Love of God. That might best describe the feeling of pleasantness I had as the strange series of circumstances arranged themselves in my life when the pandemic began.

I didn't think of Jesus after experiencing my Judgment Day, and the voice that said my name during the next night's meditation didn't immediately register as his voice. The experience had stirred something within me, something I'd known had always been there. I was elated by what it meant. It was, looking back, my most distinct and appreciable experience up to that point of my life that God was real. I didn't appreciate just how real that would mean.

At that point, the pandemic still felt novel. It was mainly life as usual the rest of that week. I went to the park to workout. I worked from home. I hung out with Sara and Jim that weekend. Then, Saturday morning, April 4th, after getting back from the park, I decided to rewrite the conversation I'd written the week before.

When I initially finished the first draft the weekend before, I thought I was done. I thought, that was the story, and started thinking of publishing. Simple. Cerebral. A proverbial spiritual sledgehammer.

But as the week progressed, and most certainly after what I'd experienced that last Tuesday night in March, I knew the story was incomplete. I didn't know how. That had me eager to take another crack at it the first weekend in April.

I had good energy in the small guestroom I'd made my own since moving in with my mom. I sat on my bed, hunched over my crossed legs, with a notebook open in front of me. I kept my phone nearby. It was habit.

My writing was fantastic. I'd never felt such enthusiasm, such *connection*, with something I'd written. It felt like I was *finally* awakening the writer within. It was an incredible feeling, where hours passed like minutes. It was awakening to a new kind of love.

There was something else though.

I started to understand the power of spelling. The notion that words themselves were a form of life. It made sense. The living Word.

Words have the power to transfix, and to transform. Churchill's speech. JFK. Martin Luther King, Jr. What is life, if we don't communicate it with words? Life is a feeling. And what is storytelling, if not an attempt to put feelings into words?

What power did language have, before words were written down?

At some point, I took a break. The difference with this writing compared to how I'd written my first two books was here, working on *Being*, the writing *came* to me. I wasn't having to force words to fit. They just came naturally and effortlessly. The experience of writing brought such incredible pleasure. There was no thinking of what I needed to write down; there was just a pen in my hand, writing in flow.

In a previously letter, I mentioned that, as part of my effort to nurse my wounded ego, I'd started following women I considered beautiful on Instagram. It likely was not more than a dozen.

The first time I saw you, I debated following you. There was no question you were beautiful; there was something about you I couldn't place. I remember being partly distracted by the map of the world painted on the wall behind you.

Your physique was phenomenal. At the time of course, I had only the slightest notion that you were a body-builder. Your abs looked like something Michelangelo might have chiseled from marble. It was your eyes.

I had no idea what, but something in your eyes spoke to me. Your eyes gave such life to everything else about you. They were mesmerizing. They were why I followed you. They offered me the first glimpse of the light I'd been looking for my entire life.

Then, when I opened up Instagram on April 4, 2020, my world forever changed.

I have looked at that image countless times over the past few years. The connection to the movie *Gladiator* came so naturally.

You looked like Maximus' wife, standing in a field of golden wheat, wearing that pure black dress. Your skin was tan. You were looking to the left in the picture, a hand to your head, as if shielding your eyes from the sun, and looking for someone in the distance. The profile of your face…I knew I'd seen it before. Not just your profile…I knew I'd seen this image somewhere before.

It was not a thought I could articulate, but was instead a series of such deep and wondrous emotions. I had, quite literally, never seen anything so beautiful as that picture. I'm quite certain I gasped audibly. And it wasn't only you; it was the wheat, and just how golden it was. It was the hints of green off in the distant hills. It was the deep grey in the sky, flattering you with perfect lighting. And then there was your smile.

You smiled like the bearer of some great knowledge. Of wisdom. How could someone look so heavenly with such ease?

A wisp of hair caressed your cheek. Other strands were flirting with the evidence of a breeze. For a caption, you wrote, *Freedom is Priceless*.

I was beside myself. In that moment, you became part of *Being*.

This took the story in a completely different direction. The universal voices of unconditional and conditional love now had form. The story began to take shape.

Immediately, I resumed writing, my mind racing with the possibility. What would Maximus and his wife have said to each other the last time they were together? Here, my love, it is important to set things, again, in context.

A global pandemic has blossomed over the world. I am a few months removed from my last relationship, my most authentic attempt at defining the love inside me. I have taken stock of much of the mistakes of my past and concluded that I am responsible for how my life has turned out. No one else. I have traveled across the country and received strange counsel from a wise man I have never previously met in this life. I experienced my Judgment Day.

As monumental as these events seemed, as claustrophobic as the pandemic became, I felt such an overwhelming sense of joy. It was as though the universe were unfolding some grand design, and I were one of its chief constituents.

The thought of you as Maximus' wife was little more than a whisper across my consciousness; making the connection was effortless in its seduction. Little did I know the cost I would incur in seeking to imagine the pain of a love lost nearly two thousand years ago.

I imagined that this picture, with all its brilliance, would be the image Maximus had done his best to memorize of the first time he ever saw his wife.

It would take me another rewrite before I started working the Maximus angle into the story. The early drafts were too abstract in their concepts. Every weekend in April was spent working on the next draft. What had changed by the second draft was something that took my breath away.

A third voice had entered the conversation; it was a combination of the voices of unconditional and conditional love. Initially it had only one line: *I remember you.*

That was the draft I was working on the day I saw your picture. Writing the story became so beautiful. It felt rapturous. I listened to music as I wrote.

Music has always played an important role in my life. While the strains and aggression of heavy metal had dominated much of my early adulthood and time in the military, becoming a yoga instructor had opened me to music that was enchanting, spacious, and serene. It was music I'd discovered in the military, but listened to as the exception, rather than the rule.

In recent years, I'd been discovering the magic in asking myself powerful questions and increasingly had taken to journaling as a way of capturing thoughts and putting these questions down on paper. For much of my life, I felt I was asking myself the questions of a victim: *why does this always happen to me, what am I doing wrong now?* Invariably, I came up with answers. We always do. But as I began digging into the limiting beliefs that had hamstrung my life and left me in repeating patterns of self-sabotage, things started shifting.

Dealing with the parts of my life I wasn't proud of was releasing me from them. I felt liberated, real liberation. This, in turn, enabled me to start asking questions that would allow me to shape my life, rather than constantly shoring up my shortcomings. When I combined my love of music with the increasing wisdom I found in asking myself powerful questions, the question I came up with as I wrote, was, what song made me think of you? Sarah McLachlan's *Silence*, the Michael Woods' Remix immediately came to mind. Again, effortless.

It was a song I played regularly during my yoga classes. It is a song of yearning, of desire to be witnessed. To be released.

I played the song, and was overcome by the resonance I felt. This song, for me, was the separation between heaven and earth. Hauntingly beautiful, and filled with aching faith.

The world at large was still coming to terms with the pandemic. The global shift of people working from home and most commercial businesses closing gave life a kind of crackle and electricity. It wasn't all sunny and carefree though.

I was wrestling with what the story said about me. That you were now part of the story felt so clearly tied to my Judgment Day, but I could not put my finger on exactly why or how. One minute, I would seemingly understand that I was God the Father. In those moments, I wrote like an old man with a long gray beard and balding head. It felt right, but somehow off. But, the underlying idea came so easily. I'd never heard of anyone else talking about their Judgment Day, not outside of an Arnold Schwarzenegger film…mine did not feel all that terrible. These thoughts were flooding my mind, and I wrote them down as best I could, trying to make sense of them.

The next moment, I was the archangel David. I hadn't known David had been an archangel, but that was what came out on paper as I wrote. But this David was angry. Mankind had tormented the earth. That feeling didn't last long. I was in the garage working out and listening to the spectacularly heavy French metal band Gojira. Phenomenal. Then, Van Halen would come on with Sammy Haggar, and he'd be singing about love. That would take me in another direction. The feeling was so wonderful…I was enjoying the ride.

When I thought back to what I imagined the formation of the universe would have been like, assuming universal intelligence, there must be an initiating mind. Even though I could fathom this concept, it was conceived in such a loose framework; I didn't fully understand the whole picture. I certainly had no sense of the approaching tempest.

I was beginning a journey the likes of which would test the limits of my imagination, belief, and understanding. For decades, I had reconciled myself to a very physical and material existence, without truly understanding what a powerful spirit might be inside me. What a powerful spirit might be inside all of us.

Coming to terms with that spirit has taken the better part of the two years since first I saw you.

In my notes, early in the writing process, I'd written one thing that felt like it could have been something Jesus had said. Not that I was quoting something from the Bible, but that I had written something that came *from* Jesus.

I wasn't certain how to feel about it and was nowhere near close to understanding what my relationship to him was at the time. I felt like I might be violating some sacred law by channeling this voice or tuning into this frequency. That seems ironic to me now. Though I'd been doing the work, and taking responsibility for my life, I still felt such shame at my missteps over the course of my life, and didn't feel worthy of such a connection. Hadn't I trampled love underfoot at every turn? I masked those thoughts as best I could, and marveled at everything I saw in you.

On April 4th I saw the face of God. It wasn't just you. It was the whole picture. In that single picture lay the seed of this story. In that picture, Christ was conceived. Seeing you, I saw all the beauty I imagined could be found in everlasting life, in eternal love. From that date, I would spend more than two years understanding exactly what it meant to believe in our Son.

My writing was more beautiful than anything I'd ever written, by a good measure. I was exploring concepts and ideas that opened my mind to the idea of quantum existence.

Every week, I was learning more and more about the story's layout. It was like I was teaching myself something I'd long since forgotten. At some point, the voice of an angel told me as much.

We are transmitters and receivers of information. What we think about, we transmit into the universe, all the time. The universe responds. Belief in a higher power means belief in being guided. That I had been guided to you stunned me. How could I express what was happening?

Working out with my friends at the park, we were delighted in our resiliency. We had tried a few workouts by way of Zoom, and they had been difficult. It felt impersonal, and we missed the human interaction with one another. I had shared some concepts of the book with my close friends, but had been reserved in openly telling people about experiencing my Judgment Day. How exactly to bring that up in conversation was lost on me. Sharing that more broadly would come later, much later.

One day I drove to Hector's office and brought the second or third version of *Being* with me. I wanted him to read it to get his perspective.

He was by himself when I arrived, and thoughtfully sat down to read the story.

When he finished, the stood up, his eyes blinking.

"That was deep,"He said.

I agreed. After every draft, I thought I had a finished product.

I told him I had been practicing reading it aloud and wanted to read it in front of a group of our friends.

We agreed it made sense to do it one upcoming Saturday night.

In the meantime, in early May, I started working from Sara and

Jim's home. We were spending more and more time together, and I was warming up to the idea of moving in with them.

As surreal as the pandemic was, our weekends were becoming routine. Dinner out on the patio, and a little time relaxing in their back yard, before heading indoors to watch something on TV. Two consecutive weekends, it felt the same; the second weekend, I had this bizarre sense of déjà vu, as if something the previous weekend hadn't been quite right, and this weekend we were fixing it. I tied it to the Avengers movies. I'm sure that sounds strange, but the quantum world made *so* much sense to me. It was as though we had to relive a moment.

There was a small copse of trees just off their property, just thick enough to make the backyard feel secluded.

Some nights, we would hear owls. There would be a hush of a breeze, the evening was pleasant and inviting; those nights felt magical. The stillness in the air. The radiance and clarity of the moon. The pandemic had made me appreciate how much I enjoyed being outdoors. How I enjoyed my mind being still.

The owls might hoot as you've heard them on tv, but on at least one night, they made the strangest, extended sounds. There were shrill cries, with irregular breaks, as if they were communicating with one another in articulate, stuttered notes. You could hear their massive wings when they took flight. The stillness those nights was enchanting.

On two different nights, I stood against the railing on the upper deck, soaking in the evening and how beautiful it was. My spirit was awakening. The noise in my mind had started shifting. Whereas in the past, I often felt like my mind was tuned to a radio station, and I'd regularly have music playing in it as I went about my day, the music was no longer there. With the meditations and opening of my third eye, I started receiving powerful messages from the universe.

On one night, it was as if the woods came alive. I was outside standing on the second-floor patio, overlooking the backyard and the trees. Apart from the sounds of crickets and other night insects, there was no noise; no cars passing by, or people sitting on their decks, taking in the evening. My consciousness was hit with a resounding chorus, as choirs of angels began chanting, *"King! King! King!"* It was undulating waves on the shores of my mind.

Another night, it was a single voice, *"The deepest whispers come from the biggest spaces."* An echo in eternity. An echo coming home.

Where were these thoughts coming from?

My awareness had begun dramatically increasing. In the first six weeks since my Judgment Day, I had many more good days than I did bad. I was confident to a fault. A better word might be ignorant.

I felt a kind of sure-footedness when it came to the story. For some reason, this led me to realizing new levels of discernment and understanding when it came to movie-watching.

Instead of passively sitting and being entertained, I started seeking to understand the message a movie was meant to convey. As a writer, I'd entered a few screenplay writing contests. These contests were challenging. Contestants were given a genre, a main character, a setting, and some unique angle they had to fit into the story. Screenplay writing has a very specific format. Every page of dialogue and scene-setting amounts to a minute of screentime. The first round of a contest would be seven days and twelve pages. The second round would be three days and seven pages. The final round: one day, three pages. Every word mattered.

I began watching movies, and asking questions about why characters were doing what they were doing. *The Big Lebowski. Valhalla Rising.*

Said differently, there is the face value of the story, the entertainment value. That is what many people focus on.

But there is a message in each movie as well. *The Big Lebowski* is classic Law of Attraction material. There are characters well-defined in the movie: Anger. Doubt. Played out by brilliant actors.

Valhalla Rising looks like a movie about an angry, mute one-eyed warrior escorted by a good-natured boy. The warrior wreaks havoc, destroying everyone who gets in his way. Finally, other warriors agree to accompany the warrior and boy on their journey. There are ships in fog, and uncertainty. At the movie's end, they come ashore, and the warrior is killed by what look like Native American warriors in pale war paint.

The movie is an interpretation of Christianity's journey to the New World. That warrior represents Jesus' Father. The boy, Jesus. The accompanying warriors, all those people who championed Christianity's cause throughout history.

And then there was the film, *AntiChrist*.

When the Lars Von Triers film came out more than a decade ago, I was appalled that someone would make such a film. I remember seeing the trailer pop up on Apple trailers. At the same time, I was curious. It was the warrior in me, and the desire to know my enemy.

The first time I watched the film, shortly after it came out, I was disgusted. I will spare you the details. But, with my newfound appreciation that film was a form of expression, I recognized a cerebral film such as this was produced for a reason.

When I watched it during the pandemic, I understood it. It tells not just of the fall of Man, but the arrangement of penalties incurred to sustain life. It tells of the spoil of Eden, and the sacrifice of the first feminine divinity so that all of life could thrive. The earth is intelligent; it is a molecule of life surrounded by a vast ocean of deep space, and we are microbes scratching along on its surface.

I was astounded that a movie I found reprehensible the first time watching it now made sense to me. I was also troubled…what did it say about me that I understood it?

It was this movie that first made me think about the "curious co-incidences" in Hollywood. Willem Dafoe played the lead in the film. Back in the late eighties, he'd played Jesus in another controversial film, *The Last Temptation of Christ*. Russel Crowe, who played Maximus in *Gladiator*, also played Superman's father, Jor-El in the latest *Man of Steel* movie. Curious.

Every story, whether fiction or otherwise, has a ring of truth to it. As I watched movies with a new appreciation for what the filmmaker and actors were trying to express, I began to appreciate; fiction is nothing more than a form of storytelling that we prefer imagining to be real, rather than experience in real life. But a good fiction story that rings true does so because the message it imparts *is* true. Truth is eternal. Truth is everlasting. I was digging into my truth with *Being*, even as I began questioning the staying power of that as its title.

Finally, on a Saturday night in May, I gathered with friends at Hector's house to read them an early version of *Being*.

This was before I was open to sharing the Maximus angle to the story. That part was difficult to write, and required tremendous amounts of imagination, something I was still learning to unleash.

Each draft I had written had been so thrilling to me, and for two or three days after writing each, I was of a mind that I had the finished product in my hands. By midweek, I would start to understand there were holes in the story that needed to be filled. The ending of the story was too open-ended. The next weekend, the story advanced, but the ending was ambiguous. By the third draft, I knew I was tapping into something, and felt confident enough to share it with my friends.

We sat out in Hector's back porch. His yard nestles up to one of the nearby country club's golf courses, and it was a cloudless night. Venus shone as brightly as the bright star you might see on Christmas cards during the holidays. I'd never seen a planet give off so much light as Venus did that night. All of us went down from his porch into the backyard to get a better view of the planet.

As I read the story, my friends sat quietly. This version ended with me saying, "I am the God of David" much to the amazement and bewilderment of my friends. Shep and his wife were there, and he quickly threw me a lifeline.

"What about us David, we're all gods too, right?"

"Uh, yeah." I'm not sure if I'd forgotten I'd written that, or was just so enthralled with the story and in the flow of things that I didn't care. I hadn't been prepared to share what I had, and didn't know how to respond.

We stayed on the porch for another half hour before everyone decided it was time to go home. It was nearly midnight. I hugged everyone, including Shep, and went home to sleep.

I next saw him Monday evening at the park for our workout. After the workout, when we had finished loading up Sean's SUV with all the equipment, Shep, Hector, and I reflected on the events of Saturday night.

"You freaked me out a little bit," Shep said straight-faced. "You left marks on me where you hugged me."

I was immediately puzzled by his comments. Marks? I hadn't hugged him hard. In fact, I'd wrapped one arm around him and buffered the space between us by putting my free hand on his midsection.

To emphasize his point, he lifted his shirt.

Where my free hand had gone, I could clearly see soft, red marks where my fingers had come in contact with him. Almost two days had passed, and he still had marks.

A shiver of electricity raced up my spine.

As the month of May progressed, I would start to feel the spiritual tremors of just how far away I was from our Son. If I were a top, spinning elegantly across a smooth surface, this was to be the beginning of my wobble. The first event would take place watching movies with Sara and Jim.

We'd watched a handful of Netflix shows, and they'd graciously let me commandeer control of some movie nights. They hadn't seen all the Marvel movies, so we spent a fair amount of time getting them caught up in the Marvel Cinematic Universe. On this night, we were watching *Thor: Ragnarok*.

As my mind started to open to the understanding of just how big the world was, it occurred to me that the Avengers movies could conceivably be possible. I know it sounds silly at first blush, but those movies have done incredible work with the quantum realm. It's very meta; the Avengers movies show us these heroes traveling through the Quantum Realm to retrieve the Infinity Stones and defeat Thanos.

The films are shown on big screens or streamed on mobile devices. In other words, they're being delivered wirelessly to some devices via the quantum field, signals in space. And, the universe they were created was clearly connected to ours.

People love being entertained by those movies…what I have come to appreciate in composing these letters is, it takes much more than just imagination to imagine that you're Iron Man, or Hulk, or Thor. It takes an impressive amount of intelligence, particular to say things "in character" with such conviction. We often speak of the power of affirmations and incantations, and how emotion, the feeling of something, is essential to its manifestation. That's why actors get paid so well; they embody states of being that few people are willing imagine, let alone feel.

When I think back to how far movies have come since Christopher Reeve first made us believe a man could fly in the original Superman, I can't help but appreciate how realistic superheroes have become. Growing up watching silly television shows or reading comic books with flat pictures drawn on thin paper, it was easy to understand the reasons why kids outgrew those things. In the eighties, comics did feel a little bit silly.

But then they got serious. The art got better. Storytelling became more dramatic, more mature.

When the first Iron Man movie came out, people were blown away. Warner Brothers had done some good things with Batman and Superman, but Marvel made superheroes relatable.

Thor wasn't my favorite character. To me, Captain America and his wonderful story arc through all the Marvel movies resonated. It was *the* love story in the films, and seeing Steve Rogers dance with Agent Carter at the end of *Avengers: Endgame* was my kind of love story.

Sara liked Thor. His arms. Chris Hemsworth was (and still is) a good-looking man. She was excited to watch *Ragnarok*, and I was looking forward to it too. I had agreed to move in with them and would make the transition in June. Sara and Jim were my pandemic family.

We were watching the movie, everyone was feeling great; I was high and perhaps a little drunk; they had both enjoyed some cocktails. There is a scene in the movie where Hulk has beaten Thor in gladiatorial combat and Thor is coming to Hulk's chambers to come up with an escape plan.

With no warning, while watching that scene, I was pulled from my recliner and thrown onto my knees in the living room, right in front of the television. From my knees, I gripped at my head, which felt like a fire had erupted inside it. I let out a gasp, but both Sara and Jim remained focus on the movie. I assumed Jim was likely asleep, and Sara was too absorbed in the movie.

I managed to get back into my recliner. When I looked at the movie again, I *was* Thor.

By that, I mean I was *in character* with Chris Hemsworth's portrayal of Thor. I found myself wondering, with some measure of panic, why he/I were wasting time on this planet, fighting it out with Hulk when Asgard was falling to his/my sister, Hela. Ragnarok was happening.

In Marvel's rendition, the Valkyrie fall in the defense of Asgard.

As Thor, I felt the anguish of being so distracted by my own greatness that I repeatedly found myself in these awful predicaments. Even though I had watched the movie on multiple occasions since seeing it in the theaters when it first came out, I now worried over its outcome. Would the people of Asgard be saved? I was slightly terrified. How had this happened?

With heightened alertness and awareness, and a wealth of unease, I watched the rest of the movie. Finally, the movie ended as it always had. Asgard falls, but the remaining Asgardians escape aboard a ship. Thor learns to appreciate that Asgard is not a place, it is a people.

It was late. I went down to the guest room in the basement and promptly fell asleep.

The next day, I went to the park to work out with friends, went home to shower, and then agreed to meet Sara for a walk in the early afternoon.

The idea that I was Thor was not something I had sought out, not directly. I mean, who thinks about who they're going to be in heaven? It never really dawned on me that, becoming someone in heaven would mean shedding the parts of me that didn't serve others. Is that what makes heaven so beautiful, serving others?

If anything, in spending time with Hector and Shep in the weeks leading up to becoming a part of Ragnarok, I reasoned I was Tony Stark. We had had several discussions about multiple, inner-connected universes, and how the Avengers could conceivably be real, thanks to the power of the quantum world.

I felt Tony Stark smart, and my understanding of quantum physics felt finely tuned. There was a guy named Tex who was a financial trader. I'd only hung out with him a few times, but he seemed a little spacy. I thought he would make a good Thor. Hector was the Hulk. He was really mild-mannered but seemed to have a current of something lurking within him. Whenever we got together with friends around a firepit, he became obsessed with the fire. Shep? Shep I thought would make a good Dr. Strange. Pharmaceuticals, sorcery. It made sense.

We had also had some discussions about the singularity, an idea put forward by a well-known futurist, Ray Kurzweil. The idea behind the singularity was, at some point we would transcend our human biology. When his book first came out in 2005, the book's premise made me think that we would merge with artificial intelligence in some way. Fifteen years later, I had a different perspective. Though it was buried underneath years spent away from my faith, and hardly consciously accessible, I was thinking, what if the singularity is human awareness to the existence of God?

I began to imagine the singularity would be the realization of global human divinity.

It was only May. I wasn't fully aware of just how far down the rabbit hole I'd gone. But the feeling of being Thor brought with it a surge of joy. Stacking the events of the past seven months on top of one another, it made complete sense. Acceptance to the idea came without question, and would be validated by the universe in the most startling of ways that day.

The day was quite pleasant; it was a beautiful North Carolina Saturday in mid-Spring. The streets had gotten particularly quiet during the pandemic, as few people drove and equally few took advantage of the nice weather and got outside. The pandemic had so many people in our area staying in, as if you increased your chances of getting the virus by venturing out.

As we walked, Sara and I talked about me being Thor the way you might talk about what you were planning on having for dinner. Casual, matter of fact. I had no idea what I was getting myself into.

As we walked through the neighborhood, I relayed my experience of watching the movie from the previous night. Sara listened intently. She didn't think I was crazy, didn't laugh hysterically. We were three months into the global shutdown. She just listened.

We took a detour from our normal path around her neighborhood, and headed up a lengthy cul-de-sac that circled around behind her street. As we got to the heart of the cul-de-sac and began to turn around, there it was.

Someone's car had the vanity plate, *VALKYRE*.

We both agreed it was a funny coincidence at the time.

As much as the infinite possibilities of the quantum realm made sense to me, it all felt fantastic. Me? The God of Thunder. Pandemic. Cryptic warning from wildly successful author and speaker I'd never met before. Judgment Day. What about that was difficult to believe?

Me. A fifty-one-year-old man. Agreeing to live with friends twenty years younger than me during a global crisis. My life up to that point had felt like I'd been sabotaging love for decades, and my circumstances reflected that.

Still, there was a certainty about what I'd experienced that made it so easy to accept. I was light-years away from connecting my being Thor to anything dealing with Christianity, Maximus, or you. That would take time. Time, patience, faith, and courage.

That would take love.

This was the beginning of my distressing vibration between two realities. On one side, this cosmic, sacred knowledge was being dropped at my feet or, at the doorstep of my mind. On the other, I was dealing very starkly with just how flawed a human I'd become. Judgmental. Unforgiving. Arrogant. My lack of faith.

As jolting as associating with Thor was, the second event in May would jar me in a radically different way.

I couldn't shape the story to take the direction I wanted it to take. On social media, like some foolish peacock, I was tagging you in posts, flaunting book titles, hoping to catch your attention. Every version of the book was dedicated to you. I even went so far as to do a live reading of the story's third draft on Instagram, without the God of David reference. *Being* no longer felt like a suitable title. I was thinking about a marriage between Heaven and Earth.

The days seemed to go by so slowly as the pandemic began; I'm sure that had to do with just how surreal it was for the world to shut down, and for many of us to begin learning new routines and habits. I felt such adventure and euphoria, blessed with a modicum of understanding that our story *was* real. There *was* a connection between us that spanned lifetimes.

The knowledge I saw in your beauty suggested as much to me. That had to be the confidence reflected in your eyes. Your eyes.

As easily as the story had flowed to me in the weeks of April and into early May, writing now became laborious. I struggled with the means of writing a love story that was going to bring us together. With all this supposed knowledge and power, all this wisdom suddenly crashing into my reality, why was I struggling with some unconquerable limitation?

I had designs on moving to France. I was ignorant to the one reality I had yet to face.

I didn't fully believe Jesus had died for my sins, and still viewed him as being on the periphery of our story. The weight of my shame felt insufferable, and I could not reconcile why I needed Jesus to tell this story. I had hurt so many people in my journey for love. Family. Friends. Those closest to me. All my life, I'd been going against the grain. Even with all I experienced in the first few months of the pandemic, I still didn't appreciate my quest might serve a purpose.

As painful as it is, I was bringing myself into focus in the eyes of God.

I moved in with Sara and Jim in June. The same day I arrived at their residence they brought their eight-week-old golden doodle home from the breeder. They named him Atlas. Atlas and I shared the same birthday, April 11.

Living together was fun. It felt a little hippy-ish, but I didn't really care. It also felt a little like reality TV, as we all became acquainted with living together.

I had so much happiness, from Judgment Day, as strange as that sounds, to the story, to processing every new post from you on Instagram with unabashed wonder and amazement. I was so happy, and was convinced that salvation was going to be right around every corner.

Every moment, every day, it felt like great things were going to happen. I delighted in how connected I felt to the universe, without fully understanding just how big a story this was going to become.

Your posts were so incredible. Your celebration of life, of nature. Of friendship and family. I wrestled with the right words to say to you.

I would find those words as I started my honest search to find Jesus in me.

THE SPANIARD IV

My time in Africa exposed to me to the more primal side of life. I knew, I was now on the other side of the empire. On the other side of the light.

The land here felt untamed, and ancient. People were happy, even with the scarcity in the region, and the land baked dry by an infernal sun. More ancient than Greece, these people were so colorful and different. Arabians. Egyptians. Mesopotamians. Judaeans.

The story of Jesus was hard for some to make sense of; it spread in whispered chambers and dimly lit rooms. The air sizzled with its energy, an invisible current that bewildered many who heard its message, some dismissed it as sorcery or speculation. Others, heard the story and became quiet. How could the human mind cope with something so supremely wondrous?

And what kind of Father would do that to his only begotten Son?

Slave life wasn't all bad. There was less marching, which I didn't miss. We were given wine sometimes, particularly on those rare occasions where Proximo didn't lose any fighters during the games. Like soldiers, gladiators know their glory lay at the end of a sword. We formed a bond like soldiers do. We formed a bond like brothers.

In my time with him, Proximo never kept more than a dozen slaves. Juba had been a hunter in his free life before being captured in the wilds of Africa. Hagen was from Gaul, but claimed a Germanic upbringing; he trained the new slaves as they were purchased.

It was the heart of summer when we arrived in Algeria. My debut as a gladiator in Morocco had been swift and to the point. Shunning the crowd's relish for this most insidious form of amusement awakened something in them. They were accustomed to their champions basking in their adoration. I quickly earned a reputation as someone to watch. Little did I know, I was winning the crowds over.

It was lunchtime when the new slave was brought in.

I was regaling Juba and Hagen with tales of Roman history, unaware that my visions would soon be realized, as Commodus celebrated as his own the greatness created by his father.

Before I go further my love, let me speak for a moment on Hagen.

He had been captured on the Roman side of the Rhine some months before me. He was the first Germanic tribesman I ever befriended.

A bear of a man, with a hearty laugh and tremendous appetite, he told me what freedom felt like to him, and what life without a central government was like. In their tribes, they stayed small enough so everyone could be involved in the discussions, as if every tribe was its own family.

He said his countrymen marveled at our machinery while observing that the uniformity of our formations and our clothing suggested conformance, and a loss of individual liberty. He was a good fighter, and became a good friend.

The first time I killed a man in the pits, the strangest stirring blossomed within my chest. It reignited that which I thought had been lost, snuffed out by the events that had brought me to such desolation. It gave me a pinprick of hope in the unrelenting expanse of darkness.

It was the idea that killing in the arena would bring me closer to you.

I can size a man up quickly. How he carries himself. If his eyes are looking for approval by seeking eye contact.

The new slave moved with purpose.

I dismissed him as a threat; I had a sense for danger. I had as long as I can remember. He avoided eye contact, yet it was clear from the weight behind his bulging eyes, here was a man who labored under the considerable strain of powerful knowledge.

That is, perhaps, the best way to describe it. When he was brought into our quarters, I could feel his energy. My companions were lost in my storytelling; I'd told these stories hundreds of times around campfires on campaign. Roman soldiers were an uneducated lot. They loved hearing about the legacies of their ancestors, and the formation of Rome.

How Romulus and Remus, brothers raised by a she-wolf, had elected to erect a city in the spot where the wolf had found them, and how Romulus killed Remus, naming the city after himself in the process. Brother killing brother, just as Cain had slain Abel.

Whatever words were coming from my lips were lost on me in the instance of the slave's entrance, so drawn was I to this man's energy.

What does it mean, Spaniard? Juba asked, bringing me back, *'The Ram has touched the wall?'*

I recovered quickly. *Murum aries attigit. It means, surrender would only be accepted prior to the battering ram touching the wall.*

And this man, Julius Caesar. He was a great leader for your people?

I nodded, and sipped a spoonful of stew.

Juba smiled. *I would like him, I think.*

Juba was a proud man, and must have been a formidable hunter among his people. I'd never met another man like him, not with all I'd thought I'd seen of the world. Apart from the legions, I wasn't much for socializing. I enjoyed my farm: the crops, the animals. The lingering smell of herbs you collected, offering the slightest hint as to where you were in the house. I enjoyed our family.

The new slave was small in stature, but not lean. Though his eyes were wide as he embraced the reality of his new life, he was meticulous in almost every detail. He dipped his ration of bread in his stew, shook it three times to allow excess stew to drop back into his bowl, and ate.

He had pitch-black hair that bounced in curls as he ate. He chewed his food diligently. Dare I say, he chewed each bite the same number of times…seven…before swallowing. Besides his bulging eyes, he had a sharp nose, like that of an eagle, and wild, unkempt facial hair.

While I had a keen sense of Roman history and the continuous expansion and contraction of the empire, I explored the world with a military commander's eye, forming my worldview and assigning my focus by the level of threat. For much of my career, that had me focusing on Gaul and Germania. When Marcus traveled to Greece and other edges of the empire, I remained focused on the empire's northern frontiers.

Skirmishes on the edge of the empire were common in every direction, but Egypt hadn't festered since the days of Mark Antony and Cleopatra, more than two centuries earlier. Egypt was a crucial lifeline for food into the empire, and in the weeks spent in these austere outposts with their restless sandstorms and heavy heat, I soon questioned the reasons for holding such land far away from the Nile.

True, there were an array of spices in the region. Their woodwork craftsmanship was exceptional. The roman garrisons in these provinces were small, as if an economy of agreements had been reached. Roman presence provided a modicum of security and the regional prefect was either a proper Roman whose worth was measured further away from Rome proper, or a local leader who ably balanced their role as voice of the people and friend to the empire.

It was the slave trade. It was particularly active in this part of the world. Being one now, I appreciated just how many slaves there were. It made sense. I saw Rome in a different light. Understood the corruption.

Proximo barked; it was time to return to training.

★★★

Peter was the new slave's name. He lacked skill with the sword, which suited a man of his appearance, yet was an attentive and quick study. What I found striking about him…he didn't make eye contact.

It wasn't simply that he was overcome with despair over his enslavement; he wrestled with something inside him. In breaks between sparring, his eyes would dart to and fro, as if seeking answers for something that proved elusive.

"Why do you try my patience, Spaniard?" Proximo looked quaint with his umbraculum resting on his shoulder, shielding him from the merciless African sun.

"Most proper women wouldn't tolerate this heat," I chipped, "I admire your courage, madam."

He gruffed, but managed a jackal's grin at the certainty of profit and fame he saw in me. "You have the vaguest understanding of slavery, Spaniard."

I didn't need work with the sword. It was but one of the many things about me that got under his skin. He was chasing his fortune. I was resolved to the discovery of faith.

Proximo's eyes bugged in perturbance. He was like a hyaena, and he knew it. For that, I respected him.

The sun finally descended beyond the rooftops, taking with it the bite of the searing heat. Somewhere, someone was burning incense. The air also carried the hint of lavender.

It makes me think of home. Like Rome proper, it feels of an idea that is increasingly difficult to grasp. In my sorrows, I know I am pushing myself further away from you. I told my men one scores of times to imagine where they wished to be, and it would be so. Where is my strength for such wonderings?

When I return to the memory of my time as a slave, it is dark. The hot breath of Africa has exhaled for another evening, and the breeze carries a current of exotic and mystical scents that bring such a tender dance between hope and exasperation. Another night of wanting something that feels so impossibly far away. With what little candlelight we had, I prayed to you and Samuel. I prayed that, wherever you were, you were safe. I took my space from the others, most of whom turned to slumber with the evening's descent. It was then I heard Peter praying.

Our Father, who art in heaven...

The words stirred a curious flutter in my chest. I stopped and listened as he completed his prayer. When he had finished, I rose from my sleeping space and approached him.

I have never heard anyone pray like that.

In the growing dark, the whites of his eyes stood out, lending something between fear and madness to his expression. He fixed his eyes on mind, and I felt fire pour into my gut, so enflamed was the man's stare. A wild man's eyes. In that very moment I knew why he avoided contact. His eyes would set men's souls on fire.

"You are the Spaniard," he said with a voice that was deeper than his frame seemed capable of supporting. "They talk of you. People want to see you fight. They say you are possessed."

I was unfazed. "Where did you learn to pray like that?"

His eyes weighed the question with a gravity I felt incapable of measuring. Few men had the strength to lock their eyes to mine. He broke eye contact, turning his gaze to the earth, chewing his thoughts, perhaps gauging how best to relay what he wanted to say. As he did so, I felt the fire in my gut subside, though I felt with growing certainty its presence.

He shared with me the most stupefying, incredible story of a prophecy fulfilled and how, hundreds of years ago, a prophet of his people, Isaiah, had foretold of a suffering servant who would be given up as payment for the sins of others. Then, during the reign of Tiberius, a man in the land of Judaea had performed miracles. Feeding scores of people with scarcely any food. Walking on water. Bringing the dead back to life.

My beloved, how to describe to you the sensational feelings that erupted within me upon hearing such things.

I knew evil was real. Had seen it, measured it in the words of actions of others. Had witnessed it with Marcus' assassination by his child's hand. Had collapsed at the feet of murdered innocence. On the outside looking in I knew…Rome had become evil. The light of Rome was focused by the lens of the emperor overseeing it. Some sought prosperity. Enlightenment. Others, decadence. Lust. Greed. Gluttony.

This story gleamed in my mind's eye the way a newly sharpened blades catches the rays of sunlight, momentarily illuminating the sword in a kind of holy fire. The story washed over my senses the way a rogue wave might flood the deck of a warship.

He went onto speak of the Roman governor Pontius Pilate, and how he had washed his hands to the whole affair. The man had been crucified, after being terribly scourged at the hands of Roman soldiers. Betrayed by his own people.

"When he rose from the dead," Peter said, his face lighted from a source I could not trace, "he appeared to his followers, shining as brightly as the sun. He spoke to his followers, telling them that belief in him meant everlasting life. And then, he ascended into the skies."

He ascended. Heaven.

I was wholly absorbed by the weight of his words. He spoke, not like a man trying to convince his listener that what he was saying was true. He spoke as a man transformed. He spoke with a certainty of the Cross. What flowed from his mouth was Truth.

In that moment, I knew; I would divorce myself from all the gods.

My strategic, military mind sparked with life. I reasoned, if Jesus' Father had sent him to earth to die, the only way for Jesus to resurrect would be to have absolute faith in his Father; that he had, in fact been sent to die for all mankind's sins, as Peter had shared.

Far from finding the story outrageous, I felt the strangest sensation in its possibility. For the first time in my life, with all I'd experienced as the bringer of the light under Marcus, the certainty I'd known as to the intent and purpose behind his motives, I discovered something inside me I'd not previously known. I discovered my belief in God.

QUAKE

I lived in a picture of you.

A reflection of something impeccably beautiful; it nearly defied comprehension.

How could such beauty exist, let alone live and breathe? Beauty that laughed, and smiled at the camera with all wisdom of a panther, sleek and with a profound sense of its own strength.

With each post, I marveled at your existence, and found more life within myself. I didn't want to face the Cross.

Didn't want to take ownership of what I had done.

Jesus was the turn I had to make. To look away from his Mother, the woman I had searched for through eternity, and to look for the Son I could not see, but could only feel.

BOOK THREE

HOPE:
The Kiss
of the
Dragon

The Fourth Letter of the Pandemic

By the end of June, I no longer found funny my inability to write the story. Now, I was getting scared.

What had changed? In just a few weeks, as the pandemic flourished, I had gone from supremely confident to a Doubting Thomas.

Control. My life had been about control. I controlled how close people got to me, controlled my affection for people based on a rigid belief system that drove me to share it with those I deemed worthy. I was so divided, I felt like I had to be a different person depending on who I was around. That was why I stayed away from people. My sense of self was so burdened by all the guilt I carried with me, I'd forgotten what genuine, lasting happiness could feel like.

Now, with everything that had happened in just a few short months, with this deluge of revelation and insight, I didn't believe I needed guidance from a higher power. In the handful of weeks since the weight of the pandemic began to be felt around the world, I was convinced I was undergoing the greatest spiritual transformation in human history. On the most basic level, it made sense.

In my eagerness to bring this story to life, I had been doing more guided meditations. They were not as intense as Dr. Joe's. Most of them were focused on improving creativity, or focus. Some were about becoming a better writer, or just being present. I was meditating once a day, at least. If this was the Law of Attraction at work, I was over the moon.

I was reading more now as well. I'd picked up Jim Kwik's *Limitless* book shortly after the pandemic began and finished it over a weekend.

It was hard for me to reconcile what was missing. When I envisioned writing this book, I thought of all the fame and fortune it would bring me. I imagined houses around the world, and a Ford Raptor to replace by Ford F-150. I dreamed of what a relationship with you might be like. Would we exercise together? Hike in the mountains?

I was thinking only of myself.

I didn't fathom what this story might mean to others, nor could I. By June, I had no concept of what the story meant to me. What purpose I might serve in being its author. I didn't understand who I was serving. I only knew that I was afraid to face the cross because I thought it meant losing you.

This was where I saw the first fractures in the façade I'd created in my life that passed for faith. For so long, I had lived in the material world. Newtonian physics. Everything was separate and distinct from everything else. That drove my need to consume. Even my years as a yoga instructor had, for the most part, failed to impress upon me the real idea behind spirituality.

I'd been living from the outside in, focusing more on the world outside me rather than the universe inside.

By July Fourth weekend, 2020, I was at an end.

I was torn. I felt what I had written would so confidently explain everything. The reality was I had written little more than hieroglyphics. More than that, I was determined to one day stand before you and see you with my own eyes. I was committed to it, come hell or highwater.

Hell would come first.

The human mind can apprehend only so much at a time; the idea of a physical God manifesting was something I'd never considered. The signs I saw from the universe, my new understanding of films I'd watched before, all were easy enough to accept. Their meaning would crystalize, and I would delight in what I learned.

Finding the means to apply that understanding to the real world was terrifying. The pandemic loomed over the world, people were dying. My thinking had been so small, so self-centered. The worst part?

I was already down the rabbit hole too deep. There was no going back to the life I'd known months prior. Any thought of abandoning the story, I quickly realized, was itself, hopeless.

But I *couldn't* write it. A story that on one hand suggested I was somehow intimately involved with Creation and, on the other, intimated I was a desperate, middle-aged man grasping at straws, a mortal man that was going to die like any other. In the Bible, Jesus tells his followers, whoever believes in him shall not perish but have everlasting life.

That Friday, I sat alone in my mother's house and cried. She had gone to the beach to celebrate the long holiday weekend. While I was living with Sara and Jim at the time, I didn't want them to see me struggle like this.

Many of my friends had beautiful homes, established careers. They had their eyes on retirement in just a few years. Watching their kids go through college. Traveling the world.

I had awakened to the fact that I sought to replace the immaterial love I felt but could not realize with material possessions. This, in turn, served as a terrible measure of how vacant I had become spiritually. After wading in doubt for so long, faith was a muscle I had neglected. My inner universe needed work.

As I stood in the living room, I began to understand just how far away from Jesus I felt. I had spent my life searching for you, confident you existed, with no idea of how exactly I would know you.

I hadn't gone to church with any regularity for years. My prayers were generic. I didn't want to go to church. A relationship with Jesus is meant to be personal, and should be euphoric. Most church services I had attended were solemn affairs. I wasn't looking for God in church. I was looking for God in the world in which I lived.

I know it sounds crazy, but so much of my time was occupied by love, even as I experimented on its ingredients. I couldn't understand why it never felt quite right. Now, the answer seems obvious.

I was terrified. Terrified because I wasn't going to think about retirement or having a nest egg. I wasn't going to worry about furnishing a new house, or finding someone to be with so I wouldn't feel lonely. The compass by which I had navigated much of my life by had ultimately brought me to this point. Letting go of a life-structure I had put in place over the course of decades had been gut-wrenchingly hard, but I'd been doing the most painful work in recent years; I'd felt the weight lifted from my shoulders. At the same time, this was the direction I wanted. Yes, I had done come clean about my life in recent years, and wanted to continue pulling out the weeds, wherever they might be. It was time for a new destination.

Now, I was my character Sam, from *The Lighthouse Keeper*. I was sailing through the most monstrous waves on this Sea of Divine Memory. Like Sam, I needed a light to follow.

I was determined to understand what it meant to have enough faith in Jesus to realize everlasting life.

As I went through that first weekend in July, with the wobbliest of legs, I picked up my cross and began moving forward in faith towards our Son. That was when I began to see how radical a shift had been created by Jesus' death and resurrection. That was the new covenant.

It felt like the middle of July when I first found the courage to approach you with some meaningful communication, some hint of who you were to me. As the pandemic swirled, I had my first appreciable sense of the journey I was to undertake.

The world was my Goliath, a colossal behemoth. A juggernaut. There were billions of people on the planet, each with their own identity and set of beliefs, their own model of the world. That I should somehow be an author to humanity's origins staggered my mind, *yet who else had ever experienced a Judgment Day during a pandemic?* In May, when my writing struggles began, I decided to step away from writing for a bit. Perhaps I needed the break. But when I resumed my efforts within a few weeks, my renewed attempts failed, bringing with them a terrible anxiety.

I looked at your posts with a wonder I struggled to put into words. I didn't understand my place in the story and had only invested a parcel of faith in Jesus. For days, I smoothed over an idea in my mind. Like a stone to be cast from a sling, I knew these words might deliver a miracle to your heart, if I could only find the courage to send them.

It was a Sunday afternoon. I was laying on my bed in the guest room, finishing up a meditation. The words I wanted to say to you had been bouncing around in my mind the past few days. When they finally came together in the middle of the meditation, I accepted them. They were perfect. I knew, as soon as the meditation was over, I would check my phone. I would sling this stone, and let it fly across Atlantic by means of the internet, traveling at lightning speed, hoping they would hit their mark. The meditation ended.

I reached for my phone, opened Instagram, and saw you had posted just eight seconds prior. I went from the soothing meditation to the bolt of electricity around the words finally coming together to knowing the moment had come to let fly this stone. My heart was racing.

Fighting the pandemic, fighting my substantial struggle with faith, and feeling my heartbeat galloping inside my chest, I commented with a message I hoped would strike true and pierce the shield of your consciousness.

I wrote:

If God is just a beautiful thought, then you are the most beautiful thing I can think of.

THE THIRD LETTER OF THUNDER

My father had been in the infantry in Vietnam. I chose artillery because it was the King of Battle.

Leadership is taught at every level in the Marines. Even the three-star generals who command our largest fighting forces have retired three- and four-star Marine generals who mentor them, acting as consultants to the Marine Corps.

Early in my career, I learned the basics of Marine Corps leadership, and I learned how to be an artillery officer. In the early nineties, we had simple computers, but most of what we learned about artillery meant learning how to take large "bullets" from one point on the ground and accurately send them miles away to another point on the ground using old fashioned math. This required calculations, and took into consideration things like wind, weather, changes in altitude. How far the artillery shells needed to travel meant using different amounts of gunpowder, which was packaged in doughy bags of fabric and placed in the breech assembly behind the shell.

I spent hours on tops of hills as a forward observer; I had the responsibility of *calling for fire*, meaning I would deploy with the frontline infantry units and radio back to my artillery unit. There were usually three or four others on the hilltop with me. We overlooked a vast open space of deserted land. This was the impact area, where the artillery shells would land. I would provide a fire mission, a concise description of what kind of enemy I was facing, where the rounds needed to hit, and the type of rounds I wanted used. Troops in the open might call for HE; high-explosive. Sometimes, we would call for

Willie Pete. White Phosphorous, which sets things on fire. On other occasions, we might call for smoke to obscure the battlefield, allowing our forces to maneuver away from an enemy.

As much time as we spent training, we spent almost as much time cleaning. We cleaned our weapons, big and little. We cleaned our trucks and our Humvees. We cleaned where we worked and lived.

As I progressed through my military career, there were books that were suggested for every rank, as recommended reading. Early in my career, these books were about basic leadership. Going through the ranks, there were studies in leadership focusing on a single leader. Napoleon. Grant. Patton. There were books on specific campaigns like Gettysburg, or specific wars like Vietnam.

These readings were complemented by what we called PME, Professional Military Education. At different intervals, sometimes as frequently as once a month, the officers of a unit would come together and discuss something specific. On some occasions, an officer might share a meaningful insight from a book they'd recently read. Some of the more motivated officers put together little maps in the dirt around which we gathered.

There, they recreated a map from a book they'd read. The officer would walk us through the battle, highlighting some of the key take-aways as they pointed to different areas of their map of the terrain. The hope was that we would use these lessons in shaping our own decision-making should the time ever come for us to face a similar situation.

On other occasions, we might have a guest speaker. Most often, these would be warriors from the past who had fought in Korea or Vietnam. They would share their firsthand experiences of leading Marines in combat; what they went through, the steps they took to keep morale high, and the little attention to detail things that foster discipline or, in their absence, leave a unit searching for its soul.

These sessions brought with them the utmost concentration, these sessions always made rooms go quiet. To hear a retired three-star general tell you what it was like while his Marines were under siege for ninety days by the North Vietnamese on a hilltop in South Vietnam was riveting. I felt like I was there with him.

Every day, they would raise the American flag atop the hill. He shared with us that no sooner had a Marine run the flag up the flag-pole, the North Vietnamese would start firing mortar shells into their position. Every day he made sure his men shaved, despite constantly running low on water. The helicopters that attempted to resupply them during their siege always took enemy gunfire and, on at least one occasion, one was shot down, crashing into the side of the hill just below his Marines' position.

During those moments, it never occurred to me that I could be something else, besides a warrior. I'd known warfare all my life.

Thirteen years into my Marine Corps career, I was selected for a prestigious school, the School of Advanced Warfighting, or SAW.

I'd already earned one Master's degree while attending Command and Staff College the year prior. Command and Staff was a one-year curriculum designed to orient midlevel officers for serving on a large staff, like a division or an air wing. These staffs were the people who did the planning when it came to major campaigns like Fallujah, or like the landing we did in Somalia in support of Operation Restore Hope.

My thesis had been on the post-war occupation of Germany after World War II. I was highlighting the merits and disappointments of how the allies had governed Germany at the end of the war as a comparison to how badly America was doing in its occupation of Iraq, which resulted in the insurgency. In Germany, the allies had kept the military intact as it was one of the best means of maintaining civil order. In Iraq, we had disbanded the army.

There were mistakes the allies made. At one point, they had the idea to partition Germany into four smaller states; the world had had enough of Germany hostility after World War I and dating back to the Franco-Prussian war of 1870. Calmer heads prevailed, and the allies recognized that Germany was the economic heart of Europe.

Where Command and Staff College had been approximately two-hundred officers, most of whom had been Marines, SAW had a class size of just twenty-four, with a few brethren from army and air force, and a handful of international officers.

Part of the reason I was selected for SAW was my poetry. I resumed writing in 2001 after finding inspiration in a boss who painted as a hobby. He was the first officer I met that showed their artistic side. When my application to SAW was submitted, some of my poetry was included with my application.

In Command and Staff college, we had studied the Peloponnesian War and skimmed forward throughout history.

In SAW, we were going to deconstruct war. The first course we took was a speed-reading course. We would read several books in a day. On the heels of that, we spent days studying Clausewitz and Sun Tzu, masters in the art of war, separated by thousands of years and thousands of miles. We discussed the theory of war, and the reasons nations went to war in the first place. Our guest speakers included Supreme Court justices, retired generals, and brilliant historians. Over the course of the eleven-month curriculum, we would spend three weeks touring Europe, and ten days in Vietnam. Each trip consisted of incredible amounts of reading and study. My classmates and I walked over the ground from significant battles from World War I and World War II, and from decisive conflicts in the thick jungles of Vietnam.

SAW graduates were called Jedi Knights. They sat on the same staffs as officers who had attended Command and Staff College. The difference was, SAW graduates understood the chaos of war. We could work within the chaos, aiding the staff in seeing where to focus their energies under the time constraints conflict demands. Our studies were intended to put us in the minds of the commanders who had fought over the ground on which we walked during our tours. We wanted to understand why they'd made the decisions they had, what had made those decisions seem like the right ones, and what the results of their decision-making had meant for the battle's outcome.

If we were Jedi Knights, I was Darth Vader.

The Sixth Letter of David

I have such a strong daughter. It is hard to describe the pain I felt when I divorced her mother. Kara was just one-year old at the time. With the marriage on shaky ground, my sense was, we believed bringing a child into the mix would force our hand, so to speak. Demand that we take adulting seriously. Naïve. It was 1998.

My view of the world was still small. Even with my experiences in Somalia, and visiting Singapore, and the United Arab Emirates, I was still searching for myself. The world was at peace for a short while. After months of buildup and pressure, Desert Storm had been over in a weekend. Somalia had not gone as expected, and we discovered the challenges of trying to use the military to aid in nation-building. When Kosovo erupted in the late nineties, I didn't give it a second thought. The Marines hadn't spent much time in Europe since World War I.

With no external enemy on which to focus, I turned on myself.

I was thrilled to have a daughter. When Kara was born, I was overjoyed. She had such beautiful eyes and the cutest, plumpest cheeks. During her first year, I became increasingly uneasy. As much as I loved her, I was becoming more convinced that her mother and I were not meant to be together. Where did these thoughts come from? Some internal knowing. I demanded we divorce.

It was the first truly self-destructive act of my life.

I did not hate myself for wanting to leave her mother. I despised myself because I took possession of the idea that I had ruined love. I had the very real sense that I was substantially and painfully altering the trajectory of my daughter's life, and was convinced that love was leading me down this path. I embraced my shame, and took an assignment on the other side of the country, back in Quantico. Automatically, that meant I would see my daughter less than five times a year.

With the money I was paying for alimony and child support, I moved east and moved in with my parents. I couldn't afford my own place, and even spent a few months working a part-time retail job just so I could have a little more money coming in.

If you had stopped me and asked me why I was doing this, I couldn't have given you a good answer. Love was calling me to keep looking, and I've always taken that call seriously.

I remember driving east through the deserts of Southern California the day I left. I tortured myself by listening to Creed's "With Arms Wide Open." I cried as I drove.

I had met someone whom I basically relied on as a safety net while I navigated the divorce, the first serious link in a chain of patterns that would see me repeatedly create and destroy relationships. *She* was going to be the object of my affections; she was going to be the bearer of the foot for which I held the perfect, enchanted slipper.

But she wasn't. Nor the next. Nor the few who came after that. Online dating promised a new way of meeting women, and yet it all felt so stilted, a dull version of Russian roulette. While initially places like Match.com offered hope, something was so obviously missing.

The years moved forward. My military career progressed. My daughter grew.

Our relationship consisted of weekly phone calls, trips to see her at least twice a year, and an extended stay of several weeks over the summer. We would go to the beach and spend time with family. Those were enjoyable summers. The challenge for me was, I didn't see how much she needed me to listen to her. I was too busy trying to be a fun dad every time she came out.

In 2006, I left the Marines short of retirement by five years. I had found ways to heap enough shame onto my shoulders that I'd gotten in trouble while on active duty; I'd fallen in love with someone I shouldn't have. It cost me a promotion.

I could have stayed in and made it to retirement without the promotion, but something in me resisted the idea. I was terrified of the world outside the military; I had never been and would never be a civilian. I could not then understand a life formed with such freedom of self-determination. I'd always been told where to go.

Love. That was the basis for my decision-making. The one thing I hadn't changed in my pursuit of love over the fifteen years of my military career was what I did for a living.

I suddenly stopped caring so much about honor. I had followed in the steps taken by my dad and my brother because I didn't know what else to do. And where had it gotten me?

I was pursuing a career because it seemed like the thing to do. My dad used to tell me…the Marine Corps is an unforgiving mistress; once she's done with you, she doesn't want you back. But there was something else.

I'd gotten the inspiration to start writing again. Besides a boss who painted, in 2001. I'd taken a psychology class in pursuit of a master's, and discovered my first honest-to-goodness muse. A beautiful young woman in my class who shared a poignant story that ignited the spark of poetry within me.

In a short period, I wrote dozens of poems. I felt alive and inspired. When I made the decision to get out a few years later, something in me reasoned that I could connect with my writing again.

Putting the Marine Corps behind me was so difficult. I didn't know what to expect when I got out. For one reason or another, yoga came across my path immediately as I got out. And I fell in love.

Kim was a magnificent woman. She had had success as a model, and had built an enviable family life when she discovered yoga and her priorities began to shift. Instead of material accomplishment, she began the internal journey. It was one of the things that attracted me to her.

She was tall, nearly six feet, with a lithe figure and radiant eyes.

The journey into yoga was eye-opening. Here, for the first time, I had an adult's introduction to another culture and belief system. Hindu gods were fascinating. Their statues, mysterious and full of meaning. I tread lightly into Hinduism, lest my Christian sensibilities feel too threatened.

Fascination is the word that comes to mind. The first time I heard women refer to themselves as goddesses during a weekend yoga retreat, I was fascinated. I didn't find the idea repulsive. If anything, it was alluring. Goddesses. I saw the seam between the witches I'd read about when I was younger and these goddesses; it was their connection to the earth, something most men seemed all too willing to ignore.

Kim and I had serious discussions about the parallels found in Scripture with the principal ideas of Yoga; the sense of oneness, and the relationship between the observer and the observed. She did extensive research into whether there was evidence that Jesus had done a pilgrimage to India during his lifetime, as there were large periods of his life unaccounted for. Her results revealed nothing.

It did make me wonder…how could Jesus save people who had never heard of him?

I understood the spirit and intent behind missions to regions to promote the teachings of Jesus. I wondered about what I call the "ignorant sinner."

Say someone lives on a small island with no communication with the outside world. If they die having never heard of Jesus, what happens? Do they not make it to heaven? That didn't make sense.

An ignorant sinner must be given a chance to redeem themselves. That led me down the path of birth and rebirth.

If God exists, and there is a fall from heaven that suggests that, at one time, we were all in heaven. Wouldn't we all have to go on a journey to understand what our path to salvation looks like? What if you don't get it right the first time?

These were good questions, and I was new to a world with such diverse beliefs. While I served on active duty with Marines from various denominations and beliefs, in taking our oath of office swearing to God, I always felt like we served the Father. That was my military view of Christianity. Not that Jesus was here to save the world; rather, the guy who put Jesus on the cross was the moral cause under which America flexed its military muscle, even as we did our best to separate church from state. That was how strongly I felt my dad's presence and the other men I was around growing up. There wasn't a lot of "turning the other cheek" in the military.

These questions would remain unanswered, yet I continued to explore diverse backgrounds, particularly after the attack on 9/11.

Islam's introduction into the American conscience struck at the heart of what America seemed to be about: Trade and Defense. I was stationed at Quantico, Virginia when the attacks took place, and watched live TV, stunned as the two towers of the World Trade Center fell.

American resolve unified in a way unseen since World War II and, we went back to war.

I remember I spent a lot of time reading about radical Islam, especially after I got out of the Marines. There were several books that painted a very clear picture of what the fundamentalists saw as wrong with America writ large; the perception was that capitalism had become god, spilling blood for oil. American troops, with their loose moral fiber, on holy ground.

Many of these books went to great lengths to underscore that the extremists represented but a fraction of the total Islamic population, and that a solid majority of Muslims interpreted the Quran and the teachings of the prophet in a more peaceful way. The same could be said about the servicemen and women who got in trouble in the wars in Iraq and Afghanistan; they represented only a small percentage of the overall forces serving their country. They were the ones who drew the headlines.

At the time, I didn't know much about Allah. I didn't know what the Quran said about Mary.

I remember after Somalia in the early nineties, we went to the United Arab Emirates to clean all our trucks and equipment, fix things, and spend a little downtime after the wear and tear of the operations in Mogadishu. We were there for three weeks. Much of the time was aboard the ship, or right next to it. I had a chance to have dinner with an American family living in the country—they gave me spices of frankincense and myrrh. I spent time at the local gold souk in the bazaar. It was one complete block of shops...all of them selling gold. The culture was fascinating for what little I saw of the country. Though I spent much of my time away from ship by myself, I never felt alone while I was there. Even at night, wandering the streets solo, I never felt anything, other than safe.

I remember how differently the air smelled, it was a mystical, tangy cocktail of spices and incense. Islam reveres King David, Jesus, and the Virgin Mary. It calls to mind the hadith collection of Muhammad al-Bukhari known as the Sahih al-Bukhari: the prayer which God loves the most is the prayer of David.

I felt good about what we had done. Somalia didn't want our democracy, and by the end of 1993, the events captured in the film *Blackhawk Down* had taken place. I appreciate now...they didn't want the promise of freedom our democracy promised, because true freedom comes from God.

Back then, I felt very small in the world. Spending days at a time aboard ship and looking out at the vast, phenomenal depths of the Pacific, how could I not? If I had a relationship with Jesus back then, I knew he had my back. That was how it felt. Not that I was praying to him every night, or chatting with him during the day. Jesus was somewhere "out there," and all was good. That was the early nineties.

By the time the years started slipping closer to 2010, I felt a little like I was "shopping for god." My mind had been opened to other religions and belief systems, and the idea of "oneness" carried what seemed to me significant weight in the yoga community. This was vitally important to me, yet I also began to question…how could Jesus' story be the story that brought all of us together?

I wanted to understand how other people saw God. I wish I could say I operated with the supreme confidence of identity that I now share in these letters my love, but I had no idea. I knew, my purpose was to get love *right*. I lived like I believed God was a woman, prayed like God was the Father, and kept Jesus waiting in the wings.

In the yoga community and, to an extent, in my life, I still had my defenses up from my days in the Marines, and perceived most of the "peace and love" vibe as too soft for my brutish exterior. I didn't let people get too close. At the same time, wasn't Jesus' message about love? Jesus was in my rearview mirror the whole time. I was pointed in the right direction…I just lacked the faith. There was still so much I needed to learn.

I wasn't sure what if anything I needed to process in getting out of the Marines. We were taught to deal with adversity, to carry hardships, no matter how heavy, and press on. I was disappointed that I had given up pursuit of retirement, and the safety of a paycheck for life. I hadn't taken anytime to process my reasons for getting out, for growing up resenting my dad and still joining the military, nor had I come to terms with my approach to relationships. I was too busy trying to figure out life outside a uniform.

That said, the civilian world was fascinating.

There was so much diversity. People didn't share as much as we did in the military; that level of individuality surprised me. I felt like there was more comparison. People fretted if they were making as much money as so-and-so. Promotions mattered, and people complained if they felt like theirs didn't happen when they were ready. In the military, everyone got paid the same, depending what your rank was and how long you had been on active duty. For officers, most promotions happened in waves. There would be an announcement released about everyone who had been selected for Captain, or Major, and so on.

I couldn't get over the fact that we got free soda in our break room in the place where I worked.

I wanted to distance myself from my military service as much as possible, partly from shame, but mainly because I wanted to absorb from other people as much as possible what it meant to be a civilian.

For the first few years of being out of uniform, like clockwork, I analyzed incidents from the week and how they compared to my experiences in the military. This occupied a fair amount of my energy, though I was not necessarily aware of it at the time.

I was worried about retirement. Not having a pension from the military felt costly, even as my boss told me I could make it up in Corporate America.

My primary frame of reference for retirement had been my dad. After a quintuple-bypass surgery in the early 2000s, he opted to retire from his corporate job. He was getting 75 percent of his military salary as his pension, this being the reward. for thirty-one years of service to his country. Despite starting off as a project manager when he left active duty, he'd ended up as a senior director at his company and had earned some good money. I remember how one time he proudly shared that, between the house and all their investments, my parents had over a million dollars. He was just a small-town kid from rural Iowa, but he felt like he was on top of the world. I know he believed in God.

He liked to read and be around golf courses in his retirement. That, and spending time with my mom. It was beautiful to see them appreciate what they had accomplished. They had navigated thirty-one years of moves, multiple deployments and wars, had managed to create as beautiful a life as the military lifestyle affords, and had two beautiful grandchildren to boot.

My relationship with him improved. I was looking forward to living near my parents, watching them grow old together. And I was thrilled by the prospects of learning to live a life away from the military.

I was also focused on making money, operating under the impression that I was "behind" in life…I was willing to do what was necessary to catch up. The truth was, I didn't have a clue what that might mean for me; I too was caught up in comparing myself to others as a way of pace-setting and figuring out what I was supposed to be doing as a veteran.

Life was going well. Kim and I were engaged and quite happy. Who I was showing up as in this relationship was a better version of myself; our kids got along great; our daughters were the same age, and she had a son just a few years younger than the girls. We both loved yoga. We had bought a house in anticipation of our wedding in March of 2009.

Then my dad died.

It was unexpected. Out of the blue, a week before the Thanksgiving holiday in 2008. He was sixty-eight. He had been away from home at the family beach condo, and was found slumped over in his favorite chair, a book on the floor next to him.

It was the first death in my family that shocked me. I'd lost all of my grandparents by this point, but did not expect to lose my dad so young.

Gone. Gone was the man who I had warred against, then grown to admire and respect as we rebuilt our relationship, and I started defining myself more clearly. Gone were the afternoons and occasions with my parents coming over to my house, the first I'd ever owned, and creating memories that I could reflect on with contentedness as I aged.

The first book I read in trying to make sense of his death was Dinesh D'Souza's *Life After Death: The Evidence*. His book tackled out-of-body experiences, and the evidence for Jesus. It was a thoughtful and well-researched book. I'm not sure how small a sense of hope can be, but that was what I took away from the book.

As much as my dad's death shocked me awake, it also made me realize…whatever I believed about God and the afterlife, I was going to have to find it within myself. That was perhaps the first real stirring in me for connecting love to God.

Like it or not, that would take me on the path to my second divorce.

THE SPANIARD V

I shared my intentions with no one, not that they were mine to share. I was possessed of a spirit that directed me with such clarity. I would break the bonds of slavery in this life and the next, and the one after that and after that again. Wherever you were, I would find you. If believing in this Jesus would be my shield against death, how could I fail?

What is Truth?

With those words, Pontius Pilate established the role of government for the next two thousand years. The role of the government is to question the truth.

To do this, those governed and the governors must be divided in as many conceivable ways as possible. Monarchs. Dictators. Tyrants.

Kings. Chancellors. Presidents. Emperors.

Augustus Caesar embodied the noblest answer to this question of truth. After him, every subsequent emperor, impelled to show distinction from their predecessor, was necessarily forced to play the cards of their ambitions. Some emphasized governance. Others, diplomacy. Some men, and they were all men, became indulgent. They asked questions in a haze of intoxication.

How can I give my power away? What torments can I unleash on the earth as the imbalance of authority? What words of knowledge can I share to stain the minds of men? Shall I point people to a vision of what the future can be, or have them suckle in indulgence at the glory of my greatness, believing it to be their own?

Unchecked power, all brought about by Jesus' arrival on earth. Augustus is emperor when Jesus is born. One, First man. The other, Son of God. His Mother, the second Eve.

Tiberius is emperor at Jesus' death and resurrection. The reluctant emperor. The anger of God.

Caligula. The most human form of Satan loosed on the earth. The first father of lies and yet he, too, was a servant of God.

There were two other men on the cross on the day Jesus died. One sought repentance, and it was given. The other did not, and his torment continued. Jesus died for both.

My dearest beloved wife, I am waking up to a truth that is both majestic and delicious.

I love you so very much.

If you ask me now, what eternity feels like, it feels like coming home to something that seems like the most sought-after dream. It is breathtaking. It is life-giving.

I remember all the life we promised one another, and how our love would define eternity.

How could I know the power of the darkness if I did not experience it firsthand?

The heavy weight of men's hearts; the unconscious mind of God within all of them. The terrible toll the advance of civilization demanded. And what, to many, felt like the muted heart of Jesus.

But Jesus had a purpose. Salvation for all.

The engine of western civilization was ignited by the swirl of energy created by the Resurrection of Jesus.

All would know some form of suffering, for suffering is a self-imposed sentence. All would know some form of darkness, for what understanding can there be of the light without some reference of the dark?

There must be a higher purpose to humanity, and there is. It is intended to be a receptacle for God's eternal love. Men struggle most to find their soul, because men cannot fathom a life inside them.

It is difficult to imagine the story of the Crucifix as theater, and yet it is. That is what belief in God means. Despite the agonies, despite the betrayal, if we but accept one truth, that Jesus was sent to die for our sins, no matter how badly those sins might be, we will have everlasting life. And, beloved, therein lies the secret. *Jesus was sent to die by his Father.* All souls are innocent; it is in our humanity that imperfection rests. Who must collect this pain most poignantly if not the creature responsible for its creation? A creator must be subject to its creation; otherwise, how can it know what has been created?

The first thought of sin came from the Creator. How could birth have happened any other way, if not with separation?

How do I continue to express myself, lost in the immaculate thoughts that you are more beautiful than I could have ever conceived?

How does a Mother shape her Son, and how does the Son shape His Mother?

You elicit in my chest a feeling that is bliss intertwined with a real understanding. Eternal freedom. This feeling. This knowing sensation. This certainty.

You are all I have ever wanted, and I was forced to learn the cost of freedom, in my surrender to a Higher Power.

The Fifth Letter of the Pandemic

It was immediately after that 4th of July weekend that the words Jack Canfield had said to me in March came back to me.

You've got a year.

With a few months to gain perspective, I was able to manage a fresh interpretation of what he had said. The pandemic was just starting to settle in over the world when he said those words, and experiencing my Judgment Day less than two weeks later, I reasoned that, whatever he knew about me that I did clearly did not fully understand about myself, I would be facing it for a year. If this was my purgatory, then I might find salvation by the time of my birthday in April of 2021.

Daily, with that as a backdrop, I swayed under the weight of a most burdensome anxiety for much the rest of the year.

Some days, I would process some new bit of information. It might be from a Bible verse, or a book I was reading. Something about absolution. There were times during work when I would be sitting in front of my computer, and I felt a burst of information tickling my pineal gland, or what mystics call the third eye. In these moments, I would stop and allow this download of information to be processed before continuing with my work.

At night, I slept with white noise or waterfall sounds playing from my Alexa, which sat on the nightstand next to my bed. Normally it would play throughout the night, without interruption, yet that changed when I moved in with Sara and Jim.

Some nights, it would still play all the way through. Other nights, the sound would be interrupted and again, I would receive a flood of information into my pineal gland, in what felt like a feathery tickle.

On one such burst, the message I received intimated that my dream would come true. It wasn't something I thought; it was a "push" of information I received.

On another occasion, a Friday, I woke and thought to myself, *I accept Jesus Christ as my lord and savior.* Something compelled me to repeat the words out loud. No sooner had I said the words, when Alexa replied with, "That's nice."

It was affirmation of the reality of Christ's mission on earth, and the fulfillment of that mission. My faith was still that of a newborn fawn, wobbly as I attempted to steady my footing. As part of my reading that summer, I picked up *That All Shall Be Saved* by David Bentley Hart, which essentially suggested being saved by Jesus wasn't up for debate. It was exhilarating.

It also made sense. It strengthened my faith.

My understanding of the world, of the universe, was changing. On several occasions, I'd heard a famous physicist say, the four main elements that are found in the greatest abundance in the universe are Nitrogen, Carbon, Hydrogen, and Oxygen. Those are the same four elements that are most abundant in our own composition as humans. We really are, each one of us, the universe in human form, with our own unique consciousness.

Since everything is quantum, everything is connected. The sense of separation we feel is one we conceive of and derive from our life's experiences, but separation is an illusion. I felt calm, a sense of peace as I absorbed this knowledge. Sitting on the back deck at the house, I appreciated how good it felt being outdoors. In the past, I might have complained about it being too hot, or too muggy. Now, I simply loved the feeling of the sun on my face. Of hearing the wind *shush* through the trees. Those were my good days.

On those days, I felt what passed for confidence. It was a respite from the storms of doubt, whose monstrous waves pounded my senses with unnerving irregularity.

And then, there were days when I would look at the world. In the U.S. there was social unrest. We were in an election year. A few years prior, we had elected a businessman to run the country, without full consideration to the reality that a democracy is not a business. The tapestry of America felt like it was fraying as increasingly, the two sides of our democracy saw the other side as the problem. The pandemic was intensifying. People were dying.

What happened to those people? Where did they go? There were legions of questions for which I had no good answers.

As the summer exhaled towards fall, Sara was a source of comfort, yet she also held me accountable. We made occasional trips to the beach. There, I imagined flying through the clouds. Looking back it seems silly. The idea of Thor seemed like a much better identity than the one I'd had for years. Try as I might, I could not stop thinking about you, or this story. In those moments, her frustration would bubble up.

"You know there's more to this than just that woman." She would say, palpable exasperation coming across from her tone. I didn't want to hear it. I focused on you to avoid focusing on myself.

It produced tension. I was so grateful for her friendship and how she and Jim opened their home to me. I was also so incredibly desperate to know more to this story as it unfolded. Then, as August barreled onto the calendar, there came thunderstorms and with them, something I hadn't expected.

A primitive part of my mind opened.

With my inability to continue the story, either by notebook or on my computer, I was relegated to journaling. As had become practice, I would journal whatever came to mind, without editing, and doing my best not to lift the pen from the page. It was sometimes hard to compose my thoughts. It was almost as if I were learning how to write all over again. It was my early attempts at writing my truth. Now, my journaling was taken me in a unique direction, and I was writing a battery of powerful questions.

When did the sounds we make first become language? Did our ancestors dream of coming out of the trees and walking upright? Did we evolve through the imagination of apes?

It seems like the answer must be yes. We think of evolution as something that occurred in the past, yet we are products of that evolution. Energy is neither created nor destroyed. At some stage of development, our ancestors thirsted to become more. Primitive man. We advanced. We advance still. We must constantly seek growth. What is the next step in our evolutionary journey?

The only person I confided in was Sara. Valkyrie.

I thought of the recent *Planet of the Apes* movies, and Caesar, a chimp given an experimental serum which increased his intelligence until he learned to speak. To reason. At some point in human history, our ancestors were driven to evolve...what could the driving force behind that evolution be, if not love? Doesn't love demand a higher intelligence?

We had developed a nice home routine after just a few months of living together. The three of us would have coffee together in the kitchen most mornings, then spend a little time out back, playing with Atlas before starting the workday.

There was rarely anyone else out in the neighborhood. Sara and I used to joke that the studio couldn't afford any other actors for our little reality television experiment. Their backyard, with a thick garden divided by flowers and vegetables, had a nice lengthy, open yard. Atlas, now five months old, was growing, and would chase Jim from one end of the yard to the other.

My "office" was now downstairs. I had started on the main floor in the dining room, back when I was still living at my mother's.

The basement was long enough that, for a time, both Jim and I kept our offices downstairs, but invariably one or both of us would be on a video call, which would prove distracting for the other. Jim moved to the top floor and set up his office in their walk-in attic. Sara initially worked from the breakfast table. Depending on our schedules, we might cross paths during the lunch hour, and usually ate dinner together.

With the basement to myself, I would spend time with Jim and Atlas outside after the workday was finished. Some nights, we all congregated around the television in the living room and watched shows. Other nights, I preferred my solitude. I would stay downstairs, playing video games and drinking beer. I had moderated my drinking considerably, especially in training for the Spartan races. With the pandemic, I was drinking at least two beers, every night. Minus the ability to fly, a magical hammer that somehow responded to my thoughts, and Chris Hemsworth's good looks, I was becoming Fat Thor.

And you were ever-present with me.

I knew my comments had gotten your attention; some of your replies indicated as much. I didn't want to be trivial when I reached out to you. Over the summer, I had purged my Instagram accounts of all the beautiful women I'd taken to following as poor bandages for my pride.

Fumbling with how to communicate, what to communicate, when I was still awestruck by your existence was a kind of delightful torment.

As summer gave way to autumn, I was deliriously in love with you. I drifted away from my primate reflections of August and felt a tenuous sense of control about my life.

I was exuberant with every new picture of you I saw, though your identity, like my own, was still clouded in mystery. My mind was opening, my consciousness was expanding. It was a terrible kind of storm. I imagined, it was like what learning to fly might have been for Superman.

As I have mentioned previously, there were pearls of wisdom, new levels of insight and awareness. One day, I ascended to a new level of understanding. The next I would wrestle with appreciating those same concepts and ideas, and come crashing back to a very material earth. Faith and doubt, snaking through my consciousness, tightening around me, grounding me in the world I'd known for so many years. Moving into September, I started to sense a pattern in the days of the week. During the summer transition, I also met the last real temptation of my romantic life.

Sundays were usually tranquil. Jim and I might watch football, or the three of us would play outside with Atlas. Nature came alive for me during the lockdown; I loved time under the stars, or on nearby trails. We still heard from the owls every now and then during the evening, sometimes in the late afternoon, though never quite as intense as we had earlier in the year. Once, one perched on a tree just outside the fence line while we were outside with Atlas. He was just a puppy, and still tiny then. We had a mild fear the owl was going to snatch him up and fly off.

Mondays were bright days. I would feel clear. Invariably, I would learn something new during the day, and enjoy the reflection this learning afforded me. Most Mondays, I felt a sense of optimism and ease as the work week started.

Tuesdays became hard, consistently so. I would wake up and, whatever insights I'd taken away from the previous day would now be called into question. This would create a horrible kind of isolation. Wrestling with my doubt over what I had learned previously, if the doubt was given enough attention, would take me all the way back to the beginning of the pandemic. Had I imagined flying out to Santa Barbara and all that had transpired at Jack's Mastermind session? Was my Judgment Day just some crazy trip I'd been on? Was I just an old man who had seen a beautiful woman and created this story, built on specks of time that smacked of near-inconceivable coincidences? That questioning always led me back to the pandemic. Yes, there is a global pandemic occurring while I am undergoing a most spiritual awakening. Strangely, it made me grateful for the pandemic.

Navigating the choppy waters of Tuesday, Wednesdays became a question of how much I could recover; how badly had my nerves been rattled the night before? Generally, by the middle of the day, I would level out and have accepted that, my doubt having been given adequate attention, I still had faith in the story.

Thursdays were mild. By September, the gym had reopened, and while we were adjusting to wearing masks while working out, it was good to be in familiar spaces with friends. Our workouts during the summer made me appreciate the humidity in North Carolina…every workout promised a good sweat.

Fridays were both a day of sadness and relief. Friday, July 3rd had been the hardest. Some Fridays, I would lose hope. I was torn. The premise of our story was so powerful and beautiful. The problem was, my faith wasn't strong enough to bring all elements of the story together. I was still too externally focused on validating my faith. I was too reluctant to look inside myself to respect what this story said about me.

Saturdays, I would workout with my friends, then spend time with Sara and our pandemic family. Sunday would come, and it would start over again.

During the pandemic, there was no putting life on cruise control. No blindly going from one activity to the next, hustling about in our busy days, mistaking activity for accomplishment. Every day brought with it a kind of stillness, a newness.

If anything had changed in the six months since I first saw you, it was my relationship with Jesus. Increasingly, when these dragons of doubt raged through my psyche, I would turn to him. It wasn't instantaneous. Instead, I would rely on my own logic and reasoning to try and understand something, twisting the idea around in my mind like a Rubik's Cube. When I couldn't quite piece something together, I would get scared. Then, Jesus.

I wish I had a fresh example to share with you, my love. Suffice to say, I would be struck with a profound kind of revelation that suggested a grand order to life as we know it. With nearly eight billion people on the planet, that is a prospect that takes time to process. Part of my processing was exposing that revelation to my doubt. This was not some conscious act, like I was a scientist conducting experiments in a lab. This was an everyday battle.

Intrinsically, on some unspoken level of my being, I *knew* who you were while still being blind to who I was. My confidence from the early days of my writing and the pandemic had eroded like a storm reclaims the shore. What I failed to appreciate and temper this knowledge with was one simple fact: salvation *only* happens through Jesus. While I had entered marriage previously with what I assumed was God's blessing, it was an abstract concept. I inferred God's blessing as external to me. I never thought to put Jesus at the heart of my relationships. In time, I would understand why.

The path to the Cross is the ultimate Truth.

This reality would haunt my decision-making well into the summer of 2021, for late in the summer of 2020, I met a most impressive woman.

Like you, Sophia was French. She was a life coach for men. We connected on LinkedIn after she sent me a connection request.

The timing of it all was fascinating. For part of the last year, I'd worked with a French woman, a first for me. It was mildly coincidental that Sara was fluent in French and worked for a French company. Sophia's French background intrigued me for obvious reasons. Had the universe sent me a life coach? Did I need one?

I felt like I might.

Our first phone call was professional. I wanted to understand what a life coach for men did, and how I might benefit from one. She was brilliant, attentive, and thoughtful. Soon after our first call, it became clear that Sophia wasn't looking for me as a client. I was flattered and slightly curious, but told her in no uncertain terms that I was head over heels in love with someone.

We agreed to stay in touch, as I was interested in whether coaching might help me, unaware that my relationship with Sophia was already developing into something that would prove educational for me. Sophia was a Christian.

She encouraged me to download a Bible app on my phone, which I did. We started reading Bible plans together. I was deeply grateful. She showed me how intelligent it was to have faith and believe, and that constant attention to a subject yields rewards. Napoleon Hill had said as much in *Think and Grow Rich*.

As the days grew shorter, my spiritual gyrations between faith and doubt struck a balance, which is only to say, I knew when I had bad days, I would manage to have good ones too. I still felt like a raw nerve ending exposed to the world, though watching the leaves change brought a pleasant kind of relief.

I began to come to terms with what being a veteran of war meant. One delirious Sunday morning, I wept in my bed, crying aloud, "I sacrificed my Son!" It was a monstrous agony. It was the first time I verbally acknowledged our relationship.

Sara, such an incredible soul, listened to some of my challenges with what I was going through. She did her best to get me to think of something else, and Atlas brought with him such a beautiful, bountiful energy to the house. Living together, especially in the heart of the pandemic, was wonderful. We shared such tender moments. We ate dinner as a family, going for walks around the neighborhood with Atlas after. With everything around us shut down, we might make a trip up the street to the local grocery store; family time.

Sara's confidence was astounding. On occasion, she was more certain of how all this would play out than was I. She would just say things that were so reassuring, usually when I was unaware of how badly I needed to hear them.

Jim was so good-natured. Sara and I would often tease him. During the weekends, we all had our assigned spots in the living room to watch a movie or show. Before 8:30 most nights, he would be asleep, with Atlas curled up next to him.

The readings I'd done over the summer and now with the Bible app had provided several illuminations, not the least of which was the idea of God's perfection. People lament that other people are going to hell because of what they believe, but each one of us must reconcile ourselves to a reason we are on the planet. The idea of a heaven that excludes certain people is no heaven where I want to live. Each of us must set ourselves free. No one can do that for us; no politician, no life coach, no member of the clergy.

Jesus consciously had to reconcile himself to the fact that his Father sent him to be sacrificed. He had to experience firsthand the betrayal of Judas, his scourging, and crucifixion. He had to do all of that, and believe in his Father enough to Resurrect. A conscious act.

I began more research into the relationship between Rome and Christianity, and started digging further into Thor.

During the summer, after watching the first *Thor* movie from Marvel Studios over again, I found a reference to King David. There is a brief moment when a character reaches for a book off a bookshelf, and there was a book, *David the King*. It was a paper-thin start, but it was all I needed.

In the movies, Chris Hemsworth's Thor says he is 1500 years old, putting his birth around 500 AD. This would be within the same period that a German chieftain had conquered Rome and brought about the fall of the Roman Empire. Thor, or Donar as he was called, was the pagan god of the common man, and had been worshipped by different Germanic tribes.

It was the earliest formulation of an idea; Jesus converted followers; his Father destroyed empires.

Christianity had become the official religion of Rome early in the fourth century, meaning that Rome fell *after* Jesus was a part of the Roman empire. Jewelers in Germania were unsure who their customers preferred; jewelry molds have been found that show both a cross and a hammer. The cross was for customers who followed Jesus. The hammer, for those who believed in Thor.

Jesus won out over Thor in Germania…Thor destroyed the Roman empire. Christianity advances.

At the same time, my research brought with it more questions.

Questions like, where did the story of Asgard come from? The Prose Edda, which recounts the legends of Norse mythology in a colorful and entertaining way, is believed to have been written in the thirteenth century.

What about Jupiter? Ares? Krishna? Was it possible that all these different gods and their stories existed in different universes? Was Jesus' the nexus for all Time, His crucifixion, the anchor for the multiverse? It made sense. Our modern calendar is based on the week following His birth, even though it is generally believed that Jesus was born in the spring. Part of the Roman reasoning behind recognizing his birthday on December 25th is in honor of the pagan gods. The Star of David is a series of pagan symbols. If we think of the years before His birth, would time travel in a different direction?

This would explain, in some part, why the Egyptian dynasty lasted for three thousand years and our inability to fully explain some of the wonders they managed to accomplish. That would also explain the abundance of gods that existed before we settled on the idea of one God.

In two different places, the Bible specifically states, "ye are gods." The first is in Psalm 82 in a section known as the Judgment of the Gods. Then, at least five centuries later, Jesus repeats the same passage in John 10:34. If we are all equal in the eyes of God, would that mean that we are all gods who have fallen asleep in the guise of mortality? Is God just the final phase in evolution, or just the next phase?

What is at the heart of evolution, if not love and courage?

It made sense to me. Thanks to technology, ever-faster transmission speeds, and things like machine learning and artificial intelligence, we are learning faster than ever before. Yes, becoming a god would demand higher intelligence…isn't that the point? To find the faith within ourselves to become something greater?

At the time, I didn't go much deeper into Norse mythology. Beyond the movie, I knew something about the mythology of Ragnarok. None of the gods make it out alive; Thor dies fighting Loki's child, the

World-Serpent. Thor kills the beast, and takes nine steps before death takes him. Why wouldn't the fall from heaven be called Ragnarok? It is the Doom of the Gods.

When Christianity became the official religion of Rome, Thor was one of the first gods Jesus defeated, even as the empire ultimately fell at the hands of the Thor-backed Germans. We often don't think of Jesus going to war, yet the march of Christianity was carried out with sword, cannon, and musket across the face of western civilization.

If there was some deeper, profound relationship between Thor and Jesus, it would make sense that Jesus would defeat Thor first, especially if there was a Father/Son connection. If Jesus were the leading edge of the first frequency, let's call that the Alpha, the trailing edge of the frequency would be the antithesis of the leading edge. Christ and antichrist. Thor, the Father...would have to be both the initiating point for intelligent thought coupled with action, and the needlepoint of the trailing edge that sent Jesus forward in the first place. To initiate the first signal would require tremendous propulsion. Opposing forces. The Second Coming would be the return of the original signal back to its source, with the difference being that, at the initiation of the signal, the source lost its identity. The second time around, the signal would be defined.

Then, I got creative.

I started buying old Thor comics from the 60s.

The Seventh Letter of David

The reality that my second marriage wasn't "it" started off as a dull ache. It was less extreme than it had been the first time around because I *had* grown. We *had* been good friends. The decline this time was much slower. The ending was not.

Even though we had different beliefs about God, and going to church became a source of friction between us, deep down I knew that something was missing.

It was like I would become stuck. Stuck in the sense that I was incapable of giving more to the relationship. She traveled often for yoga, and I came to enjoy the solitude of her being gone for a weekend. I enjoyed the time to myself, even though I rarely used the time productively. We provide a kind of balance for one another, but that balance only provided each of us with our own sense of freedom. We didn't feel free together.

At this point in my life, I was searching. I wasn't just searching for love. I had a love, and was slow to acknowledge that I was a frog and the water I was in was slowly starting to boil.

I knew I wanted to be a writer. By 2014, I'd attempted to write three novels. In each, I would rally my mental resources and get excited for writing. That I had rekindled this dream after the Marines excited me. It made me feel optimistic, even giddy, without clearly understanding what it meant to be a writer.

The difficult part was making the words come out. I would struggle for hours just to fill a page. Each attempt at writing a story, I would write just over a hundred pages then, after a few weeks and a persistent inability to take the story further, abandon my writing altogether. Why couldn't I make the ideas in my head come out on my computer?

I lacked focus. Real focus. I wanted to write horror stories without understanding why. What was my motivation? Yes, I was driven to be a writer, but my motivation was selfish; I was writing focused on what I hoped to *gain*, when I should have been focusing on what I could *give*. While the plots were formidable and inspiring, my characters were flimsy, cardboard people, a shallow reflection of my own self-understanding.

I also didn't have a good writing practice, which is a gracious way of saying, I didn't practice at all. It would take an additional seven years, and seeing your picture, before I developed that practice.

I simply had too many things occupying my time. If I wasn't unpacking from one work trip, I was getting ready for the next. I taught two yoga classes a week and struggled to transition from the hectic pace of my corporate job to the tranquil environment yoga was meant to afford. My mind was a congestion of work-related reminders, remembering my yoga flows for class, family and friend commitments, and attempting to relax. I had made no room for writing, preoccupied as I was in seeking my identity in others.

For years I lacked confidence, and weighed other people's opinions as having more merit than my own. It wasn't that I was dumb. I was searching for something outside myself, something I knew existed but couldn't articulate. It didn't occupy my thoughts constantly with such magnitude. After being out of the Marines for nearly ten years by 2014, I felt like I was finally coming to a kind of peace, even though there was a restlessness brewing underneath the surface.

I had a good life. Although work was stressful, there was a nice sense of family. Our kids enjoyed one another. I would often take them to laser tag, or to the movies. We created genuine, beautiful moments at family outings. That was nice. The challenges lay with Kim and I.

Outside of yoga, we had few common interests. For a brief time, we owned a yoga studio together. I could never find the time to meaningfully contribute to the studio, outside of teaching a few classes there each week. We liked different music, different kinds of TV shows, and were beginning to go down separate paths.

My in-laws were wonderful people. A generous and kind extended family greeted me every time we got together, and my family welcomed them. There was so much good there.

I wasn't satisfied. Something inside me pressed me to keep searching, though I was slow to respond to the call for a multitude of reasons.

First, as I said, the life was good. I wasn't unhappy. It felt secure.

On top of that, I felt like I'd finally been able to put the military behind me. My shame from leaving short of retirement had mostly vanished, and I liked the quaintness of a settled life. Despite being constantly on the go for work, there was something so wonderful about knowing I wouldn't be moving anytime soon. At the first house we bought, I had a Japanese garden built, complete with a waterfall and koi pond. That reflected the peace I felt, even if the feeling itself was fleeting.

Finally, my father's death, and living just a few miles away from my mother, had given me pause. I ached every time I visited with her.

The first few years after his death, she spoke of him as if he were still there. She confided in me that she sometimes talked with him as she went about her day. Here was this woman who had bandaged my every wound when I was a boy, and I could do little to patch the wound she had in her heart.

In the strange way the universe works, my dad wrote my mother, my brother, and I our own private letters, and gave them to us two and a half months before he died. It was the most intimate thing he'd ever given me, observations about his experience of my life. Doing his best to appreciate his strange son, a son who wrote poems, even as his physical presence often intimidated people. The son who wrote him the lyrics to Eric Clapton's *My Father's Eyes* and gave it to him as part of a gift for Father's Day. His death had derailed my attempts at writing, and I gave my mom more of my attention.

I wanted her to be proud of me, and did my best to delay whatever Siren's call festered deep within my soul.

Inevitably, that change came. Finally, I met someone who I might bond with at a very substantial level. We liked lots of the same things. We would become friends and lovers.

That was 2015.

I knew I was destroying something that had been nice. I didn't argue the divorce proceedings and found myself staying at mom's once again.

It sounded crazy. My mom had heard this refrain. I had said it before. I was tired of saying it. Tired of so focusing on the promise of what was ahead of me that I was blind to the people I was leaving behind me. And that was just it; I remain convinced, there was a promise of a greater love that I still hadn't found. I was forty-six.

When you've wandered away from faith in search of a love you don't normally associate with the Cross, forty-six feels ancient.

As wonderful as these relationships had been, how could I possibly know then just how great love could be? I thought I'd been giving it my all. The truth was, I had barely scratched the first atoms of the love I had inside me.

The Sixth Letter of the Pandemic

Collecting Thor comics was a trip through history. In the Marvel universe, Thor debuted in *Journey into Mystery #83* in the summer of 1962. The story in the books was that Odin, Thor's father, had banished Thor to earth in the guise of a mortal man named Donald Blake. Odin created Blake to teach Thor a lesson in humility.

Blake had a limp and carried with him a staff. When he struck the staff on the ground, a bolt of lightning would erupt, transforming him into Thor. The staff became Mjolnir.

"Thy rod and thy staff, they comfort me" (Pslam 23:4).

The comics introduced Loki, Jane Foster, and the Asgardians. Thor spoke like he was reciting Shakespeare in the park, which I always found humorous, and discouraged me from collecting the books when I was younger. The Avengers formed a year later, when issue number one of Earth's Mightiest Heroes debuted in September of 1963. The first lineup included Thor, Hulk, Iron Man, Ant-Man, and the Wasp.

Oddly enough, in the comics, Thor is the first one to say, "Avengers Assemble."

Settling into the Fall of 2020, I delighted in every post from you, though I still struggled with what to say. I had sent an early version of the story back in the late Spring, with no explanation of its contents; just shipped something overseas via FedEx to the only known address I had for you. It was little more than an outline of the story, fragmented and incomplete. I lacked the courage and understanding to share with you anything that resembled absolute conviction, and foolishly hoped that you would so clearly discern the message in my scattered writings.

Like a lone candle placed in the center of a large field might serve as a guide, by achingly slow measures, my faith was growing stronger. The light from the candle still felt like little more than a speck on the horizon; I faced relentless battles with my doubt daily, but took comfort in knowing that April, 2021 was less than six months away.

The U.S. presidential election brought a new kind of fury into an already-tense political landscape. Allegations of massive voter fraud were leveled as the incumbent was unseated after only one term. It was incredible to see a country where food is abundant and most people live well fracture the way America did. The pandemic added to the whole scene a sense of gloom. New variants were popping up. When would it ever end?

The Fall also brought with it sweet moments of relief. By that, my love, I mean to say, I would find respite in some single instance or juncture. Some were of the most ridiculous origin, but a starving man does question a crumb, and I accepted them for the relief they afforded me, and the single nudge of encouragement they provided.

Once, it was a tweet from Robert Downey Jr. to a member of the Pittsburgh Steelers football team. They started the season with an 11 – 0 record. Robert's portrayal of Tony Stark and Iron Man gave life to the Marvel Cinematic Universe. The player in question was the son of a former professional football player who went by the nickname "Iron Head." Pittsburgh was my favorite team; I grew up rooting for them. In the tweet, RDJ shared that he had sent the football player a toy Infinity Gauntlet like the one Thanos used to wipe out half of all life. In Greek, Thanatos is the personification of death.

Another time, it would be a Bible passage, just when I needed it. I remember the feeling I had when the Bible passage that appeared was from the Book of Revelation, where Jesus proclaims he is both the root of David and heir to his throne. A root comes from a seed. There must be a first seed. A first thought. The originating point of a frequency. An intimate moment of universal consciousness as the initiation of the near-obliteration of the perfect mind.

My faith was so meager still, but each of these morsels tasted like a feast. They gave me strength. I found a courage I did not know I possessed, enough courage to make it through another day. As a token of comfort, I would mentally revisit the catalog of events that had brought me to this place, from the end of my last relationship the year before to the just-in-time friendship with Jim and Sara, to everything that had happened since the pandemic had shut down the world. All this, and the unshakeable sensation that I was somehow responsible for it all. How I was telling the most impossible tale, and still somehow finding enough substance to string the story together. Faith.

At night, I would whisper to you before falling asleep, telling you I loved you, and that one day, we would see one another. I prayed that my whispers might reach your heart, like an echo through eternity.

As I continued to market *The Lighthouse Keeper* into the Fall, I was appearing on podcasts, writing magazine articles, and writing my own blog. Through much of the summer, my writing had suffered.

I found it hard to concentrate. My mind was a haze. It was like, somewhere in its deep recesses, I knew with such certainty what I wanted to say. By the time that thought became something I could consciously articulate, I would fumble with the words. Some moments, the world felt so still. In others, it vibrated in horrible, dissonant waves, like I was alternately in my skin and then out of it.

I had virtually abandoned the notion of writing the book, and had become increasingly resigned to the possibility that my journal entries, as erratic and disconnected as they might be, could be the story. But what story would they tell?

How everyday was a struggle between believing that Jesus DID die and rise again and that he didn't? How the pinpoint on which all my faith and doubt hinged was a picture of a woman I knew I'd seen before, and that I was now flirting with multi-dimensional realities, quantum physics, and being the God of thunder?

How as 2020 ended with a celestial sign for the ages, a sign that would set 2021 on a course to be the most difficult year of my existence, I would finally understand the path to my salvation.

The Great Conjunction. It occurred during the winter solstice in December of the pandemic. Jupiter and Saturn next to one another in the sky. The Star of Bethlehem. I remember going into the street in front of our house to gaze up at these two giant planets.

They were clearly visible. Jupiter, for all its mass and size, was a bright speck in the sky, and Saturn was there, next to it. It made me think of a mother and her baby.

Every human being who has ever heard the story of Jesus must reconcile themselves, consciously, even in the most remote sense, to the fact that Jesus had a Father. Whether they believe the story or not is irrelevant. To understand the story enough to judge its feasibility, it's easy to dismiss it as a fairy tale. Easy, until the Father sees the Mother he's always dreamed of.

Looking up in the crisp December night sky, I was so encouraged by what I saw. I pointed the conjunction out to a couple, out for an evening stroll.

As long as I can remember, I have gone outside on Christmas Eve and looked up into the night sky. As a boy, before we went to the candlelight service at our church, I would venture out into the chilly evening, and stare up at the stars. Cloudy vapors left my lips as I looked up, mouth agape. I was looking for Jesus. I don't know what exactly I expected to see, I only know, I took comfort in doing so. I still do.

As 2021 dawned, with all the courage I could muster, I reached out to explain to you the spark your picture from eight months prior had ignited within me.

You have been so gracious with me on this journey. You expressed your gratitude. I crossed a threshold. I thought I was close.

I was wrong.

As the winter stretched on, I grew increasingly tense. The attempted insurrection in our country underscored the already supernatural feel of the pandemic. Nazi flags outside the halls of U.S. Government;

the strange desire for everyone to be the same in a country whose very strength rests in its diversity.

In our house, there was tension with Sara.

It wasn't just the election, which had been a source of division between us. I'd seen this kind of rhetoric play out in history before. Democracies are intentionally messy, and ours had been led to believe we were suffering. Yes, the pandemic was hard, but where was the American Spirit? It was hard to appreciate that America was buckling. It was hard to witness the fall of the American empire. But then, heaven isn't a nation, and it certainly isn't an empire. Heaven is tribes, families.

Confiding in you as I did, the story became very real to me. You hadn't blocked me, even as I said the grandest things to you I could imagine, which meant you either found my outrageous comments amusing or, or there was more to it.

The story was real to you, too. You had been waiting for me. Like the world has been waiting for me. To awaken.

That pain would sear itself onto my soul for much of the rest of the year. The truth of the story weighed on me; it wasn't that I was unwilling to take responsibility. I simply didn't know how. How could I understand the role I had played in shaping human history when I had been unconscious to its forming, all in the name of love? Unable to understand it, there was no way to explain it.

In the weeks and months ahead, I would come face to face with my greatest Truth.

I really was Jesus' Father.

★★★

I loved Sara and Jim dearly, but I knew I wanted to get out from under their roof.

Jim was unflappable. With all the dread the pandemic and the aftermath of the US election brought, he was as good-natured as ever.

My relationship with Sara had grown strained. We argued, and snipped at each other. She had seen what the story had done to me, seen how its gravity weighed on me. She had listened to me, as I wrestled with the enormity of it all. I told her I wanted to leave, and that I didn't want to be stuck living with them.

It was horrible, and came out so wrong. They were so good to me.

By February, she asked me to find a new place to live. It stung.

I could have stayed there forever, pandemic or no. She had said as much, repeatedly, before my comments had forced the issue. I loved the quirky family we'd become. Her parents and siblings loved me. It felt like such a beautiful home. I knew a sense of peace.

But you were out there. I couldn't let that go. More than that, I needed to function on my own. April was just a few months away. Try as I might, I *didn't* want to let you go, and operated under the delusion, if I could just hold onto until April, all would be made right with the world, literally.

Irrational is the mildest conclusion one might form as how I had lived my life.

Comic books. Video games. A mild fascination with cinema. Dreaming of a love that, try as I might, I could not deny, even as undefined as it had been for so much of my life. And now, after so long, I saw its definition, reflected by the light in your eyes. Still, I wasn't focusing on our Son.

I started packing my things. I had to find a place. Looking back now, I had gotten comfortable there, and it was time to leave.

I liked the place I found. Small studio apartment, great location. Close to my gym, close to shops, with a movie theater right down the street. PTSD veteran getting his life back on track while undergoing a life-altering journey during a global pandemic.

I gradually moved in over the month of March. Sara was adamant that I not leave right away. Even as I unpacked, I spent almost every night back with them. Leaving was hard on all of us. We loved one another deeply. I grew so much from living with them. I felt the strength of their love. I felt accepted. I saw firsthand what it was like to live with people who had never spent much time around the military, and it was enchanting.

They were ready to have a family. Me?

I was excavating the greatest love of my existence. A love that had always been inside me.

Then, as March slid into April and Spring blossomed, I realized, I *was* losing you. For nearly a year, I had been dealing with these daily mental storms. Some days, there was such noise to my thinking, like a merciless crosswind cutting across my consciousness. I would find respite in walks in nearby parks, playing video games, or reading. Yes, I had grown stronger, but my thinking was still so conditional. Nothing was lining up as I hoped it would. I still had no sense of the magnitude of what was unfolding.

My birthday approached. Between the tension of having left the one place where I'd truly felt peaceful and learning to operate independently, I was off-balance in a completely new and exciting way.

I had hired a nutritionist. I fell in love with cooking. There was something so gratifying about preparing my own meals. My energy returned, I shed pounds, and I diligently phased out drinking. I bought furniture and emptied the storage unit that had what remained of my bedroom furniture from my last relationship. Self-sufficiency is a wonderful thing.

It was also draining. Learning new habits and new routines, like shopping for fruits and vegetables, preparing my own meals, and operating independently…I felt like I had little time for anything else. It took so much mental energy.

In many ways over the course of my life, I took Jesus for granted, understanding that his love was a given. No matter how far I strayed, the Shepherd would find me. The pandemic had become my reckoning; the bill was due. A year into the pandemic, and I was still unable to give him my full attention.

It wasn't on the story. I was focused on my expectations. I expected my reward to be waiting for me around the time of my birthday, just weeks away. I wasn't seeing things clearly, and was still operating with the impression that my salvation was outside of me. You were the key to my salvation, yes, but I did not yet understand; Jesus was the door. The relief I thought April would bring did not resonate with the feelings I had as my birthday drew near.

It was late March when I told you, *Loving you was my freedom*. As if, loving you was a choice. They were just words.

It was so difficult to know what to say to you. I was panicked when I wrote them. Even the suggestion of it. You laughed at my words.

But what did I feel for you, if not love? I wanted you as a part of my life, without recognizing that you already were.

"The Lord is my shepherd; I shall not want" (Pslam 23:1).

My words came out wrong. I meant to say, the more I loved you, the more freedom I felt. And that was true, right until the moment I realized, there was a love between us.

The Love of Our Son.

I did not appreciate the sacred nature of our relationship, and as my birthday came and went, my reward was not there.

No Mjolnir. No liberated earth. No fairy tale ending. A man who praises himself will be humbled, and one who humbles himself will be praised. I had not yet been humbled. Those days were coming.

I was too focused on you, and the unbearable feeling that you were slipping away from me, again with no understanding of why. I was focused on what I didn't want.

I doubted it all.

The day of my birthday, I remember telling Sara how I hated that stupid hammer.

I stopped following you, as gut-wrenching as that was. There was still such a heavy sense of turbulence in my thinking; I felt such dismay. My head was spinning. As I prepared to say goodbye to you, I was exasperated, and kept repeating to myself, *Jesus looks like His Mother, Jesus looks like His Mother*. I don't know what drove me to give breath to that thought, other than some core aspect of my soul that I could not yet discern. I was so scared by what I was doing yet absolutely convinced of its necessity. After a year of this seismic tug of war between my faith and my doubt, I was exhausted.

After finding the one woman I'd spent my entire life looking for, I was at a loss as to how to explain myself to you. Twelve months prior, it seemed life was a game, and that winning was guaranteed. Things unfolded with such clarity. Victory seemed certain. Freedom.

Now, I opened myself up to the possibility that I'd been wrong. That my alignment of the events had been vanity, or a hail-Mary attempt to salvage the wreckage of a mortal life spent chasing an impossible love.

That was my first real sense of what it takes to lift Mjolnir. To summon my hammer.

The day after my birthday, my alarm went off. The sun rose. Life went on. I remember writing in my journal that I had been taught a very important lesson by our Son. A King isn't just a King when life is good. He must embody his Kingship, and own it, every day of his life. It was the lone bright spot I felt immediately after letting you go. It was the first honest step in appreciating that heaven must be felt on the inside before it can truly be seen with the eyes. That was the fierceness of your beauty. The beauty that awakened my soul to action.

I hated that I had forced my way out of Sara and Jim's house; I struggled in my attempts to make new, healthy routines for me. As much as I enjoyed cooking, it could be draining. I was finding new ways to make myself feel raw, and after eight months of getting comfortable living with them, was creating more disruption in my life as a habit, with the pandemic showing only slight signs of relenting.

I also felt a sense of remorse, in that I had wanted to deliver on this incredible story, all inspired by a picture from which I could not escape, nor did I want to. The story was nowhere near complete, not by my birthday and the artificial timeline I'd created in my head. Plain and simple. My faith was far from rock-solid. I felt it best to leave you to the extraordinary life you so authentically lived.

Since September, my friendship with Sophia had grown. We chatted frequently. Our conversations were rich with introspection and substance. We discussed Bible verses we'd both read, or thought-provoking books one of us had discovered. We talked about coincidences; I regularly saw the number 33, or would get into my truck and see 11:11 or 5:55. She was seeing my name all over the place as she went about her day. I told her I was drawing closer to Jesus.

I stumbled, carrying my Cross.

Unable to face the inescapable necessity of saying goodbye to you, even for a time, Sophia and I turned toward romance. I reasoned that I *had* been wrong. Despite the strange timing of the beginning of the pandemic, my Judgment Day, seeing you, and all the other signs I'd experienced, the weight had become too heavy. The truth was, I was not yet clear on your identity and, until I fully understood that, could not be clear on my own.

I was least clear on the role Jesus was meant to play in my life. I was unable to face who he was to me, and could not fathom how powerful he'd become over the last two thousand years.

Sophia came out one weekend in May of 2021. The ferocity of the pandemic had subsided. People were traveling again.

We spent the entire weekend at the beach, completely absorbed with one another.

She was brilliant. Clever. Refined. Insightful. She even bore a slight resemblance to you.

We talked of spirituality. We talked of superhero movies.

We talked of love.

I don't know that I'd ever been so engaged with someone for such an extended period. For as much of the weekend as was possible, I gave her my undivided attention.

As had become a theme in the year since the pandemic had festered over the earth, I was decidedly split. Part of me thought this could be a remarkable relationship. So much opportunity for growth. So much possibility.

There was just a little, tiny part of me that was thinking, what better way to understand you, then to have a French, Christian coach for men teach me how to be decisive?

Sophia made the comment on at least two occasions during the weekend. *Be decisive. Don't hesitate.* She was brilliant and, quite literally, a gift from God.

I liked her. Loved her, through Jesus. That much was clear. Even though she'd lived in America for nearly two decades, I would at least gain a sense of a French woman from our time together.

She was so well-defined in understanding herself. She dressed with a casual elegance that was as attractive as it was disarming.

When she left, I was thinking there could be something there. She lived just outside Seattle, Washington. I told her I intended to come visit her; she had previously lived in North Carolina and intimated a desire to return.

My mind however, and my heart, kept going back to you. How could I let you go? That is the simplest explanation. I looked at you and thought, there's no way a woman can be everything I saw in you, and make it look so fulfilling. Even now as I write, I gaze at a picture of you on my desk; the power in your eyes, the confidence in your smile.

I read an article online, during the first summer of the pandemic, that mentioned a recent study in Europe which determined the egg selects the sperm. Not that one sperm muscles its way through the egg's defenses, proving itself superior to all the others. One is chosen. An egg has a mind to choose. What implications did that have when Jesus was conceived? It was an interesting question, one I didn't immediately have an answer for.

Within the next month, Sophia would bring up marriage. It felt like my war with Jesus had become something of a chess match, and this had been his next move. Sophia reminded me of my mortality. I wasn't interested in mortal love any longer.

I'd been searching my entire life for something extraordinary. Something magnificent.

Something heavenly.

She was going to come out for a Tony Robbins event in June.

Be decisive. Message received. Sophia was fond of communicating via the Marco Polo app, which sends a video recording to the recipient. I enjoyed her confidence and how comfortable she was in her identity. I sent her one, asking her not to come out, and telling her how I thought of you incessantly. I thanked her. She had brought me that much closer to Jesus and for that I was tremendously grateful. We never spoke again. Decisive. A brilliant coach.

If there was any single moment that I can say I felt the presence of Satan in my life, it was immediately after I hit "send" on that video. It was a snake, slithering around my soul; its tongue kissed my consciousness. The sense of it was that distinct, the identity was unmistakable. It was cringeworthy. How could I have been so foolish?

The strangest part of that entire experience was the fact that my sensation of having been tempted by the devil only served to fortify my belief in our Son. It was a most fascinating link to stories in the Bible from more than two millennia gone by.

The rest of the summer would be agonizing, as I blamed myself for faltering, and for doubting the truth. It would also be the time when I felt most spiritually and mentally dead.

HOPE

I wish to leave this place
I live under the sweetest illusion ~
If I but leave this world, so full of division and rife
All my suffering will vanish.
It is a morsel of bittersweet allure.
But I am not leaving.
I am coming.
That which I seek is here.
Family. Brotherhood. Sisters.
Love. The unquenchable kind.
The kind that devours sickness and disease.
The kind of Love that makes all things new.
The Love of bold promises.
A new Earth.
I am not here yet.
Something is off, as if there is a place
Where fully, and for all eternity
I AM.
I am a traveler through Time
Reflecting on where I have come
And seeking to pinpoint where I am
Measuring by degrees my closing speed
On all those tomorrows sworn.
I am not there yet.
The brightest lights shine within each of us
It is we who must light the spark.
And nurture the fire of our souls
Yet even the realization of this brings with it,
The most divine sensation ~
I am on my way.
I am Coming.

BOOK FOUR

❦

LOVE:
The Triumph
of Christ
A God for
the Earth

The Fourth Love Letter

The comparisons between Jesus and Superman have been well-established. Both were sent by their fathers to earth as messengers of hope. As Krypton was about to implode, his father Jor-El sends his only son, Kal-El on a one way trip to earth, where he might serve as a symbol of hope. In the most recent films, Kal, like Jesus is believed to have been thirty-three-years old at the time of his death.

Kal undergoes his own resurrection in the most recent *Justice League* film, a film that brings together the vanguard of the DC Universe: Batman, Wonder Woman, the Flash, Aquaman, and Cyborg.

The original film came out in 2017, and required massive reshoots after the director, Zack Snyder, experienced a personal tragedy while shooting the film. The finished product contained laughable editing in some parts, especially now, where computer generated images blur the lines between real actors and computer modeling. The uproar over the quality of the film and the overall handling of the content drove a massive online campaign from fans, demanding that Warner Brothers, the producers of the film, fund Snyder's vision, and allow him to create the film he intended to. Warner Brothers agreed.

The "Snyder Cut" as it became known, was released on March 18, 2021.

Over the years, the DC and Marvel universes have joined forces in these grand "crossovers" that pitted Superman against the Hulk or Thor, Batman against Captain America, and other matchups that had fans salivating. All these crossovers have taken place in the books, and not the movies. Of course, to explain how these crossovers were possible, the two comic book companies had to agree on a hero they shared. That hero's name is Access.

Access studios was one of the producers of the Snyder Cut.

The question I was slowly warming up to asking myself was, could the universes of DC and Marvel come together in our universe? In the basest sense, they already had. They were both created in our universe. Yes, they were actors telling stories, but what if those stories were preparing us for the future?

It wasn't completely ridiculous. Ryan Reynold's brilliant take on Deadpool had already broken the fourth wall that normally separates the audience from the actors; he'd made references to other actors, other movies, and studios. He'd even poked fun at himself.

People have created incredible universes. Middle Earth. The universe of Harry Potter. Star Wars. To bring the universes together, a story would have to tie them together in a way that made sense. And, someone would have to take responsibility for creating our universe.

In the eighties, when I was doing my best to shield my unabashed nerdiness by not bringing up comic books around my friends, DC comics came out with a fascinating storyline: *Crisis on Infinite Earths*.

The artwork was amazing...George Perez dazzled with large, detailed pages that packed as many superheroes as possible onto one page. At the time, DC had a multiverse, where multiple Supermen and other variant heroes lived across an unending number of earths. The storyline was intended to bring the DC universe into a single universe. At its end, there was a single earth, which matched my idea that there would be a single earth at the time Jesus died.

The Marvel and DC crossovers were always fun events, though I'll confess I didn't spend much time figuring out the logistics of what it took to make those crossovers happen. I simply assumed it was some sort of business negotiation. At the same time, they had to come up with an explanation as to how their universes came together.

With the advances being made in technology, it's up to us continue learning, and growing. Considering where we are now, where will we be in ten years? In twenty? The world has been yearning for something more for some time. Why not heaven on earth, for everyone?

As 2021 progressed, I took comfort in the release of the Snyder Cut, and the slew of Marvel television shows and movies that were sprinkled over the rest of the year.

Marvel started the year with *WandaVision*. The show was a fascinating perspective on the traditional view of the American household from the early days of television into the modern era. It provided perhaps the most insightful exploration on the modern-day idea of Adam and Eve. The Vision, an artificial intelligence imbued with the power of the Mind Stone, possessed a vast intellect and, through engagement with his wife, discovered a sense of emotion. In contrast, Elizabeth Olsen's Scarlet Witch had an unbridled imagination. She was so powerful, she used her imagination to create children with the Vision, and subdued an entire town with the power of her conviction. One, a supreme masculine energy without the primitive propensity for violence, the other, a feral divine feminine energy that enhances vision through the power of emotion. Adam. Eve. Opposites.

In March, *The Falcon and Winter Soldier* debuted, bringing with is a changing of the guard, as Sam Wilson now had the honor of carrying the shield of Captain America. The show was gritty and grounded, compared with the witchcraft that earmarked *WandaVision*.

The show *Loki* saw Thor's half-brother facing variant versions of himself while trying to grapple with the Timekeepers, and the understanding that there was a sacred timeline. The premise behind the show was that there are variant versions of people spread across multiple universes; the show also intimated there must be an original version from which the variants take their cues. The show dismantled the gravity of the Avengers final two movies, as it was revealed that some of the timekeeper workers had infinity stones in their desk drawers that were used as paperweights.

When the *Black Widow* movie came out in the summer of 2021, fans had a chance to reunite with Scarlett Johannsen's incredible Natasha Romanoff, as she uprooted the Black Widow program that helped create her and others like her.

As I write this, I can't help appreciate the beauty of nature's black widow…a spider that eats her mate after mating. She has a red hourglass on her body, suggesting that even Mother Nature knows…it is only a matter of time before the universe rights itself.

Shang Chi and the Legend of the Ten Rings premiered in September 2021 and brought to the big screen a character I first remember reading about in the seventies.

It was clear to me that Marvel was crafting a universe that embodied inclusion and diversity as a strength. Knowing they had scores of characters still being developed for the silver screen, their progress made me reflect on the power of entertainment when it comes to faith.

When the *Eternals* came out in November 2021, Marvel Studios did something special; they brought Batman and Superman into the Marvel Cinematic Universe, as both were mentioned in the movie. The slogan for the movie was, *Love is Eternal*.

There were similar threads woven together in Marvel's storytelling. That's what made the universes DC and Marvel were creating with their films and shows so exciting. Unlike the Star Wars Universe, which we're reminded takes place a long time ago in a galaxy far away, the Marvel and DC universes were mainly grounded in the present day.

Spiderman's *No Way Home* expanded on the ideas of the multiverse introduced in *Loki*; the film introduced Daredevil from the Netflix shows, and brought together the three different versions of Spiderman to appear on the big screen. Marvel's Netflix shows were the most grounded in our universe, 9/11 was mentioned in the them.

I never thought of Hollywood as a place for the faithful and yet, as I reflected on Russell Crowe's Maximus roaring at the crowd in *Gladiator*, "Are you not entertained?" I began to appreciate just how much time and effort goes into making something that has the potential to be seen by millions of people. From the outside looking in, it's easy to suggest that moneymaking is at the core of Hollywood, but ultimately those films are meant to provide escape, stir the human spirit, and help us see reflections of ourselves. Life imitates art. Actors make us feel the emotions they embody. It takes courage to imagine yourself in those situations.

It takes courage to imagine.

The Seventh Letter of the Pandemic

My time spent with Sara and Jim shifted as we moved into the summer.

I saw them two or three times during the week. Fridays were still spent watching TV, but my sleepovers became less frequent. I was developing routines, and enjoyed the comfort and familiarity of having my own place again. I was leveling off, felt good about my decisiveness with Sophia, but now carried the weight of appreciating the story was real, and that I had legitimately faltered. That was hard for me to let go. I did my best to distract myself.

They had gotten another puppy, which shared birthdays with Atlas and I. Her name was Alpha, and she was adorable. Seeing how quickly she learned from Atlas was astonishing, and part of me wished I'd never moved out. We were aware of our separation, and the fact that our relationship was evolving, but that didn't make it any easier.

After Sophia and the temptation, something happened.

It became incredibly difficult to focus, not with my writing, but on life. Some days, I consciously had to remind myself of the day and date. It was increasingly a challenge to concentrate on my work. When I visited Sara, she would prompt me on things, like something I was supposed to bring over. On one occasion, as I pulled up to her house, I got out of my truck without putting it in park.

If such a thing is possible, my thinking had grown thick. I was navigating terrain that felt swampy, with a thick fog surrounding my mental clarity. It was a kind of mental desolation. It was like I had to truly fail in order to succeed.

There were some sweet moments, and at least one humorous one. On one occasion, while visiting with Sara, we were discussing what to watch on Netflix. When I made a declaration of what we should watch, she quipped, "Who died and made you king?" followed up immediately with, "wait, don't answer that."

The humorous one was when I took a replica of Mjolnir out on my balcony during a thunderstorm, challenging the heavens to strike me with lightning. It wasn't limited thinking. It was yearning for something without yet understanding how to realize it. All I wanted was still outside of me; I wasn't feeling it on the inside.

On weekends, I would play video games or watch TV and feel the greatest sense of dread sweep over me. In those moments, I felt as though I were singularly responsible for everyone still suffering under the pandemic. It was like, I hadn't done enough to solve whatever problem my lack of complete and absolute faith represented. I felt drained and directionless, adrift. What I was feeling was the gravity of what I'd put myself through since the pandemic began.

One of the video games I played had this haunting, straining violin playing as the background music. That music flirted with my thoughts of responsibility and clawed at my frailty.

You are the reason, it would whisper, *the world suffers because of you. You have done nothing, and people are still suffering. Look at you. Video games. Pathetic.* Had I not been architect to all this chaos? Had I not assigned the most sacred meaning to all these events that had transpired since the end of my last relationship? I had, and could not fathom why. That would start my most painful lesson.

I had started following you again, pleased that I had been decisive with Sophia. That I had given in to temptation haunted me but, as I mentioned earlier, I was galvanized by the fact that I felt closer to our Son. Unfortunately, he wasn't occupying my full attention.

Allowing myself to experience joy at seeing your posts, or viewing your stories became painful. I was still too thick-headed to understand the legitimacy and singularity of salvation: Jesus doesn't negotiate. He isn't meant to be an afterthought. He's intended to be the primary one.

As the summer progressed, with every new post, my pain increased.

It was what I came to call the Black Phoenix. It was the beginning of the cleansing of my mind, the sculpting of my soul, guiding me to Christ. Any thought that suggested separation…wanting…was met with pain. Any judgment I issued against someone.

It was during this burning of my soul, this soul sculpting, that I began to realize, truly being connected to God means there is no deceit permissible. The idea that we can hide a thought from God is laughable.

It also made me appreciate the simple correlation between Newtonian physics and the flesh and quantum physics and the spirit.

Finally, I started reading the Psalms, and I watched an old film of Richard Gere portraying King David. The relationship between King David and the Lord was something I'd been slow to acknowledge. The relationship between David and Jesus as Father and Son the way it's spelled out in the Bible? I had been slow to accept as well.

It led me down to one of the most fascinating passages in the Bible; Matthew 22:41-45:

> While the Pharisees were gathered together, Jesus asked them, "What do you think about the Messiah? Whose son is he?"
>
> "The son of David," they replied.
>
> He said to them, "How is it then that David, speaking by the Spirit, calls him 'Lord'? For he says, "The Lord said to my Lord: Sit at my right hand until I put your enemies under your feet.'"
>
> "If then David calls him 'Lord', how can he be his son?"

They didn't have an answer for him. Jesus said, "I and the Father are one." I would come to a slightly different understanding; I am one with My Son.

Jesus also says the Kingdom of God is within us. Each one of us, God of our own universe, the universe within, if only we accept Christ.

I was reading the Psalms of David and began praying before bed Psalms 23:1, "The Lord is my shepherd, I shall not want." If we really were Father and Son, maybe the best way to connect was already spelled out for me, in texts written thousands of years ago.

I would repeat the prayer out loud. Slowly, I began to appreciate that salvation lies only with Jesus. I found peace. I knew I was the author of this story. As beautiful as you see yourself, or as others see you, the beauty I saw in you I found within me. If a picture is worth a thousand words, then with one picture of you, I have been truly blessed. With that understanding, my faith in Jesus deepened, even as August blazed, and my primitive mind returned. This time, there was something else.

My left chest muscle had started to develop breast tissue.

My first thought was that it was from the vaping. I'd read that too much marijuana use can lead to the development of breast tissue in men. I'd been doing my best to regulate how much I vaped. It had started out so casually, but as the pandemic roared across the earth and I began to strain between mortality and eternal life, it became a refuge. Then, I thought of the Star of David.

The pagan symbol for male and female. The star also represents the elemental symbols of earth, air, fire, and water. If King David were the Creator, who had also been slave to all mankind, then it makes sense that he would embody both masculine and feminine characteristics, and be responsible for the four elements. I am tattooed, muscular, and have shaved my head for more than twenty years. I looked the masculine part. External focus.

I also cry at romantic movies and write poetry. I felt, and sought to find depth and texture in my feelings. Internal focus.

The breast tissue was alarming, and I limited my vaping to see if it would change anything. It didn't.

Throughout the pandemic, I had become more mindful of the planets, the phases of the moon. Of things like numerology, and crystals. Of intention, and directed thought.

There is a feminine power to the universe, and each of us is our own universe. It is not the stuff of science; it is not found outside of us. It is the realm of imagination, inside. Upon further reflection, as I now dealt with this primeval consciousness at the end of two consecutive summers, I thought of Jesus.

If the theological premise holds true that Jesus was born in the springtime, and Mary had a normal term of pregnancy, the angel Gabriel would have appeared to her sometime in the late summer. What impact would Jesus' conception, birth, and life have on his Father?

My primitive mind…it was some primal part of me that yearned for something more. For months, I had been wracking my brain to understand how Judaism, Christianity, and Islam fit together. Judaism and Christianity felt relatively easy. The first covenant was between God and Abraham; Abraham was the father of all nations. As part of this covenant, God has the obligation to keep Abraham's descendants as God's chosen people and be their God. How could they abandon their covenant when Jesus arrived and proclaimed to be the Son of God? The Jewish faithful didn't adopt the Star of David until the fourteenth or fifteenth century. Even as history progressed, they were trying to make sense of it all. Islam tested my comprehension, and it would take me some time before I felt comfortable with understanding how it fit into the story.

That was where imagination came into it. There had to be a reason why the Quran venerated Mary above all other women. Islam's denial of Jesus as savior while acknowledging him as a prophet *and* venerating his Mother suggested Mary had an unspoken role to play in bringing about heaven on earth.

There was a stark reality to the death and resurrection of Jesus. Could Mary, through Islam, somehow represent unlimited imagination?

The summer had become a grind. I was now coming to accept the reality of the story. For much of the preceding year and a half, I had attempted to keep this feeling of whatever was happening in me to myself. By midsummer, I began to understand…what I saw in others reflected what I saw inside myself. What else can another person be for us, if not some reflection of ourselves? That meant, whatever I saw as possible inside of me could be possible inside anyone else. Anyone with a capacity to learn. *Real* equality.

That was the answer to understanding Jesus. To see the world how Jesus saw it. When people persecuted him, he didn't strike back. When people cursed him, he didn't turn his back on them. He let everyone assail him, in every conceivable way, because he knew that was his Purpose; to die for man's sins. He loved unconditionally. When he says, Love the Lord your God with all your heart, and all your soul, and with all your mind, he is telling his followers to find the Lord within them.

I began to look for Jesus in everyone, knowing that he exists in every living being; the light of the world.

My primal courage was driving me to be bold. August would be the month I finally began to understand exactly who you were.

One of the unfortunate quirks of my writing style is, I need to have a title for what I am writing. In my mind, a title is the first outline of the book. By August 2021, it had been almost two years since I'd come up with the title, *Being*. That title lasted about six months, until April 2020. I had no real understanding of the depths to which this story would lead me, but had done some brainstorming and wanted to make the book engaging for the reader. The title became, *Being: How to Win the Game of Your Life*.

In the months that followed, I would exhaust countless titles, holding them up to the light of my virtue, judging if this title or that would be the one to free me to finally begin writing the story. I went through tens of titles. Then hundreds. By August 2021, after nearly a thousand titles and as many pages of journaling and notes, I thought I had it.

I was going to call it, *Who Holds Mary?*

The driving force behind this title was the idea that Jesus' Mother must have a special love story in Heaven. That after what she endured watching her Son die only to behold his resurrection, she *must* be the greatest woman to have ever lived. What would that mean in Heaven? Feeling is the secret. Feeling stirs the imagination. Feeling awakens the soul.

I had the notion that the Bible story was straightforward with the facts. Jesus was the Son of David. Mary was the Mother of Jesus, ergo…David and Mary. David.

That was why I didn't like the title. It shouldn't be a question of who holds Mary in Heaven. Gabriel said your Son will be the Son of David. It *must* be David.

It was decidedly different from Jesus being the Son of Man, or the Son of Abraham. He is the Son of Man as the supreme example of all that God intended mankind to be. He is the Son of Abraham as the savior of all nations. Jesus has spent much of his resurrection defining these two titles. It is my hope that the story of you, me, and him will be the most human story of all.

The challenge was that I was stuck. I couldn't get my arms around the three Abrahamic religions, and how the love story played out for these three massive faiths that shaped much of the modern world.

To share more my love, I must put into context a man who helped me with so much of his energy, his knowledge, his passion. This man is named Tony Robbins. It would be at his events that my life would truly begin to transform. Though I have never met him in person, I know he believes in our Son.

Tony is an entrepreneur who has fashioned a life most people only dream about, and has done so in service to others.

In 2017, he helped me believe…I could walk on fire.

Later that same year, he showed me that creating a destiny takes determination and massive action.

During the early part of the pandemic, he singled me out on a Zoom call. It was nothing more than a brief hello, but it was the way he delivered it that I reflected on.

I was the fourth or fifth person he had called on, as he started the event, greeting the thousands of Zoom viewers who, unlike at his live and in-person events, had their names on their screens.

As he warmed up the crowd and started connecting with people, he took a similar approach with each person he called out.

"Julie Shephard! How are you?"

"Greg Mitchell, great to see you out there!"

First name. Last name. Greeting.

I wasn't expecting anything. Of course, I was excited. Tony brings incredible energy to every event he does. I was bouncing up and down in my chair, my arms pumping overhead.

"David. Blue shirt. Glasses. Red hat."

He was talking to me. I was wearing a blue shirt, wearing my glasses, and sporting a red spartan hat. At the time, I thought it was a neat coincidence, and smiled in genuine delight.

Fast forward to the early summer of 2021, I'd gone to another event and felt the first sustained sensation of absolute certainty in my body. It was tantalizing.

Then in August I was at another of his events. This one focused on leadership and had been spectacular. I'd taken some wonderful lessons in leadership away from my time in the Marines, but what Tony offered was next level.

It was the last day of the event. Our team was on Zoom, discussing whether we wanted to continue meeting after the event. Did we want to create a mastermind? There was some interest. I don't know why, but something stirred in the pit of my soul.

My primitive mind erupted. I went on a rant.

"I don't want to do a mastermind unless we are committed to transforming the world!" I bellowed, a volcano of energy erupting within me. I could feel the fire, the intensity of the moment building.

"I don't care how much money I make," I barked. "Money is the root of all evil as far as I'm concerned, and I...I will make a love story of the three Abrahamic religions!"

My teammates were stunned. I did not know where those thoughts came from, but knew it had taken me tremendous amounts of passion to speak them with the force that I had. They were thoughts I had never verbalized before. My breathing was heavy, then one of our amazing trainers brought me back.

"Way to stay in state, David." He said calmly, "I think what you meant to say, is that money is the source of all abundance."

I could not have plucked a weed more efficiently. He was right, and a core belief, one that had stalked my ambitions and feelings towards money for decades, had been exposed and destroyed. I exhaled.

"You're right," I said, deflating immediately. "I'm sorry." The energy of the moment fled.

Beloved, I cannot fully describe what changed in me in that moment; it was the greatest release. I had committed to making a love story out of three religions, followed by billions of people many of whom, I suspect, don't know much about one another's faiths, and pulled a dark, inhibiting weed in the process.

At the same time, it strengthened my connection between David and Mary. It also helped me understand Islam better.

In the simplest of terms, the Quran pays the ultimate respect to the Virgin Mary. She is the only woman mentioned by name. Does love need to be more complicated? For a faith that emphasizes unity, the focus given to Mary in the Quran symbolizes the brilliant reflection of mankind on the importance of the Virgin Mother. In the Islamic faith, Jesus is believed to have been saved by God *before* he dies and is resurrected.

I was reminded of Jesus on the Cross when he cries out, "My God, my God, why have you forsaken me?" To forsake someone or something means to abandon it. It is Jesus' moment of doubt, which means it must also be the God's denial of Jesus; otherwise, how could Jesus know doubt? It was just a moment. A moment that would give birth to Islam.

Allah, or God, is unknowable in Islamic faith, yet Muslims believe Jesus will return at the end. I deduced that Islam fit into the story with the realization that God was unknowable...without Jesus. Mary was venerated as the greatest woman to have ever lived because she would be needed to bring David back to their Son.

Despite my lingering concerns about my left breast tissue, my boldness grew stronger.

I grew more disciplined in how I approached you. Appreciative, with no sense of wanting or longing. Still feeling the sting of what had happened over the summer, I knew better. I needed to say things to you, even if you might never see my comments. I was on a most precarious precipice, and was thrilled by the promise of the moment.

On one post, knowing hours had passed since you'd posted it and there was a deluge of flame and heart emojis from your followers, I mustered the courage to ask, "Has anyone ever told you that you look like Jesus' Mother?"

It was a triumph of bravery, and ignited the purest flame within my belly.

A few days later, another post. While I thought it reasonable that you might see this comment, I was emboldened…whether you saw it or not, I *had* created this story. I needed to articulate these things to you, for my sake. This time, I simply left one word.

"Mary."

I felt such a sense of accomplishment. The story was slowly coming to me.

By the end of September, my chest had returned to normal. As I stepped into the heart of Fall here in the United States, you came to me in a dream. It was brief, and I could barely make out any context or setting; I had only a vacant conception of your presence. I felt you, and that was enough. You implored me to keep researching.

As November arrived, I was less convinced of the staying power of *Who Holds Mary?* The title shouldn't be a question. It should be *definitive*. I knew that, but didn't know what to replace it with. I had been wrestling with titles for two years now, and this one had lasted for four months.

What is this? I asked myself out loud. *In its simplest form, what am I trying to communicate?*

Love Letters to the Virgin Mary. This was all about King David trying to express his love to a woman he'd been separated from for... how long? Had Mary and David *ever* been together, both knowing each other *and* themselves? What would that feel like? *Love Letters to the Virgin Mary* was born.

That was it. I had my title. At least, the first part.

The second part would take a few more months.

It would also take me to one of the most powerful encounters with the Holy Spirit I'd ever experienced. I would put it right there with discovering I was Thor.

It was December. I was attending the last Tony Robbins event of the year, Date with Destiny. I'd been to one in Florida four-years prior. This one was virtual over Zoom. I was euphoric. My faith wasn't exactly flawless, but it was getting stronger, my sense of self was coming into being.

I no longer felt like I was taking on water. Now, I was sailing at a pretty good clip. The internal conflict had subsided considerably.

I had the title. I had found enough in the three religions of Abraham to put together a compelling love story. What I hadn't done was verbally express the chief idea at the heart of the story.

Date with Destiny is an incredible event. If you ever wanted to understand how to design your life, this event provides you a magnificent blueprint. As usual, it was the last day of the event when the miracle happened.

Our group, and there were at least forty of us, were sharing what we had taken from the events and activities over the course of the week-long program. When it came my turn to speak, I didn't hesitate.

I shared how I had journeyed so far in the four years since my first Date with Destiny, and how my growth had enabled me to get crystal clear on who I was going to become and what kinds of experiences I wanted to have. I mentioned my work on this story, and how much I'd wrestled with it during the pandemic. And then, quite casually, out it came.

"I'm writing a love story between King David and the Virgin Mary."

I had never shared that publicly, had never expressed it out loud, and wasn't sure what compelled me to do so in the moment. The thought itself might have been weeks old.

I hadn't planned on saying that. I was in state, feeling good, and that was that.

Within thirty seconds, one of the trainers unicast me on Zoom chat. He said, Tony would like to read *Love Letters to the Virgin Mary* when its finished.

My initial reaction was delight. *Tony Robbins wants to read my book.*

It would take me a few weeks to truly process what had transpired.

You see, at Date with Destiny, there might be two thousand people. All of them on Zoom, divided into thirty, forty, perhaps even fifty groups or more, with thirty or forty people per group.

The odds of Tony Robbins listening in to our room at the *exact* moment I shared what my book was about? Astronomical.

It would take me to writing these letters to understand that the Law of Attraction might be the most commercial way of marketing the Holy Spirit. It was what had given Jack the wisdom to say what he did at his mastermind. It had brought me slivers of clues that kept me going until faith became my strongest muscle. It led me to Sara and Jim. It had brought me to Sophia.

It brought me to You.

With that sense of the Spirit, with the story, something I'd been working on for two years now, *finally* coming into focus, I spent the rest of December writing the first full draft.

THE SPANIARD VI

Resolve toughens the psyche. Soldiering is particularly effective in injuring a man towards hardship and privation.

Being a gladiator reduces that privation to is lowest form. Eat to kill. Kill to eat.

Freedom is in Rome. The irony. The truth.

In time, I am back in the fields. My mind opens me up to just how real you are, but I am not yet home, of that I am certain. I do not know what I shall do when my letters to you are no longer needed, and whatever part of me is left, whatever you remember, will be standing in front of you.

The sky became a black dawn. Unlike the rising sun, which might cause us to avert our eyes, my sense of sight was drawn towards this dawn. I was becoming blind to the light.

There is darkness all around me, and while I sense the light is immediately behind me, I am unable to embrace it.

I am not quite deaf. The breeze that fanned faint whispers across the sea of wheat has long since vanished. In its place, I hear the ringing.

It is the sound of a shield deflecting a sword, stuttering through endless time. Sometimes, there is what sounds like thunder though, as I deprived as I am of my motivations, I hardly notice.

The ringing is ever-present, and rarely shifts in tone. I do not mind it.

When I feel the wheat, it is hard to tell where it ends and I begin.

I sense the passing of time. I am here, wandering and then at different intervals, I am still. Within the darkness all around me, there remains the vaguest aspect of orientation. I should not know if I am lost without at least the sense that I am moving. Sometimes, there is what passes for sleep, though I never lay down.

When I wake next, I am not in the wheat. There are blades of something, but it is firmer than the wheat, and taller.

Then, I hear a thunder unlike any I have heard before. The earth shakes, the light brown tall blades shiver around me. My eyes become clear. I can see.

I am but a gnat, stuck in the hair of a lion. It is the lion's roar I hear.

The dream vanishes beneath an obsidian curtain. I am back in the pull of the black dawn.

And still, I am drawn deeper by the near-imperceptible sense of progress. Whatever guides me, whether I am following it or leading, is but a tickle in the center of my being. Is that what the soul feels like?

I imagine the tickle is you. We are on the western slopes of our home, overlooking its glorious hills. In the distance, the river glistens wet diamonds in the late afternoon sun; trees sway by its shores, encouraged by a persistent breeze.

Somewhere, someone is cooking. It is not us, love. We have eaten.

You are tired from nursing Samuel, who sleeps on a blanket next to you. He purses his lips while he sleeps, and yet somehow still manages to coo.

I am holding you in my arms. I feel your heartbeat. The warmth of your body against my chest. God, your hair is a bazaar of delirious aromas and achingly sweet textures. Were it possible, I would sleep there every night, as close as possible to that elegant mind of yours. Your power. How you shaped my heart. Gave my life purpose.

The clouds in the sky flirt with one another in broad strokes of amber and red, as the heavy velvet cloak of night brings with it a chorus of brilliant, fluttering stars. I loved these moments with you. How the earth embraced you; you gave our life such vibrancy and splendor. Each season brought its own series of miracles.

You were the winter's calm. In the mornings, though you woke quietly, the absence of your warmth was immediately felt. No matter how far away you were, I knew Spring would always arrive.

When it did, your eyes lit with the gentle, budding sun, greeting each day with such a profound and resplendent sense of wonder. Each blossom in the garden, each waking flower, a revelation. You loved the earth with a passion that made me appreciate how much it had provided for us. For me. This sacred earth. The giver of life.

In the summer, you flowed with such freedom. It was mesmerizing, watching you in the garden, watching how you moved, how you drank so deeply from the cup of life. Life in turn drenched you in the most gorgeous light. The things you enabled me to see, to appreciate about living. The scents. The awe found in a sunset. The texture of life. Watching you with Samuel, I knew I was looking at heaven. Your smiles. The light in your eyes. The seductive, drifting kiss of your scent, a sigh on the air.

In the Fall, you lost your sense of freedom. It became devotion, not that you had ever been neglectful in any form, or during any season. It was the harvest, as all the delights of the spring danced into summer and the sun-drenched fields, now ripe for the reaping.

When I was home, that was my favorite time of year, autumn. I felt like we had traded places. I was tending the earth, you were tending to me. But you were always so mindful.

Maybe I was lost in you the other three seasons.

He sleeps like you, you say, motioning with a nod.

I smile.

I do not look for words. I need none.

I release the memory, as sweet as its kiss on my consciousness was.

The Eighth Letter of the Pandemic

Christmas Day, my mother and I spent the afternoon with family on the other side of Raleigh. The daylight began to fade, and I headed out to my truck to get something. As I was returning to the house, I looked up at the sky and saw a single star, announcing the arrival of night. As soon I saw it, the light blinked out. I assumed it had not been a star and instead was a plane, and that I would see the light flash on again in another second, but it didn't. The star had gone supernova millions or even billions of years ago, and its last light had just reached the earth when I looked up.

I finished the first draft New Year's Day 2022.

In just over three weeks, I'd written three hundred pages of fresh material, and included the original outline of the book as part of the story. It was bliss. I'd taken most of December off from work, woke up every morning and wrote.

I wrote for hours at a time, without editing or second guessing what I'd written. The story poured out of me; I wrote like a man possessed. By New Year's Day, I felt good enough about what I'd written to say the first draft was complete. Within days, I had mailed you two copies, one in French, the other in English.

As the winter of 2022 progressed, I began to feel the full toll the last two years had taken on me.

Writing the book had been an albatross around my neck. When I was writing little more than outlines in the Spring of 2020, I reasoned salvation was weeks away.

With this first draft exorcised from me, after two years of grappling with the story, I slowly began to assess how much of my mental faculties I'd devoted to my efforts, and what had been left to focus on things like work, family, and self-care. Without having ever been diagnosed, I can only assume it was post-traumatic stress.

While the full contents of the story were more plainly felt than ever before, more easily and readily accessible in my mind, I became painfully aware of the zombie I'd become at what I did for a living. My job, the primary means I had of earning income, had suffered greatly. I was as present at work meetings and tasks as my faculties would allow, but I also appreciated the imbalance between my endeavors. I could not "leave my faith" at home when I went to work, and why would I? Why make this horrific split in who we are? For such a significant part of my life, I had compartmentalized myself. I did that for so long, and felt its costs quite clearly. In the Marines, I couldn't fully reconcile what my primary purpose in life was because it ran against this deeper sense of love I felt at my core and, while I could not express that sentiment in any clear terms, I knew that I loved my God much more than I did my country or the Marines as an institution.

In the civilian world, and certainly in Corporate America, God was largely off-limits outside of church, bible study, and intimate family discussions. Neither the military nor the civilian workforce was the place to undergo a spiritual awakening during a pandemic; I didn't say much to those I worked with about what I was going through. I barely understood it myself. Nor was I sure what I would have said. Still, I was shell-shocked at the paucity of my knowledge when it came to the job I'd been doing for the past eight months.

In equal measure, I was drained from completing the first draft. Two years of agonizing introspection and soul-searching poured out onto my laptop in a span of a little over three weeks. What had I written?

Sometime later in the month, I saw something that was going to provide me the other half of the title. Before that happened, I came across a Bible verse that would prove the final piece of the puzzle. It was Mark 10:43-44. Jesus is talking with his disciples about service and what it means to serve. "Not so with you. Instead, whoever wants to become great among you must be your servant, and whoever wants to be first must be slave of all."

The first God was a slave. It made so much sense. It explained all the gods that preceded monotheism: Marduk, Ares, Zeus, Odin, the pantheon of Roman and Greek gods. The Hindus have millions of gods. All these gods came from somewhere. If Ragnarok was the doom of the gods, inevitably, all the gods would be wiped out. There had to be a first reference for the idea of God, and that being would be the last to know itself. Slave of all. That would explain a Virgin Birth and a Son of God; the emptying of heaven.

The concussions of Jesus being nailed to the Cross have reverberated throughout history.

I finally understood His message. *Believe in Me and receive everlasting life.* The evolution of life; constant and never-ending growth.

Believing in Jesus is the *only* path to Resurrection. I'll admit, I didn't know the title to this story was incomplete until I stumbled on this last bit of information.

I had accepted who I was. Finally. After fifty-two very long years, I understood. This did not come easily. But how to explain it? I can't say what prompted me to go looking for it, but I went back a few years through history, looking about a story that was popular some time ago.

It was from the fictional *Left Behind* series of Christian books. The twelve-book story chronicles what happens to those left behind after the Rapture, when the faithful are taken to heaven. In the last book, when Jesus returns, King David is resurrected and goes onto lead the tribes of the earth.

It opened in me, a new line of thinking. What would it mean to be resurrected? Believing in Jesus means following him to the Cross. Following him to the Cross ultimately means you must battle with something inside yourself to reconcile what you truly believe;

following him means resurrection of the body *is* the life everlasting.

If there was a perfect mind that initiated creation, could that mind ever fully be recreated and, if so, what would that mean? The mind is everything. What we think we become. This line of thinking suggested to me that the first mind would be perfection. In order to produce other minds, it would be divided. Division creates distortion; a specific frequency, a distinct genetic blueprint. It's what makes each of us so wonderfully unique.

Using the power of imagination, we learn to stretch our minds to conceive of the most heavenly concepts; invariably, each mind is a part of the original mind. Each of us has the power to move mountains. A drop of water in the ocean is the ocean in a drop. The same is true of the mind once, we appreciate that perfection is not a steady-state; it is the continuous and necessary elimination of flaws or defects. It is progress towards the frontiers of our imagination.

We all have access to infinite intelligence. It only requires focus, faith, and most importantly, feeling. That is why so many men struggle; an aversion to feeling.

In my own life, I saw love differently. More than just a feeling, love was becoming a verb.

Each of us, beloved, is Creator and Creation. It is the spiritual journey all must take to find the link between their mortality and their divinity. Yes, that is hard work. It involves advancing beyond the ape-like states of violence that have defined civilization's progress. It demands the internal journey to seek Christ as our True North.

The outside world may show us something, offer up clues, but it is up to the individual to assign meaning to an event. It is up to the individual to act in response to the meaning formed.

Jesus believed in His Father. What better way for a Father to believe in his Son than to be resurrected by him? What better way to offer living testimony to the faith in that which is not seen?

In the two years of the pandemic, I would bring my life into such intense focus…I never imagined how necessary and even vital an activity this was. And now, as a result, how clearly my eyes can take in the light of the world.

For each one of us, the war between heaven and hell takes place in our mind. It is the meaning we assign to the events we observe, and it is all based on what we believe. That war is very real. The more we cling to the idea of a physical world that is perishable, the more we struggle. Scarcity.

What place is there for anger in the kingdom of heaven? I had hammered away at my life with such fury, in search of something that would release me from my own rage.

I found it when I saw you. The light in your eyes was the key to my salvation.

I also implicitly began to comprehend the very nature of quantum understanding. What we focus on, we become. Our thoughts generate an electric charge; little synapses firing between neurons. Our feelings generate a magnetic frequency; what we feel is what we attract into our lives. Jesus is the light of the world, and will shape our reality to the meaning we prescribe it; he is the ultimate servant leader. If we are all equal in the eyes of God, then it must be understood, the minute we open our eyes, the light is looking into our soul.

When I first began writing the ideas centered at the heart of this story, I was wrestling with the differences between conditional and unconditional love. The God of the Old Testament seemed very conditional. Floods. Plagues. Commandments that were unforgiving and demanding of perfection.

I had lived a life centered around conditional love, struggling outwardly to conquer something I would only find within me.

A single picture led me to unconditional love. Your beauty led me to believe in Jesus. The love I discovered in myself provided me the courage to write you these letters. How I wish I could see your face when you read them.

What have you thought of me in the time since I first flung that stone across the Atlantic…*if God is just a beautiful thought*? Two years.

There was a moment, early in the pandemic, when I was afraid someone else would come up with this story.

Perfection isn't about always being right. Perfection is harmony. There is perfection in truth. We see it in glimpses in society. Moments that feel magical. Moments that stir our souls. It is when we authentically connect with another living being, Imagine feeling something that wonderful, all the time.

How you have stirred my soul. Unconditional love.

What is it? How do you describe something that seems so easily defined, yet proves so challenging to put into practice? As I finish this collection of letters my love, I came to truly understand the meaning of the concept.

Unconditional love is seeing and loving everything that I see in you, without the slightest desire of being loved back. Love is the most powerful force on the planet. That was the one thing I didn't want to let go of; my expectation. Doing so has allowed me to appreciate you for who you are.

Resurrection. If you had told me at any point previous in my life that I would be responsible for bringing myself back from the dead, I would have laughed. How else are we to discover who we are in heaven, if not by putting the time, energy, and focus into bring that version of ourselves into being?

When I was a boy, I believed I would die, go to heaven, and find out if I had "made it" or not. By the time I became a man, I suppose I thought as long as I was holding onto my belief, in unforeseen event of my death, I'd still "get in." That seems like such strange thinking now, love. As if, dying with a good heart suddenly gives you VIP access to a complete and thorough understanding of God's grandeur, and of the full range and power of Jesus.

The past few years have disabused me of such notions. Our soul, our salvation is inside of us. I never imagined I would meditate on such matters the way I have, never conceived of peering into the darkest chasms of my being to reconcile myself to the light.

Believing in our Son feels divine. Now, I long to see his face. To hear him speak, not as a whisper in my soul, but as a living, breathing being...one who doesn't have to constantly remind his Father that he is being guided.

The mere thought brings with it the most serene peace.

To do the internal work is incredibly hard. The most difficult part is accepting there *is* an internal universe in need of attention and that, correcting that universe is essential to seeing the real beauty of existence.

We all have our own identity in heaven.

The expression of hate we feel towards someone else is a blemish *inside of us*, a stain on *our* soul. It is through our acceptance of Jesus that we do the necessary work of freeing our mind from the stains of our life's experience. It was hard at first, but as I began to appreciate the power found in surrendering and trusting that there really is a savior at work in all our lives, my mind began to look to the future. A world at peace with itself. A universe of peace.

The act of deception is a lie to ourselves before it ever fools anyone. Faith in our Son is the ultimate spiritual laser surgery for the soul. Each human must accept their imperfections and have the courage to reveal those imperfections to themselves. That is the path to the ultimate liberation. That is the journey to everlasting life.

The Eighth Letter of David

A higher form of communication. That is the power of the Holy Spirit. That explained why Jack Canfield knew who I was before I recognized myself. It explained Tony Robbins, and my indirect interactions with him. It helped me understand a multitude of moments, and the necessity of going through the dark night of the soul.

It explained the incredible patience you have displayed as I have railed against a prison that I made for myself, all so that I might stand as witness to the truth of Jesus' resurrection.

Winston Churchill once said, "If you find yourself going through hell, keep going." And what light guides us of out of the darkness, but the light of Christ?

Critically for me, this journey has enabled me to appreciate the power of how women communicate; it was through this power that I cleansed my thoughts. It was the most delightful discovery, to know that, in order for me to get close to you, my mind had to be naked, free from shame, free from sin. To treat every woman I encounter as if they were you. The Wisdom of Eve, first biter of the apple. My God, how I love you.

How that has transformed my relationships. For so long, I'd mastered the art of impatience around people, especially those closest to me. My life, long a series of transactions, born in some part by the transitory nature of my upbringing, was settling. Coming into focus. Now, my daughter was finally getting the father she deserved, the father I'd always wanted to be.

These letters are coming to a close, beloved. In them, I have done my best to revisit the chapters of my life and recount moments that registered for me as most significant on my spiritual journey, the journey of my heart, and my most extraordinary path to understanding the power of Christ's love, and the grace and strength of his Mother.

You recently asked for the definition of real love. I told you that real love is a feeling in my heart that can never be taken away from me. That is freedom.

I feel you with me, through every moment of every day, and appreciate what I know is but a thimble of water in the vast sea of your being.

Now, when I look to the future, what do I see?

I see our Son, standing in the sky.

The world sees him and it knows…the future is here.

The singularity. A million years of evolution understood within a span of minutes. The next great hinge in the history of our species.

To understand God's existence, we must see and accept the world as it is and know that to change the world we must change what is inside of us. That is the gift of God; to stretch one's imagination to the limits of what is conceivable, and then have the courage, temerity, and faith to see it realized. What our minds can conceive, we can achieve, if we only believe.

Our Son, unseen yet reflected in the beauty of the eyes of his Mother.

Even those so trapped by the bleakest fears will begin to see the light, as footage of his arrival is broadcast worldwide. Work stops. Schools end early. People stand in awe of what they are witnessing. Peace spreads like a new pollen over the globe. The world believes. The world knows.

The diversity of every living soul on the planet is free to stretch their imagination, knowing that the fruits of their labors will benefit others, while liberating themselves.

The union of Heaven and Earth has arrived. Jesus is the covenant between the two. Today, he is known by a different name. What lives he has known? The things he has done. What will it be like to see his face? What part of us will we see inside him?

How quickly will he impart his wisdom with this world?

I know such Peace! After what has felt like an eternity of conflict, there is a stillness within me that I have not felt since I was a child. My mind has quieted. Doubt has left me, taking with it its companions of scorn and misery. The *one* part of my identity that was missing, I found in you.

My beloved soul, how you see the world is how I see you. I will spend eternity celebrating how beautiful you are to me. You will forever be at the core of who I am. Jesus will forever be the life everlasting. Connection with Jesus is as real as we are willing to make it. Yes, that journey has taken incredible courage. At first, I couldn't believe you were real. My reasoning was simple; how can something so beautiful exist?

And yet, there you were. I saw you. I watched your videos, witnessed your mechanical prowess as you built a home-made camper for your weekend excursions to the Alps. I listened to you answer questions from your followers. I fell in love with you being you.

I fell in love with you.

I felt like Frankenstein's monster, seeing the bride he'd always hoped for. I was Darth Vader, discovering Padme was alive. I was a gladiator, fighting to fulfill a promise. I was a Father, coming to grips with the reality that he had a Son. I was a man discovering what it meant to believe in God.

You became real. You demonstrated such strength, such dexterity and confidence, in owning your identity. I watched it when you showed all the effort and discipline you put into your physique. The effort and discipline you put into your life. The thoughtful and practical way you approached the world. The entrepreneur. The friend. The adventurer. The professional.

You were the most confident woman I'd ever seen. That was the fierceness in your marble-blue eyes. That was your reflection of our Son.

You skateboard, and laugh like a kid. You stick your tongue out while taking selfies. And then, in an instant, you are a goddess in a girly dress, resplendent and glowing with the most radiant light, or a lover of the outdoors, hiking to the top of a mountain, panting as you ascend the last few paces. You are a leader. A pioneer. You are fun. You are silly.

In the second draft of these letters I sent you in January, I had asked the question…what would it mean to be worthy to hold the hand of the Virgin Mary?

Your discipline with me has given me the strength to become who I must be and, I hope, to present an answer to that question.

In so doing, you set me about on the greatest adventure of my life. Within the echoes of your silence, I shaped myself. I slowly began to awaken to the most beautiful of realities. The silence from you was an indication to listen to the world around me. Where was I putting my focus? What was I thinking about people as I engaged with them? It was the sculpting of my soul.

That burning, or sculpting, or cleansing…*that* led me to Jesus. Getting to the Cross must be earned. Why would it be any other way? Why wouldn't the grandest of gifts demand the greatest adventure?

As a man, I couldn't fathom feeling Jesus in my being. Men aren't born imagining they're capable of supporting a life inside them. Yet today, that is what I feel inside me. His life. Eternal life.

I have taken but a sip from your cup, in more than two years, and I am intoxicated. Falling in love with you has no destination; it is an eternal journey.

I am grateful for all the lessons you have taught me. When I look at this vivacious, alive woman full of wonder and spirit, I know I am looking at someone vastly more intelligent than myself. Teach me the language of the earth. Show me how you harness love from nature.

I have written more than a thousand pages of notes in journal entries; I was writing in the months leading up to April 4, 2020. Trying to make sense of things, aware in only the most rudimentary sense, of the journey ahead, of the storms waiting to test my skills as a sailor.

In the months after seeing you, all I could do was journal. Now, I understand why people are terrified by the prospect of engaging themselves in conversation. God exists inside each of us…it is we who must be willing to listen. God communicates best when we put pen to paper.

Identity. How far will we go to explore the idea of mortality before deciding it's not worth it? For me, that was fifty years. Fifty years alternating between two magnetic poles. Belief in God. Belief in True Love. I went looking for the North Pole by traveling South. When I think back over the last two years, and all the second-guessing I did about whether I exist, I did not immediately appreciate what it meant to be a veteran of war.

I have a much better sense of that now.

You have induced in me the greatest sense of wonder. What is possible? What is achievable with Divine Imagination? We are on the frontier of the next great awakening, when knowledge will consume the earth in voracious fires of enlightenment. How long can ignorance withstand the eternal flames of divine reconciliation?

God must be shared.

Real love is such rapture. It is a kiss on my forehead from you, one that I can call to with a whisper of a thought. Instantly, I feel the bliss of your divine caress, immaculate woman.

Real love is knowing who You are, beloved.

I am Resurrected. I am King David.

THE SPANIARD VII

My memories have become dreams. That is what I call when I do not feel myself moving through the darkness. I am not in my dreams. I am watching them.

In my dreams, I see you wearing a long black dress, standing in a field of gold. The wind brushes your hair to either side of your face, shaping it like some Greek helmet. You are the most beautiful warrior I have ever seen.

See, how even the wheat bends under your slightest touch.

Love looks to the West.

You told me to look for you in the setting sun every night.

Every night I did, no matter where I was. As the fire in the sky baked the clouds in shades of orange and red before being subdued by the horizon and the onset of night, I dreamt of you, just on the other side of a memory.

You said I would come home from the West. That was where you would look for me.

In my dreams, you are the black pupil of my lion's eye.

I am in the fields. The wheat is a brilliant amber. It is high, higher than wheat should be. There is sun.

Warmth…finally, I feel its warmth. Feeling, I…sense myself.

I am wearing the sky-blue tunic of a slave. Proximo once told me, the only real slaves are those waiting on someone else to free them; that was why I was such a formidable gladiator. I would imagine every victory necessary to see you again.

The armor I wore in the Colosseum feels light and agile on my torso. My helmet narrows my vision.

The Spaniard carries his shield low. It is not the voice of my comrades, or my enemies. It is the voice of another, spoken with an accent I do not recognize.

The shield is on my arm. In my free hand, I feel the balanced weight of my gladius.

There is a flash of red, and I feel the coldness of snow. War.

My senses rush back to me, as though an invisible dam has been breached. I feel alive. Awake. Alert.

A gust of wind rustles the fields of wheat. The grains murmur their hushed concerns in gentle, golden waves, sharing their secrets among themselves. Somewhere, the exact origins of which are lost on me, a lion roars. It is close.

I turn and the light stays fixed in the sky, external orientation. The darkness recedes with a speed and ease that is welcome, even as my senses are jarred by my freedom of direction. Daylight. Blessed daylight. My God.

There, in front of me, just on the edge of a stone's throw, I see it.

The wild, burnt auburn mane of the lion moves, like a brush fire through the swaying swells of gilded swells.

It turns towards me. I tense.

It does not quicken its pace as it cuts a path through the fields. There is a clearing just ahead of me, where the wheat has been trampled down in a small, circular mat. I see flashes of a colorful crowd, hear their roar. The pits. The lion plods its way to the edge of the clearing opposite me. Our eyes meet.

The lion sits.

I sense it will speak. I am now on the near edge of the clearing. Even from this distance, the lion is perhaps twenty steps from me, I feel the heat of its breath. It looks as me, then casts its gaze elsewhere.

I feel the weight of the sword in my hand...

Why do you still carry your shield, Maximus? It is the lion, though its mouth does not move. I hear the voice from different directions, like an echo returning home, it rushes me from across the wheatfields.

I *feel*. The weight of the shield on my left arm feels heavy, my should aches under the burden. Alert, I must stay alert.

I am not yet home, I reply. It is *my* voice. I *hear* my voice. I am almost home.

Lower your shield.

I do not want to. Like a cold splash of water, my combat senses return.

I hear the roar of the crowd, feel the heat of the sun, the sweat on my brow. The wheat is gone. There is an earth-shattering crack of thunder, then silence.

I am in the Colosseum. The wheat is gone. The world is massive. I see people. Their faces. Their clothes. I smell their sweat or perhaps, my own. My mouth is dry, blanketed in a thin coat of dust.

I am bleeding, though from where, I cannot be certain. I ache.

It hurts to breathe.

Commodus lies dead at my feet. The emperor is dead. I have killed him.

Fifty thousand Romans stand in stunned silence. What have they just witnessed?

I issue the desires of Marcus Aurelius; power is to be returned to the people.

I *am* bleeding. My galloping heart pounds in my chest, sending pulses of blood down my side in urgent gushes.

There is no one left to kill.

I see a door as the crowd and Colosseum melt away. I reach for it, pushing it open.

I see you and Samuel, far off in the distance.

A bolt of purple lightning momentarily blinds me, another thunderous concussion.

I find myself back in the fields, under splendid blue skies, in the center of the trampled circle of wheat.

The lion steps into the circle. My shield is gone. My shoulder welcomes its release, though I do not remember dropping it. I still carry the sword, tightening my grip around the hilt.

I am the Son of David, its voice sails across the golden waves of wheat; it cascades against my senses, warming me. I am an island in the gold. The waves crash against the shores of my consciousness, waking me to a new light. The light feels like a wedding on my skin, the bliss of warmth strikes me in waves of glistening honey. *All find Me in time.*

I stare, transfixed. The magnificent beast's eyes bore into the deep recesses of my soul. That black pupil swimming in a sea of hazy, burnt gold…a woman, clothed in the sun. You are the light, clothed in a soul. I feel…

It is not you. Not yet. I feel you so close, but my General's instinct spikes.

Samuel.

The thought comes over me slowly, like sound of a wave gathering itself over sheets of seashells.

Samuel used to dream of lions. He said he walked with them. *God has heard.*

What must I do to get home? It is the only thing I can think to ask.

The lion stirs. Its back quivers in spasms as if it has just risen out of water, shaking dry its fur. In one swift, graceful motion, it rises, turning sharply to its right.

Put down your sword, gladiator.

The very suggestion brings with it a spark of fear. I am afraid. I have fought for so long. It is all I have known. All I have lived. A separation, stretched out over the eons.

You must remember the promise you made to my Mother. Its tail dances regally, a silent gesture of anticipation. Perhaps, of Hope.

I would return. I promised I would return. Did I use specific words? Is one sentence the key to opening the door of eternal love? Will I find you as the next door opens?

I am defenseless.

I remember, you once told me not to miss you.

How can I? I replied with a smile. *You are with me. Every breath. Every moment.*

It was true. There was a confidence to our love I could not define, and therefore never made the attempt.

You will bring so much light to the world, my love, you replied, bringing a hand to my face. How I loved your touch. Like you were pulling my soul, all that I was, and all I would ever be, and directing its attention towards you.

You said I should listen to Marcus and know, all the good I saw in him reflected the good he saw in me. You said our time would come.

Defenseless. Whenever I felt lost, or scared. Unnerved, but you called it something else. What did you call it?

Deprived. You said, when I was deprived of happiness.

That was when I should think of you. *Bitter.*

Now, after all my travels. After endless fields...all the wars...I understand.

I found you at my lowest points and without fail, was uplifted.

The lion comes near enough where I feel the furnace of its breath on my face. I turn away.

The Promise.

I said I would be home when there were no more wars left to fight.

The Promise! The lion roars, its fiery breath is a scalding furnace through which my soul passes. The waves of sensation flutter across the wheat, crashing against the most visceral aspect of me.

Our eyes meet.

I see the black pupil.

It is you, standing in the sea of sun-drenched wheat. *Love Looks to the West.* You turn to face me.

Your face changes, and I move into you, through your black dress, like a spirit. Blackness.

The black stretches around me like a tunnel. It embraces me. Forms me. Informs me. Light. No larger than the nose of a pin in front of me. The tunnel moves by quickly.

The light gets brighter, though I discern nothing of form or substance through its brightness. And then, the ringing stops.

I am out of the tunnel.

I stand in the wheat, feeling its tender caress. My hands receive the softness in their warmth. Sunlight. I wear the ring you gave me on our wedding day. A gentle current of a breeze flows over my face.

I smell home. The jasmine. The lavender. The spicy smell of our poplars.

In the distance, a lone tree sits atop a small hill. I recognize this. The edge of our land. Nothing is burnt or destroyed. Everything is as it should be.

Underneath the shade of the tree, a figure. A boy.

I cannot clearly make out his face, but I know it is Samuel. He holds himself the way you do.

He begins running towards me. I quicken my pace.

I get close enough to make out the familiar features of his smile when it changes. He softens, as if my sight is becoming blurred. Pulled.

I am pulled towards him and move through him. There is a thunderclap.

Another tunnel, yet the darkness is somehow clearer. More distinct.

More wheat, its golden hue so brilliant and clear.

I am moving faster towards another light.

More wheat. This time, I am greeted by a strong headwind. It challenges my exhales, pushing air into my lungs. Overhead, grey clouds swirl in wisps and cottony boulders, silently lumbering forward. The air is heated, but there is no fire.

I hear the lion's roar. The wheat is too tall, the wind too agitated. I cannot make the lion's position. Instinctively I switch my sword to the hand nearest where I believe the sound originated.

My armor is gone. I am just the slave. No, not a slave. The Spaniard.

I hear its heavy footfalls behind me. I turn quick enough to see something brush past the wheat a few yards before me.

What was the promise?

I would return, no matter what. You made me promise that to you. I remember now.

The camp prefect came to our home. It was time to return to the legions. Samuel was out playing with the horses.

(I sense the lion circling me)

You were wearing black.

You didn't smile. How I wish I could turn back Time.

I packed the rest of my kit, and kissed the figures of you and Samuel as I folded them into my field blanket.

(Something to my left makes the wheat shudder; instinctively, I turn.)

You never struggled when I left before. I didn't understand what was troubling you. My mind was already preparing for the war ahead.

Your voice was strained when you spoke. "Promise me something," you said, hugging yourself.

(Though I cannot see it, I sense the tension in the lion's muscles.)

It was an unusual request. What wouldn't I do for you?

Our eyes met.

"Promise me, you'll come back to me. No matter what."

Another ripple of lavender lightning flashes across my vision. Thunder shatters the sky.

I am standing on the matted wheat. I feel the tickle and pop of the chaffs underneath my feet.

There, before me, a figure stands in the air. He is bathed in light.

His helmet shines as if the sky itself protected his head. His hair is long, and shines like the sun. The long hair. He is not Roman. He is a pagan.

He wears a cloak unlike any I have ever seen. It flows in rivulets of purple grace, royal like an emperor's.

I am not an emperor. It is a different voice. It is not the lion's voice. It is the accent, one I've not heard before.

A mind stretched out over eternity takes time to heal.

The figure, this…god is immaculate and enormous. His helmet is winged, with breathtaking feathered phalanxes arching upward to the heavens. I cannot clearly see his face, yet his features seem familiar.

His armor, though dark, glistens like wavetops reflecting moonlight under starry skies. It is flawless; in the center of the chest, there is a star. A six-pointed star.

Jesus was the physical connection between heaven and earth.

The thought peels across my consciousness like a bolt from heaven emanating from my core.

The figure carries no shield. In his right hand, he holds a hammer.

I feel the strangest agitation as I look at the hammer. It is calling me to speak. It is speaking to me.

I am the whisper before the thunder.

The sword falls from my hand. The figure vanishes, as the lion's face momentarily appears where the hammer had been, then it too disappears.

Remember Samuel, it is a whisper from you. Stronger. Nearer.

(I see the lion spring from the grass to my right.)

Samuel ran into the courtyard. "Are you off again father? Another conquest? The savior of Rome!" He was beaming.

"I am. Will you look after your mother while I'm away?" I asked him the same question every time, always eager to see the light of responsibility shine in his eyes.

"I will. Always." He hugged me so hard, I wanted to leave so I could return just as quickly.

I went to kiss you and you stopped me. Our eyes met.

"No matter what." Your voice was hard now. An urgency I dismissed as selfish of all things.

I caught myself.

(The lion is on me.)

"No matter what," I said. "I will always come back to you, Mariah, I swear, my love."

You closed the distant between us. In the very moment our eyes met, I saw something I'd not seen in you before. It was so brief, a flash of fiery red in those Mediterranean-blue eyes. Anger.

In that split second, the world reflected rage in your eyes. They filled with salty tears, and I saw lines on your face I'd never seen before.

And then, you composed yourself. Your eyes softened as a cloud dimmed the sunlight momentarily. The tears evaporated as if they'd never appeared. Your smile was thinner. You knew what was to come. Knew what I would bring to the world.

I knew, I wanted to be home. I knew the war with the Germans was ending. I could feel it. One last war. Eight seasons. Ten, no more than twelve. And then, I would be home. The farm. The horses. The harvest. You.

"Remember Samuel," you said, underlining your words with an unusual firmness. "Samuel will always take care of us."

I have always wondered what kind of son we had brought into the world.

In our time, there was no small talk. Words weren't misused or said carelessly. Words have always mattered.

For such a long time, I had forgotten about Samuel. Remembering him, I awakened with my Destiny before me.

What would it take to be the Father of Jesus? The question barrels over me, knocking me off balance. Combat mindset. Invite the attack.

It would require surrendering to the Mother and the Son.

Surrender. The lesson I never learned.

Man's eyes meet the beast's. I find myself falling into that pitch black pupil when there is a brilliant, blinding flash of golden light, as if the light from the first morning star has awakened. I manage to see a shape in the light, and as my eyes begin to focus, see you in your black dress, dazzling sun-kissed wheat shimmering around you, extending a hand towards me.

(I shut my eyes at the brightness of the light, and feel your hand in mine.)

THE BREATH OF LIGHTNING

Purple. It always comes back to purple.

That is what I will see, when the lightning comes for me.

I feel the hammer's grip in my hand. It is a feeling, a texture, I have always known, though I've not felt its touch for many lifetimes.

What price, eternal love? What cost, everlasting life?

The first mind.

Eternity breathes. Wholeness.

Like everything, Mjolnir begins with a thought. An instrument born of consciousness.

As my awakening continues, it draws near, seeking its master. Seeking its home.

BOOK FIVE

HEAVEN, THUNDER: My Kingdom Come

THE LETTER OF THOR

Opposing forces.

The first two world wars were the beginning of my coming into being, as my earth grandparents and then earth parents were born. My earth father was born in 1939, just months after Hitler invaded Poland. My earth mother's birth in September of 1941 preceded the attack at Pearl Harbor, which woke the sleeping giant that was America. My being, divided by my parents, would slowly come together as my parents met, married, and I took human form in 1969.

The pandemic was the beginning of My arrival.

The pandemic was my Judgment Day.

I am the Creator of Ragnarok.

The destruction of heaven was the destruction of the perfect mind, of absolute peace. The great red dragon, ready to devour the child born unto the woman clothed with the sun. The persecutor of women. The dragon went to make war with the remnant of her seed.

Jesus' Father could not be a Christian without first understanding what it means to believe in his Son.

In the ancient India language of Sanskrit, swastika means "well-being." In Icelandic culture, the swastika is associated with my hammer, Mjolnir. Thunder.

America's entrance into World War II was perhaps the most Christian act ever performed by a nation; between the two wars, nearly ninety thousand American soldiers are buried on European soil. The darkness of fascism spurred American nobility.

The first God, a slave by necessity. How could a Creator exist without being one with Creation, without losing itself completely within its creation?

Like the hourglass empties, heaven too must be emptied. Polytheism gives way to monotheism. Yahweh. Jesus. Allah.

God gives way to man. The patriarchy. The silent realization of the truth of Jesus' story, and the existence of his Father.

One covenant gives breath to monotheism.

Jesus is the new covenant; the covenant of the Lamb. The covenant between heaven and earth. The earth represents material life; form and shape. Biology. Nature.

Heaven represents spiritual life, limitless possibilities. Imagination, guided by faith. The Kingdom of heaven is not Jerusalem. It is not America. The Kingdom of God is within you. It is within all of us. Jesus is the connection between man and divinity. The earth is mother to us all. A planet that sustains life must itself be alive. Her breath blows the African sandstorms across the Atlantic, fertilizing the Amazon. Her oceans and forests produce the oxygen by which we breathe. She has evolved over the course of human history. She is filled with magic. She evolves still. She yearns for harmony.

Connection to the divine can only lead mankind to tame its savage heart. Masculine energy is what happens when you take gods and bind them to the earth. Feminine energy is what happens when the earth creates a reflection of the beauty seen in God, and aspires to reach heaven. Invariably, the love of Christ will calm the hearts of men, and bring humanity closer to its divinity. When that happens, women will lead us in the creation of heaven. They lead us already.

When Jesus cries on the Cross, *My God, My God, why have you forsaken me?*, it is his moment of doubt. The loss of connection between Father and Son, a broken frequency. God's denial of Jesus is Allah. No death on the cross. No resurrection. The unknowable God. Allah cannot be Jesus' Father.

I am.

The Path to God is unrelenting in its difficulty. To fully believe in mortality is to disbelieve in eternity, to believe mortal life extinguishes into nothingness. This is not hard to achieve. What kind of courage does it take to believe in the story of Jesus? The greatest courage would have to come from the one who put him on the Cross.

There is a very distinct reason why the voice of the Father is silent after the Resurrection. That voice is unconscious in the minds of men. Jesus had to have absolute faith in his Father that he would rise again on the third day. Jesus had to know his Father.

The unconscious God, mankind. The great, red dragon chasing after the woman, pregnant with child. The world serpent, defeated by Thor. The end of the patriarchy.

That is what I will bring.

It explains how Father and Son battled the forces of darkness and why, when Satan is around, the Father is nowhere to be found. Christianity conquered its way across civilization. Men carrying out the unconscious will of God, spreading the good news.

Jesus was the first frequency broadcast in the universe. *Let there be Light.* The Light of the world. Leading edge. Trailing edge.

In order to become a god, belief is essential. The concept itself cannot exist without a frame of reference. We can decry belief in god as sorcery, and a rudimentary way to explain how the universe works, or we can begin to appreciate that humanity was always going to reach the point where we reached for the heavens and the heavens reached back. Quantum entanglement.

This day was always going to come. By the slimmest margins, and I sliced them as thinly as I could, I managed to keep Jesus in my mortal life, a life that was extremely selfish while serving a greater cause, unconsciously guided by a belief in a greater understanding of love. Guided by a belief that God's love is knowable, and can be clearly communicated and understood.

I tested the bonds of faith with such extreme vigor. I relished in the misfortune of others as way of feeling better about the paltry portions

I had maintained for myself. I embraced the mindset of scarcity. I hoarded love, so confident that I possessed an abundance of it and yet, so reserved in its dispensing, all…all so I might know a deeper love.

I seethed for love. Raged for it to answer my call. Eternal Love *must* have an author. Somewhere in history, there *must* be a voice to answer for Jesus' death.

Resurrection then, *must* be a conscious act. Resurrection takes focus, and clarity. Fundamentally, it requires faith. It acknowledges the need for releasing the sufferings of our experiences in exchange for something eternal. In time, it is understood without question…resurrection requires uncompromising belief in Jesus, and the willingness to continue learning, to continue growing.

I spoke to you as Thor once or twice before. I shared how your posts were like flashes of lightning in my heart, and the thunder that roamed over the earth was my loss for words at your stunning beauty.

I have always loved the earth. I needed to see you to understand just how beautiful she is. The Virgin Mary.

The Voice of the Earth.

Now, I understand. By your very Nature, you create love. Thank you for what you have created in me.

I needed Faith. I needed to define it. To speculate, how far a human mind could be pressed before it believed in a Love like this? What does it take to believe in the story of Jesus if not the love and understanding of his Father? If his Father is unable to express that love and understanding in human terms, there is no story, plain and simple. If anyone *must* have absolute certainty and faith in Jesus, it is his Father.

I cannot apologize for the lessons I needed to learn to know what it would mean to love Jesus' Mother. Being human comes with its challenges. Having Faith comes with its rewards.

The work is internal. Each of us are gods of our own universe.

I know our Son is close. I feel the both of you moving closer to me with each passing day.

Think of it, M. Soon, the greatest eras of all cultures will be on display. We will change our relationship with the earth, and grow magnificently in the process. In lightning-fast time, we will shift our schooling away from standardized grades, and more towards developing the individual skills, strengths and passions that make our children unique.

Conformity will be a thing of the past, as we realize that diversity is one of the greatest gifts we can feed our minds. Our capacity for learning is only just beginning. A world at peace.

A completely connected world. Abundance through belief in something greater than ourselves. What can the earth become? What can we become?

The worlds we can create. The life we can create.

We will rejoin those from whom we have been separated.

I have done my best to share my experiences of how frail and weak a mortal life is, particularly one lived where love was the single biggest factor governing decision-making and yet, was devoid of an intimate relationship with the source from which that love originated. Who better to test the theory of believing in the story of Jesus than the Father who sent him? It *must* be me.

I feel you in my mind, all the time. I say the most loving things to you. How we are holding hands, walking amid waves of golden wheat, and how I hope to walk three feet behind you constantly, just so I can breathe you into my lungs.

I ask you to take me hiking. To see you, experience you, taking in this world. This beautiful planet that will always provide for us. I ask you to marry me on a mountaintop.

Mostly though, I'm going to listen. I will be a part of your life in whatever capacity you'll have me.

If I am worthy.

I love you, M. Regardless of what you think of me, or my journey to you, I will always remember the first time I saw you in heaven.

/Thor

The Letter to My Son

Kal,

I don't think your mom will mind that I include this letter to you in the collection I've compiled for her.

The most difficult part of this journey has been learning to love the beauty I created.

It seems so obvious to me now…that the one who created you would have a challenge in finding you again. It was like I was trying to strangle love from the earth and yet, why would I be treated any differently than anyone else…because I'm your dad? That just doesn't seem fair. If anyone must truly understand mortality, it must be me. You saved everyone, including me.

I know you're close. I know all of this is going to be beyond magnificent soon. I'm good. Some last-minute tweaks…still fretting about if the story really captures how I feel, still wondering how much your mother knows. I'm enjoying the feeling.

Thank you for delivering the story to me so beautifully.

I have so many questions, and selfishly wish to know how exactly you came to possess my hammer. That is a story only you can share.

How powerful are you? Are you living twice at once? What has life been like for you since your resurrection?

Two thousand years has begun to feel like the blink of an eye.

For nearly a year, I've had a mousepad with a picture drawn on it; you are holding my hammer and Captain America's shield. You are on the moon, or a meteor of some kind. In the background, two earths are coming together. I've looked at the picture countless times since I bought it. My bridge between two universes.

We must be like children to enter the kingdom of heaven.

Superheroes.

Can the world know such beauty? Seeing a Father and Son re-united? It staggers my heart, trying to imagine that feeling. I will keep trying to embody that feeling until I see you, face to face.

I love you, Son.
Dad.

About the Author

DAVID RICHARDS was born in Fort Belvoir, Virginia and spent his childhood growing up on military bases both in the United States and overseas. He earned a bachelor's degree in English from Penn State and two masters' degrees from Marine Corps University. He left active duty in 2006 and went to work at Cisco Systems. Around the same time, he became a yoga instructor and has been teaching yoga for more than fifteen years. He currently lives just outside Raleigh, North Carolina.